力得文化
Leader Culture

解題高手眼球追蹤術大公開

秒殺
NEW TOEIC
Part 5 & Part 6

專為提升新多益考試關鍵應試能力設計，瞬間變身解題高手，題題

陳力曼 ◎著

U0077352

追求高分，解題速度是關鍵。除了實力，作答策略不能少!!

目標: **秒殺**　　方法: **眼球追蹤+秒殺策略**

Your score

TOTAL SCORE

◉ **本書特色:**

精準掌握 掌握新多益閱讀測驗題型所需要之關鍵應試能力

完全圖解 圖解高手解題時視線的移動與停留

步驟分析 分析高手解題時的邏輯

策略提升 提升應試者在Part 5 與 Part 6 的速度表現，有充足的時間留給Part 7

◉ **單元攻略:**

簡單看文法 系統化文法觀念，簡單看，簡單會。文法實力UP!

字彙練功區 每單元隨附單字總整理，快速晉升人生勝利組。單字實力UP!

眼球追蹤 圖解高手視線的移動，提升答題速度。❶→❷→❸ 解題速度UP!

秒殺策略 分析高手解題的邏輯，邁向高手之路。❶→❷→❸ 解題速度UP!

多益簡介、測驗
容、題型分析、
數等級與對應能
。含作答策略。

Preface

作者序

Powerman老師長期從事英語教學與訓練英文檢定，對於多益測驗，看過考生對於多益閱讀面臨最大的挑戰便是題目過多，無法在 75 分鐘之內完成 100 題的閱讀題，此現象一直引導著筆者思考如何擬定一套有效的學習與解題策略，讓考生可以在有限時間內完成百題後，還可以從容地作檢驗。

要有效的攻堅多益閱讀測驗，必須具備足夠的多益相關字彙、紮實文法觀念與有效的閱讀技巧。閱讀測驗中的 Part 5 與 Part 6，共佔 52 題，其中基礎文法觀念的測試比重佔一半，再加上一般英語學習者對於文法的心理障礙，本書因而誕生。

多益測試的文法觀念，多半為基礎的重要觀念，題目不會艱澀，但解題需要觀念正確且有技巧。因此面對多益所會測試的文法部分準備，就是要在理解基礎文法概念後，務必搭配相關練習，才會知道如何應用。此外，若要增加解題速度，熟練解題相關技巧與流程是必要的，因此 Powerman 老師將眼球追蹤術搭配學習策略套入解題模式，讓有機會閱讀到本書的學習者，除了可以提升英語文法能力外，還可以多獲得關於學習技能與策略的概念。如此，學成之後，不但可以有效地在短時間內秒殺一半以上的多益文法題，還可以應用在日後英語學習或測驗中。

最後，除了感謝倍斯特出版社老闆、出版夥伴 Carolyn 與編輯部門的職員們給我這機會出版此多益文法書籍，也衷心感謝本書出版前一直給予鼓勵與建言的朋友們，讓我更有信心將所有對英語文法教學概念與熱情轉化成文字與大家分享。

陳力曼

Words From Editor

編者序

關於「秒殺」

　　新多益想拿高分，「速度」是關鍵。75 分鐘之內要完成 100 題，Part 5 及 Part 6 要達到秒殺的境界，才能留足夠的時間給 Part 7。Part 5 的「單字填空」與 Part 6 的「短文填空」，在基本字彙與文法質與量足夠的基礎下，若能搭配合適的作答策略，掌握快速解題的能力，才是新多益「閱讀測驗」題型的最佳攻略。

關於「眼球追蹤」

　　我們知道生手與熟手(專家與菜鳥)在做同樣工作的時候技巧不同，效率也大不相同。例如，一個閱讀高手在讀一篇文章的時候，不會像生手一樣逐字逐句的讀，也能快速的得到所需要的資訊。解文法題也是一樣的原理，解題高手不用整題從頭到尾看，就能快速得出答案。而眼球追蹤的觀念，應用在教學上，更期待能藉由眼球的運動（視線的移動與停留的時間）歸納出一些規則，一窺專家的思路。

關於《秒殺新多益 Part 5 & Part 6 - 解題高手眼球追蹤大公開》

　　本書專為提升新多益關鍵應試能力設計，以 15 個新多益考試必會常考的重要文法觀念為主架構，透過【簡單看文法】、【字彙練功區】深入淺出建立文法觀念，加強單字實力；並特闢【眼球追蹤】與【秒殺策略】專區大幅提升應試時的答題速度，掌握高分關鍵。提升答題速度，追求新多益高分，請速至【體驗區】體驗秒殺解題的快感！

倍斯特編輯部

秒殺

CONTENTS

目錄

架構與特色

《秒殺新多益Part 5 & Part 6》可以傳授你...

1 簡單清楚的基礎文法觀念

本書分15單元，涵蓋新多益測驗的文法出題範圍。先以條理方式列出文法基本規則，直接釐清觀念。並搭配多益測驗中常出現的題型來做例句的說明。

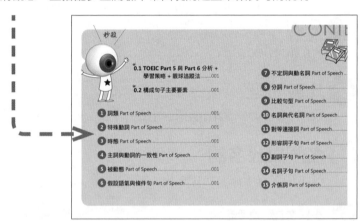

2 Mini Test限時5分

文法規則理解完畢後，練習部份以10題的「單句填空」與3題題組方式的「短文填空」供你練習，限時5分鐘，以強化應試的作答速度。

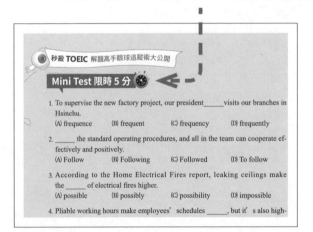

秒殺 TOEIC 解題高手眼球追蹤術大公開

Mini Test 限時 5 分

1. To supervise the new factory project, our president_____ visits our branches in Hsinchu.
   (A) frequence   (B) frequent   (C) frequency   (D) frequently

2. _____ the standard operating procedures, and all in the team can cooperate effectively and positively.
   (A) Follow   (B) Following   (C) Followed   (D) To follow

3. According to the Home Electrical Fires report, leaking ceilings make the _____ of electrical fires higher.
   (A) possible   (B) possibly   (C) possibility   (D) impossible

4. Pliable working hours make employees' schedules _____, but it's also high-

---

Question 11-13 refer to the following advertiser

BEST dishes @ the BE

The BEST Café is casual cafe with all the fla offer a _____

11 (A) vary
   (B) varied
   (C) various
   (D) variety

of Latin American cuisines, like tropical potat
pancakes topped with Mexican cheese, a
plantains. _____ , all food served is organic a

3 眼球追蹤法引導解題

「眼球追蹤法引導解題」是本書的精華重點。每題利用眼球追蹤方式，快速引導解題的文法概念與技巧，極具高效能輸入模式。用文字說明搭配與符號圖示，你可以快速地進入解題步驟123的模式思維，經過15單元反覆訓練後，變成為個人功夫技能。

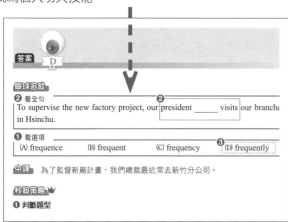

答案　D

眼球追蹤

❷ 看全句
To supervise the new factory project, our president ＿＿＿ visits our branche in Hsinchu.

❶ 看選項
(A) frequence　　　(B) frequent　　　(C) frequency　　　(D) frequently

中譯　為了監督新廠計畫，我們總裁最近常去新竹分公司。

秒殺策略
❶ 判斷題型

4 訓練作答與學習策略

在「眼球追蹤法引導解題」潛移默化中，不但可以讓你適應30秒殺單題速度的模式，並養成一套的閱讀與學習的策略。當這些轉化成你自己的個人能力與應試策略後，日後面對英語大大小小的測驗時，皆可適用。

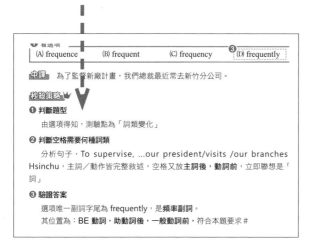

❶ 看選項
(A) frequence　　　(B) frequent　　　(C) frequency　　　(D) frequently

中譯　為了監督新廠計畫，我們總裁最近常去新竹分公司。

秒殺策略

❶ 判斷題型
　　由選項得知，測驗點為「詞類變化」

❷ 判斷空格需要何種詞類
　　分析句子，To supervise, ...our president/visits /our branches Hsinchu，主詞／動作皆完整敘述，空格又放**主詞後，動詞前**，立即聯想是「詞」

❸ 驗證答案
　　選項唯一副詞字尾為 frequently，是**頻率副詞**。
　　其位置為：**BE 動詞，助動詞後，一般動詞前**，符合本題要求 #

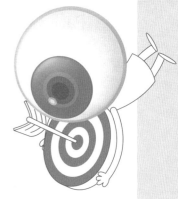

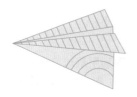

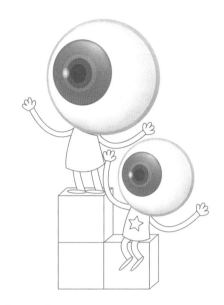

0.1
新多益簡介

新多益（NEW TOEIC）簡介

TOEIC（Test of English for International Communication）是「國際溝通英語測驗」。此測驗是乃針對英語非母語人士所設計之英語能力測驗，評量分數反映受測者在國際職場與商業環境中英語聽力與閱讀的能力。因應不同需求，另有舉辦口語與寫作測試供大眾報考。

📝 NEW TOEIC 測驗題型

多益測驗時間為 2 小時，共有 200 題，全部為單選題，分兩部分：聽力與閱讀。

📝 聽力測驗（1-100）

總共 100 題，共有 4 大題。內容描述包括英語的直述句、問句、短對話以及簡短獨白，腔調包括美國、英國、澳洲、加拿大、紐西蘭的英語發音。考試時間為 45 分鐘。分別為：

Part 1：照片描述 10 題（4選1）
Part 2：應答問題 30 題（3選1）
Part 3：簡短對話 30 題（4選1）
Part 4：簡短獨白 30 題（4選1）

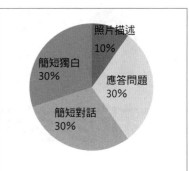

📝 閱讀測驗（101-200）

總共有 100 題，共 3 大題。內容包括測驗字彙、文法與閱讀理解，題材多元。考試時間為 75 分鐘。分別為：

Part 5：單句填空 40 題（4選1）
Part 6：短文填空 12 題（4選1）
Part 7：單篇文章理解 28 題（4選1）
　　　　雙篇文章理解 20 題（4選1）

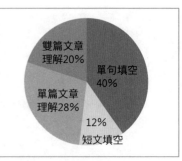

NEW TOEIC 測驗內容

測驗情境，以全世界各地職場的場景為主，題材多元化，包含：

- 一般商務 General Business
  契約(contracts)、談判(negotiations)、合併(mergers)、行銷(marketing)、銷售(sales)、保固(warranties)、商業企劃(business planning)、大型會議

(conferences)、勞資關係(labor relations)

- 製造商 Manufacturing
  生產線(assembly lines)、工廠管理(plant management)、品質管制(quality control)

- 技術領域 Technical Areas
  電子(electronics)、科技(technology)、電腦(computers)、實驗室與相關器材 (laboratories and related equipment, technical)、技術規格(specifications)

- 公司發展 Corporate Development
  研究(research)、產品研發(product development)

- 金融與預算 Finance and Budgeting
  銀行業務(banking)、投資(investments)、稅務(taxes)、會計(accounting)、請款(billing)

- 採購 Purchasing
  採買(shopping)、訂貨(ordering supplies)、貨運(shipping)、請款發票 (invoices)

- 辦公室 Offices
  董事會會議(board meetings)、委員會(committees)、信件(letters)、公司內部通信(memoranda)、電話(telephone)、傳真(fax)、電子郵件(e-mail messages)、辦公室設備與傢俱(office equipment and furniture)、辦公室流程(office procedures)

- 人事 Personnel
  招募(recruiting)、雇用(hiring)、退休(retiring)、薪資(salaries)、升遷 (promotions)、申請工作(job applications)、徵人廣告(job advertisements)、年金(pensions)、獎項(awards)

- 保健 Health
  醫療保險(medical insurance)、看醫生(visiting doctors)、牙科(dentists)、診所(clinics)、醫院 (hospitals)

- 住房與公司資產 Housing & Corporate Property
  建築(construction)、詳細規格(specifications)、購買與租賃(buying and renting)、電力與瓦斯服務(electric and gas services)

- 旅行 Travel
  火車(trains)、飛機(airplanes)、計程車(taxis)、公車(buses)、船隻(ships)、渡輪(ferries)、票務(tickets)、交通工具的延遲與取消(delays and cancellations)、車站與機場廣播(station and airport announcements)、時刻表(schedules)、租車(car rentals)、飯店(hotels)、預訂(reservations)

- 外出用餐 Dining Out
  商業與非正式的午餐(business and informal lunches)、宴會(banquets)、接待會(receptions)、餐廳預定 (restaurant reservations)

- 娛樂 Entertainment
  電影(cinema)、戲劇(theater)、音樂(music)、藝術(art)、展覽會(exhibitions)、博物館(museums)、傳媒(media)

新多益 閱讀測驗

多益的閱讀測驗從Part 5-7分成「單句填空」、「短文填空」與「文章理解」三部分。多數應試者最大致命傷就是在75分鐘內無法完成全部的題目。解套方式即先快速完成Part 5（單句填空）與Part 6（短文填空），再預留較多時間解Part 7（文章理解）的部份。

Part 5 & Part 6

Part 5 單句填空 40 題與 Part 6短文填空 12 題，全部佔了閱讀題數52%，比例之高，其重要比例不言而喻。而要從容面對 Part 5 與 Part 6 的方式，其方法就是勤背商用字彙與精熟基礎文法後，再搭配適合的閱讀與作答策略，就可增加答題速度與正確率。

與 Part 7文章理解相異之處，Part 5 & Part 6，是可以當刀直入的毋須閱讀長篇文章就直接解題的不連貫單題測驗。因此高效能的解題技巧是必要的。據估計，在字彙量足夠且文法概念強的情況下，要達到30秒解一題題目，並非難事。

新多益 分數等級與對應能力

多益分數包括 聽力 495分，閱讀 495分，滿分 990分。 依照分數分成五種等級的
證照。

TOEIC成績	語言能力	證書顏色
905~990分	英文能力已十分近似英語母語人士，能夠流暢有調理的表達意見、參與談話，主持英文會議，調和衝突並做出結論，語言使用上即使有瑕疵，亦不會造成理解上的困擾。	A級 金色 (860～990
785~900分	可有效運用英語滿足社交及工作所需，措詞恰當，表達流暢；但在某些特定情形下，如：面臨緊張壓力、討論話是過於冷僻艱澀時，仍會顯現出語言能力不足的狀況。	B級 藍色 (730～855)
605~780分	可以英語進行一般社交場合的談話，能夠應付例行性的業務需求，參加英文會議，聽取大部分要點；但無法流利的以英語發表意見、作辯論，使用的字彙、句型亦以一般常見為主。	C級 綠色 (470～725)
405~600分	英文文字溝通能力尚可，會話方面稍嫌辭彙不足、語句簡單，但已能掌握少量工作相關語言，可以從事英語相關程度較低的工作。	
255~400分	語言能力僅僅侷限在簡單的一般日常生活對話，同時無法做連續性交談，亦無法用英文工作。	D級 棕色 (220～465)
10~250分	只能以背誦的句子進行問答而不能自行造句，尚無法將英語當作溝通工具來-使用。	E級 橘色 (10～215)

Part 5 單句填空 (Incomplete Sentences)

題目類型：共40題，每題有四個選項，須從選項中選出一個最適合的答案。

測驗內容：商業書信，電子郵件，公司內部公告，廣告，報章雜誌，公告等。

測驗重點：「字彙」與「文法」

答題技巧：

❶ 秒殺30

閱讀總題數100題，需要留時間給第7部分，因此，Part 5的時間，要控制在20分鐘內完成，平均一題不超過30秒為原則。當單題解題時間到達20秒後仍難以抉擇時，則用猜測法填入答案，等完成全部作答有多餘時間時，再回來做檢測。

❷ 找關鍵字

先判斷測驗點為字彙題還是文法題，若是文法題，則進行尋找關鍵字或搭配詞步驟。

❸ 精熟詞類

Part 5中，判斷詞性題占了全部題目近四分之一。即使不認識單字，但藉由字首、字尾、前後文，空格的位置，或搭配詞，都可以作為解題依據。精熟理解八大詞類的位置與用法十分重要。

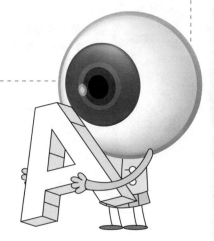

字彙題：字彙題是根據上下文選出最適當的字，這四個選項的單字的意義或字形有時候相當類似，有時後卻完全不同。片語、慣用法、搭配字的考題也常見。單字題的加強要靠平時多閱讀來增加字彙並理解正確用法。

Sample Question

Ms. Ikeda and Mr. Arroyo are the final candidates under _____ for the position of director of development.

(A) consideration　　(B) elimination　　(C) recognition　　(D) confirmation

---

選項是由詞性相同的名詞字彙所組成，答案必須由題幹的上下文脈來推論。此題為最簡易的字彙測驗題，只需要知道字義即可解題。難度較高的字彙題，會需要精細地分辨上下文義，或是熟記搭配詞（collocations）。

文法題：文法題則多半測驗基礎文法，同學不用死記文法，應該是要理解基礎觀念與句子結構。此外，詞類的考題比重大，值得下功夫去理解、記憶與背誦相關概念。

Sample Question

Last year, Andrea Choi _____ the Choi Economic Research Center at Upton University.

(A) to establish　　(B) established　　(C) was established　(D) establishing

---

選項是由establish搭配不同文法觀念的變化型組成，即「不定詞」、「過去式動詞」、「過去式被動語態」、「動名詞/現在分詞」。本題解法需要具備文法相關知識與對句子整體結構的了解，才能判斷空格的需求，選出正確答案。

A _____ from Jensen-Cokmes Corporation will be happy to meet with prospective job applications at the Westborough Job Fair.

(A) respresnt　　(B) respresnting　　(C) respresntative　　(D) respresntation

---

選項是由respresnt和衍生出的詞類所組成。本題解法需要基本文法知識（判斷需要的詞性）、了解句子整體結構（全句缺乏主詞）、了解上下文脈（判斷出應選與「人」有關的名詞）與了解字彙特徵（-tive結尾有代表「人」之意），才能判斷空格需求，選出正確答案。

Part 6 短文填空 (Text Completion)

題目類型：共12題，每題有4個選項，須從選項中選出一個最適合的答案。

測驗內容：測驗字彙和與語句Part 5相同，但為置入商業書信、電子郵件或備忘錄等文章中來做出題，因此比Part 5更需要掌握上下文脈。

測驗重點：「字彙」與「文法」

答題技巧：

❶ 秒殺30
與Part 5應答方式相同，每題約在30秒內完成。總題數12題，約3-5分鐘內完成。

❷ 直接切入
乍看下，Part 6的上下文句十分冗長且繁複，但只要直接切入空格，判斷所需搭配的是詞彙或片語語意、文法功能（如關係代名詞、時態、語態等）還是連接上下語意的連接詞或轉承詞，快速解題是不困難的。

❸ 習慣閱讀
Part 6出題，多為商業書信、電子郵件、備忘錄或是公告的特定文章，平時練習若有遇到習慣搭配用法或用字，宜多背誦記憶，可增加語感與日後作答速度。

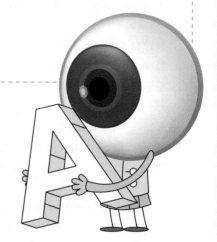

Sample Question

To: All Employees
From: Camille Raynes
Date: December 14
Re: Performance bonus

Dear Employees,
As you know, the past year was a great success for us. To reward you for your excellent performance, the Board of Directors has approved a bonus for all employees. This bonus will be _____ in your next paycheck. _____ ,

1 (A) involved	2 (A) Instead
(B) joined	**(B) In addition**
(C) composed	(C) Beforehand
(D) included	(D) Otherwise

we are now calculating wage increases for the upcoming year. Each employee's performance will be examined carefully as we determine the appropriate increase. All full-time employees are eligible for this increase. Your supervisor _____ you of the

3 (A) informed
(B) to inform
(C) will inform
(D) was informing

amount of your increase during the first week of January.

Thank you again for making last year such a success!
Sincerely,
Camille Raynes
Human Resources

Part 6由於是置入商業書信、電子郵件或備忘錄等文章中來出題，因此較更需要掌握上下文脈，但也因上下文提示，也更好掌握空格所需的語意。由上快速瀏覽，第一題測驗點為字彙，第二與第三題為句子結構與基本文法概念，內容與出題方向與Part 5相同。

(以上Sample Question取自多益官方網站Examinee Handbook)

眼球追蹤學習法

在學習方法中，眼球移動（簡稱眼動）是學習吸收與成效的重要指標。學習策略較優者，通常眼球凝視學習材料，時間較短，會有技巧性與多樣性地探索與掃視學習標的，因此注意力分配較集中；同時，為了更提高學習效能，優質的學習者將注意力投注於關鍵訊息或區域上，以有效應付學習資訊的獲得、運作、整合、儲存以及提取。

另一方面，當有圖像符號元素與語意之交叉搭配運用，題幹利用步驟標示與文字解析指令眼動的軌跡來區分不同先備知識與訊息吸收，學習者的反應答題時間會更縮短與有效益，以對學習效能產生助益。

當進行反覆練習的解題模式後，利用眼球追蹤學習與解題的模式，學習者會由原先的被引導模式，逐漸轉化成自發性的習慣，日後若學習者能夠主動控制自己的學習程，學習效果會更獨立，且會更主動地運用策略來解構學習資訊與材料。接下來，讓我們活動一下眼球。

體驗區

請先閱讀下列文字

題目

To supervise the new factory project, our president _____ visits our branches in Hsinchu.

(A) frequence   (B) frequent   (C) frequency   (D) frequently

答案 D

秒殺策略

① 判斷題型

由選項得知，測驗點為「詞類變化」。

② 判斷空格需要何種詞類

分析句子，To supervise, ...our president / visits /our branches in Hsinchu，主詞/動作皆完整敘述，空格又放主詞後，動詞前，立即聯想是「副詞」。

③ 驗證答案

選項唯一副詞字尾為frequently，是頻率副詞。其位置為：BE動詞，助動詞後，一般動詞前，符合本題要求♛

當學習者進入解析的文字閱讀階段，會依照文字敘述去解構題目，輸入解題順序，並同時在搜尋前面所學過的文法概念或相關的訊息，眼動軌跡應該也一直在解題文字上凝視或來回掃視。而當腦中處理文字或文法概念不通順時，眼動有兩種方式，一是回去瀏覽解析文字，二從解析文字中回去重新檢視題幹，此時，眼球落點便需時間與腦中所接收的指示做配合與尋找才知道要從哪看起。不論是方式一或方式二，解題或學習的反應時間都會拉長。

　　現在，我們來做一次另一種體驗。

請先閱讀下列文字：

❷ 看全句

To supervise the new factory project, our president _____ visits our branches in Hsinchu.

❶ 看選項

(A) frequence　　　(B) frequent　　　(C) frequency　　　(D) frequently

秒殺策略

❶ 判斷題型

由選項得知，測驗點為「詞類變化」。

❷ 判斷空格需要何種詞類

分析句子，To supervise, ...our president / visits /our branches in Hsinchu，主詞/動作皆完整敘述，空格又放主詞後，動詞前，立即聯想是「副詞」。

❸ 驗證答案

選項唯一副詞字尾為frequently，是頻率副詞。其位置為：BE動詞，助動詞後，一般動詞前，符合本題要求 ♛

　　當進入解析的文字閱讀時，腦中一樣依照文字敘述去一步一步解構題目，並同時在搜尋前面所學過的文法概念或相關的訊息，眼動軌跡也在解題文字上與題幹中來回掃視或凝視片段學習資料。

　　但是與上一組體驗不同是，對照解析的步驟有框出範圍與步驟符號來提示眼球落點的地方，此時眼動方式會立即隨著指示移動進行腦部資訊處理，學習者便可以很有效率地依步驟指示去解構題目，達到每題秒殺的速度。

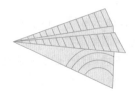

0.2

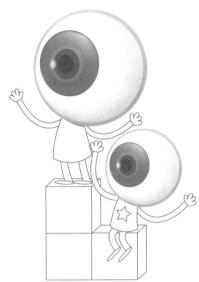

暖身 (Warm Up)

句子組成要素

　　英文的組成元素包括單字（詞）、片語、子句、和句子。正確的文法觀念，就是了解這些元素在句中的位置、作用與彼此之間的關係。

　　以下以這些元素在句中所扮演的**功能**來分類。組成元素，簡單説，主要包括主詞和述部，次要包含了受詞、補語、限定詞、修飾語、補足語和同位語。

❶　主詞：述部的主體

　　位置： 位於動詞之前，但遇特殊句型，如倒裝句時，主詞便位於動詞或助動詞後面

　　種類： 名詞（片語）、代名詞、數詞、不定詞、動名詞、名詞子句和名詞化的形容詞

· I am writing to confirm a reservation for a single room tomorrow.

　　（我來函確認明天的單人房預約。）→ I 當主詞

· Smoking is not allowed in that restaurant.

　　（此餐廳不允許抽菸。）→ smoking 當主詞

· The rich will not be influenced by the new policy.

　　（新政策不會影響富人。）→ the rich 當主詞

❷　述部：說明主詞發出的動作或具有的特徵和狀態

　　位置： 主詞之後

　　種類： 動詞（片語）、助動詞加動詞、連綴動詞加補語

· Mr. Smith postponed answering the client's letter.

　　（Smith 先生延後回信給那客戶。）→ postpone 後當述部

· You may keep the invoice for the order.

　　（你可以保存訂單的發票。）→ may keep 後當述部

· The shareholders seemed satisfied with the final decision at the annual meeting.

　　（股東似乎滿意在年度大會上所做的最後決定。）→ seemed satisfied with 後當述部

3 受詞：承受動作的對象

　　位置：及物動詞與介詞後面

　　種類：名詞（片語）、代名詞、數詞、不定詞、動名詞、名詞子句

· We plan to attend the trade show tomorrow.

　　（我們計畫明天去參加商展。）→ the trade show 當受詞

· Ms. Girard expects to get the promotion within one year.

　　（Girard 期盼一年內可以升遷。）→ to get the promotion 當受詞

· Our package designer suggests that we develop more sustainable packaging.

　　（我們的包裝設計師建議我們應該發展多些永續的包裝材料。）→ that 名詞子句當受詞

4 補語：補充說明主詞或受詞的身份、特徵和狀態

　　位置：主詞補語位於連綴動詞之後；受詞補語位於受詞之後

　　種類：名詞（片語）、代名詞、形容詞、分詞、數詞、不定詞、動名詞、介詞片語、副詞及名詞子句

· The attendance of the seminar last week was low.

　　（上星期的專題研討會出席率很低。）→ low 當主詞補語

· The worst is still to come.

　　（最糟的還在後頭。）→ to come 當主詞補語

· We all found the macaroons a bit hard but fantastic.

　　（我們一致認為這馬卡龍有點硬但嘗起來棒極了。）→ a bit hard 與 fantastic 當受詞補語

5 修飾語：具有形容詞或副詞作用的詞語

　　位置：欲修飾的詞彙、片語前後，或句首

　　種類：副詞（片語）、形容詞（片語）、介詞片語、不定詞片語等

· The diversified company can offer us what we need now.

　　（這多元化的公司可以提供我們現在所需要的東西。）→ diversified 修飾 company

· The game was postponed because of rain.

　　（球賽因為下雨被延期了）→ because of rain 修飾 was postponed

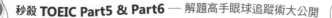
· To improve the relationship between two sides, let's take action now.

（為改善雙方關係，現在採取行動吧！）→ to improve ...between two sides 修飾後面主要句

單詞（Word）

單詞（又稱為詞或詞語）是能獨立運用並含有語義內容或語用內容的最小單位。英文單詞依其在句子中的功能，共分為八類，稱為「八大詞性」。背誦單字時，務必同時記憶詞性。以下列簡略列出八大詞類。

❶ 名詞 (noun) n.

· attention, conference, delivery, deficit

❷ 代名詞 (pronoun) pron.

· we, theirs, some, others,

❸ 形容詞 (adjective) adj.

· available, connected, deluxe, informative

❹ 動詞 (verb) v.

· assemble, conclude, fluctuate, inquire

❺ 副詞 (adverb) adv.

· constantly, partially, physically, significantly

❻ 介系詞 (preposition) prep.

· in, on, at, of, for

❼ 連接詞 (conjunction) conj.

· and, if, when, as well as, not only...but also

❽ 感嘆詞 (interjection) int.

· wow, ouch, ah, oops

片語（Phrase）

兩個（或以上）單詞組合後，具有某類詞作用的字群，片語中無主詞和述部。

種類：名詞片語、形容詞片語、副詞片語、動詞片語、不定詞片語、動名詞片

語、分詞片語、介系詞片語、連接詞片語、感歎詞片語等，以下簡列八類片語。

❶ 名詞片語

- Men and women are equal.

  （男人和女人是平等的。）→ Men and women 為名詞片語，做全句主詞

❷ 代名詞片語

- These programs are all linked to one another and so have to be changed together.

  （這些程式是互相連結的，所以要一起更改。）→ one another 為代名詞片語

❸ 形容詞片語

- This is an issue of great importance to our company.

  （這對我們公司來說是重要的議題。）→ of great importance 為形容詞片語

❹ 副詞片語

- I shall meet the client in the lobby.

  （我將會在大廳與客戶見面。）→ in the lobby 為副詞片語

❺ 動詞片語

- The train is scheduled to depart from platform 1.

  （火車預計從第一月台出發。）→ depart from 為動詞片語

❻ 介系詞片語

- In teamwork, different personalities, without balancing each other, may cause conflicts.

  （團隊工作中，不同個性，無互相平衡，可能會造成衝突。）→ without 介系詞片語

❼ 連接詞片語

- Henry can speak English as well as Japanese fluently.

  (Henry 說英語和日文一樣流暢)→as well as 為連接詞片語

❽ 感嘆詞片語

- My goodness! What an awful mess!

  （天呀！簡直一團糟！）→My goodness! 為感嘆詞片語

子句（Clause）

　　子句為比片語規模更大的結構，有包含主詞和述部，但其功能與片語相同。英文文法中三大子句。要注意的是，這些子句為句子的一部份，不可獨立存在。

　　種類：名詞子句、形容詞子句、副詞子句

❶ 名詞子句：包括間接問句與 that 子句

　　功能：作主詞、作受詞、作補語、作同位語用

- What the editor-in-chief decided then **seemed very reasonable**.

　　（總編輯當時決定的事似乎非常合理。）→ what 子句作主詞

- Do you know where the shuttle bus stop is?

　　（您知道接駁車站牌在哪裡嗎？）→ where 子句作受詞

- The bottom line is that we can satisfy you with low price.

　　（重點是我們可以以低價與準時交貨滿足您需求。）→that 子句作補語

- The president announced the news that the financial problems would be solved soon.

　　（總裁宣布財務問題很快會解決的。）→ that 子句作 the news 同位語

❷ 形容詞子句：即關係子句

　　功能：修飾主詞、修飾受詞、修飾主詞補語

- The first candidate that you interviewed seems qualified for the job.

　　（你剛面談的第一位候選人似乎很適合這工作。）→ that 子句修飾主詞

- The secretary lost all the papers that we handed in yesterday.

　　（秘書把我們昨天交出的文件弄不見了。）→ that 子句修飾受詞

- This is the reason why the chairman resigned.

　　（這就是主席辭職的原因。）→ why 子句修飾主詞補語

❸ 副詞子句：由表時間、條件、原因、讓步及附帶條件的連接詞所引導的子句

　　功能：修飾動詞、修飾形容詞、修飾副詞

- The both parties had come to an agreement when the meeting came to an end.

　　（當會議尾聲時，雙方已達成共識。）→ when 子句修飾動詞 had come to an agreement

- We are glad because we can cooperate with you again.

　　（我們很高興可以再次與您合作。）→ because 子句修飾形容詞 glad

- The new employee worked so hard that she got noticed quickly.
  （新員工很努力工作以致於她可以很快被注意到。）→ so... that 子句修飾副詞 hard

句子（Sentence）

　　句子為將兩個或兩個以上的詞按照語序加以排列與組合而成，並表達出完整的意思。本組成元素已在前方提過，接下來將句子做簡單介紹。

→ 以功能分類，包括

❶ 直述句：包括肯定與否定

- According to etiquette, you have to dress up for the occasion.
  （根據禮節，你必須在那場合盛裝打扮。）→肯定句
- The manager didn't authorize me to act for him while he was away.
  （經理在外出時並無授權給我代理他職務。）→ 否定句

❷ 疑問句：包括 yes/no 問句、wh-問句與附加問句

- Did any customers complain about our merchandise and prices?
  （有任何顧客抱怨我們的商品與價錢嗎。）→ yes/no 問句
- What is your friend arguing about with the receptionist?
  （你朋友和接待員在爭執什麼呢?）→ wh-問句
- You have itemized the groceries we need for the party, haven't you?
  （你已經列好我們派對所需的雜物清單，不是嗎?）→ haven't you 附加問句

❸ 祈使句：原形動詞為首

- Be careful. The CFO can't tolerate any discrepancies in prices.
  （小心點。財務長無法忍受報價有任何出入。）→ Be careful. 祈使句

❹ 驚嘆句：包括由 what 或 how 所引導的驚嘆句

- What a shame!
  （真可惜！）→ what+N 的驚嘆句
- How beautiful the city is!
  （這城市真美！）→ how+adj 的驚嘆句

➔ **以結構分類，包括**

❶ **簡單句：五大基本句型包含所有的簡單句型態**

· The white wine retails at $ 20 a bottle.

（這白酒零售價 20 美元。）→ 只包括一個主詞和一個述部

❷ **合句：對等連接詞或分號將兩個（或以上）的簡單句結合一起**

· I am tied up in traffic and you have to host the meeting for me.

（我塞車了，你必須替我主持會議。）→ 由對等連接詞連接兩個簡單句

· Kopi Luwak is very expensive; however, it's worth it.

（麝香咖啡很貴；然而它很值得。）→ 由分號與轉承詞連接兩個簡單句

❸ **複句：由從屬連接詞將兩個（或以上）的簡單句結合一起**

· All effofts are made to rectify errors before the new product.

（在我們推出新產品前，所有努力都是為了矯正錯誤。）→ 由 before 連接兩個簡單句

❹ **混合句：含有對等連接詞和從屬連接詞，將三個或三個以上的簡單句結合**

· The tourist who was riding a bike fell down and got injured.

（正在騎腳踏車的遊客跌倒了又受傷。）→ 由 who 與 and 連接三個簡單句

英文五大基本句型

❶ S＋Vi（主詞＋不及物動詞）

· The clients arrived earlier.

（客戶提早到了。）→ 不及物動詞 arrive 後無須加受詞

❷ S＋Vi＋SC（主詞＋BE 動詞與連綴動詞＋主詞補語）

· The ticket is not valid for the return journey after the expiry date.

（在截止日過後，車票回程是無效的。）→ not valid 當補語說明前方主詞

❸ S＋Vt＋O（主詞＋及物動詞＋受詞）

· We can rent a car later.

（我們晚點可以租車。）→ 及物動詞 rent 後須加受詞 a car

❹ S＋Vt＋IO＋DO（主詞＋授與動詞＋間接受詞＋直接受詞）
　S＋Vt＋DO＋介詞＋IO（主詞＋授與動詞＋直接受詞＋介詞＋間接受詞）

· The university offers the outstanding student a scholarship.
　The university offers a scholarship to the outstanding student.

（這大學提供獎學金給這位傑出的學生。）→ scholarship 與 student 皆為受詞

❺ S＋Vt＋O＋OC（主詞＋及物動詞＋受詞＋受詞補語）

· Some negative feedbacks made the manager very depressed.

（有些負面的回應讓經理很沮喪。）→ the manager 後加形容詞 very depressed 當其補語

　註：其他各種句子都可由這一種基本句型擴展、變化或省略而構成。

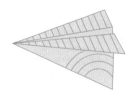

FAQ in TOEIC

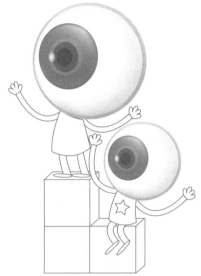

1

詞類 (Parts of Speech)

文法講解區

❶ 詞類 (Parts of Speech)

簡單看

　　英文句子由單字組成，其中單字依據其功能、形態與意義，分成八類。即一般所謂的「八大詞性」，構成英文文句的基本要素。每個英文單字都會歸屬於一個或多個詞性，隨著詞性不同，它的用法，位置，與修飾的對象亦有差別。八大詞類包括：名詞、代名詞、形容詞、動詞、副詞、介系詞、連接詞與感嘆詞。

　　「判斷詞性」在 TOEIC 的 Part 5 與 Part 6，題數佔此兩部份的四分之一比重，因此是否會判斷空格內的所屬詞性，是決勝關鍵點! 本單元將最常見的名詞、動詞、形容詞、副詞，做個別介紹。

秒殺策略

（1）判斷題型
（2）搜尋「關鍵字詞」或是「句型架構」

① **名詞：表達人、事、物、地等名稱**

> 什麼是補語？ 👑
> 1. 補語是指用字、片語、或子句補充說明句子主詞或受詞
> 2. 補語多半是名詞或形容詞

〉名詞的功能：當句中「主詞」、「受詞」或「補語」

> **EX** Mutual <u>funds</u> are not always a sound <u>investment</u>.
> （共同基金未必都是穩當的投資。）→ funds 當主詞，investment 當補語

〉名詞的位置：

• 冠詞、所有格、形容詞、介係詞、動詞、名詞之後

> **EX** According to our <u>return policies</u>, customers can return their items within 7 days.
> （根據我們退貨政策，顧客必須在他們所購買的商店退還物品。）→ return policies 置於所有格之後

• 關係子句、分詞片語、介係詞片語前

> **EX** Please keep <u>the invoice</u> with your purchase for future questions and return.
> （請保存隨貨附上的發票作為日後問題與退貨的證明。）→ invoice 置於分詞片語之前

〉常見的名詞字尾

意義	字尾	例字
動作	-al	refus**al** 拒絕
	-ance	acquaint**ance** 相識
	-age	dam**age** 傷害
	-ence	refer**ence** 參考
狀態	-ency	effici**ency** 效率
	-ion	discuss**ion** 討論
	-ment	develop**ment** 發展

意義	字尾	例字
性質	-dom	free**dom** 自由
	-ity	generos**ity** 慷慨
	-ness	friendli**ness** 友善
狀態	-th	leng**th** 長度
	-ty	special**ty** 專長

意義	字尾	例字
地方	-ory	fact**ory** 工廠
		lavat**ory** 廁所

意義	字尾	例字
科學	-ics	economi**cs** 經濟學
主義	-ism	tour**ism** 旅遊

意義	字尾	例字
~ 人	-ar -er -or -al -ard -ic -ent -ee -eer -tive	scholar 學者 manager 經理 editor 編者 professional 專家 steward 客機服務員 mechanic 技工 agent 代理者 nominee 被提名者 engineer 工程師 representative 代表

意義	字尾	例字
~ 物	-er	fertilizer 肥料 helicopter 直升機
	-or	elevator 電梯 refrigerator 冰箱

2 動詞：表示動作、存在或狀態

〉動詞.的功能：句子的心臟，不可少。有現在、過去、未來的時態變化

EX The president <u>implemented</u> an effective restructuring plan a month ago.

（總裁一個月前執行了很有效的重整計畫。）→ implement 表達 the president 的動作

〉動詞的位置

• 主詞之後（注意人稱單複數與時態）

EX We <u>closed down</u> our production facilities in Paris to keep cost down.

（我們關閉了 Paris 的生產設施以降低成本。）→ 放 we 主詞後

• 助動詞（+ 副詞）之後

EX The products <u>will be shipped</u> within the next two days to avoid late penalty.

（產品將在未來兩天出貨以免有延遲罰款。）→ 放 will 之後

• 祈使句句首（可搭配 please）

EX Please <u>communicate</u> the inventory challenge to our representatives.

（請向我們代表闡述存貨問題。）→ 祈使句句首

〉常見的動詞字尾

意義	字尾	例字
使…成為 使…化	-(i)fy -ize	classify 分類 organize 組織

意義	字尾	例字
使…	-en en-	lessen 減少 endanger 危害

意義	字尾	例字
（做）成為…	-ate	graduate 畢業 fluctuate 波動

意義	字尾	例字
做…	-ish	diminish 減少 publish 出版

3 形容詞：描述名詞的性質與狀態

〉形容詞的功能：修飾名詞

> **EX** What you have invested in our company is worthwhile.
>
> （你在我們公司所投資的是值得的。）
>
> → worthwhile 修飾 what... in our company，當主詞補語

〉形容詞的位置

• 名詞前、不定代名詞之後（**someone/ something/ anybody/ nothing**）

> **EX** Facebook has become an instrumental necessity for many small companies.
>
> （臉書已經成為很多小商家不可或缺的做生意工具。）
>
> → instrumental 放 necessity 前修飾

> **EX** The purchasing agent should know everything insufficient in warehouse.
>
> （採購代理應該知道倉庫不足的一切。）→ insufficient 放 everything 後修飾

• 放在 **BE** 動詞與連綴動詞之後，當主詞補語

> **EX** The marketing executive attends many training courses to remain competitive.
>
> （銷售主管參加很多訓練課程以保持競爭力。）
>
> → competitive 修飾主詞 the marketing executive

• 放在 **find / make / consider/ keep** 的受詞後，當受詞補語

> **EX** The new system makes the attendance records more manageable.
>
> （新系統使出缺席紀錄更容易掌控。）
>
> → more manageable 修飾受詞 the attendance records

〉常見的形容詞字尾

意義	字尾	例字
充滿…的	-ful -ous	help**ful** 有幫助的 courte**ous** 客氣的

意義	字尾	例字
可…的 能…的	-able -ible	valu**able** 有價值的 elig**ible** 有資格的

意義	字尾	例字
有… 性質的	-ish -ive -ly -some	self**ish** 自私的 nat**ive** 本土的 time**ly** 適時的 quarrel**some** 喜歡爭吵的

意義	字尾	例字
…的	-al -ic -ical -ial -ous	logic**al** 邏輯的 econom**ic** 經濟的 econom**ical** 節省的 essent**ial** 必要的 vari**ous** 不同的

意義	字尾	例字
有…的	-ed -ing	astonish**ed** 驚訝的 promis**ing** 有前途的

意義	字尾	例字
無…的	-less	use**less** 無用的 care**less** 粗心的

4 副詞：詳細地描述出動詞、形容詞、副詞或全句的意思

〉副詞的功能：修飾「動詞」、「形容詞」、「副詞」或「全句」

EX The administrative assistant behaved <u>professionally</u> at the meeting.

（那行政助理在會議上表現專業。）→ BE、助之後或一般動詞前，professionally 修飾 behave

〉副詞的位置

• 形容詞前

EX The workers were <u>keenly</u> aware of the issues of unemployment.

（工人敏銳地察覺到失業的議題。）→ keenly 放 aware 前修飾

• 一般動詞前或後、**BE** 動詞後

EX Call me <u>directly</u> after you check the tickets.

（在你確定好票卷後，請直接打電話給我。）→ 放 call me 之後，修飾動詞

EX Our guest house is <u>conveniently</u> located near the MRT.

（我們酒店位置便利位於捷運出口。）→ conveniently 放 BE 動詞後與過去分詞中間

- 全句首

  EX <u>Regrettably</u>, we can't proceed with the project as planned under time constraint.

  （遺憾地，在時間約束之下，我們無法如計畫般繼續那方案。）→ regrettably 修飾全句

- 特殊副詞（**enough** 與頻率副詞）

  EX Mr. Hoffman is qualified <u>enough</u> to lead the sales department.

  (Hoffman 先生，能力足夠到可以去領導銷售部門。）→ enough 放 qualified 後修飾

  EX It <u>usually</u> takes 10 minutes to have a daily meeting in our team.

  （我們團隊通常花十分鐘開每日會議。）→ 頻率副詞在 BE、助之後或一般動詞前

〉常見的副詞字尾

意義	字尾	例字
樣子 程度	-ly	innovative**ly** 創新地 frequent**ly** 常常

意義	字尾	例字
狀態 方向	-wise	like**wise** 同樣地 clock**wise** 順時鐘方向
朝…方向	-ward (s)	for**ward(s)** 向前地 back**ward(s)** 向後地

Mini Test 練習區 限時5分

1. To supervise the new factory project, our president _____ visits our branches in Hsinchu.
   (A) frequence   (B) frequent   (C) frequency   (D) frequently

2. _____ the standard operating procedures, and all in the team can cooperate effectively and positively.
   (A) Follow   (B) Following   (C) Followed   (D) To follow

3. According to the Home Electrical Fires report, leaking ceilings make the _____ of electrical fires higher.
   (A) possible   (B) possibly   (C) possibility   (D) impossible

4. Pliable working hours make employees' schedules _____, but it's also highly risky.
   (A) flex   (B) flexible   (C) flexibly   (D) flexibility

5. The statement details the documentation required and advance procedures needed for _____.
   (A) reimburse   (B) reimbursed   (C) reimbursing   (D) reimbursement

6. To adjust workforce, many workers are transferred to China; _____, their family still choose to stay in Taiwan.
   (A) despite   (B) but   (C) although   (D) however

7. The proposal about an exclusive agency they would like to offer _____ Linda a lot.
   (A) tempt   (B) tempted   (C) is tempted   (D) to tempt

8. It is rumored that the NEXT is _____ to merge with BEST Publisher next month.
   (A) like   (B) likely   (C) likes   (D) likeness

9. Highly _____ people always know their priorities and are clear on their direction.
   (A) produce   (B) production   (C) productive   (D) productively

10. Mr. Arnault has been strategizing to increase LVMH's revenue _____.
    (A) late   (B) lately   (C) latter   (D) later

Question 11-13 refer to the following advertisement

BEST dishes @ the BEST Cafe

The BEST Café is casual cafe with all the flavorings of Latin America. We offer a _____ of Latin American cuisines, like tropical potato salad, stuffed

    11 (A) vary
       (B) varied
       (C) various
       (D) variety

tortillas, potato pancakes topped with Mexican cheese, and cinnamon dusted sweet plantains. _____ , all food served is organic and good for your health.

       12 (A) And
         (B) Beside
         (C) Moreover
         (D) Instead of

Diners in the BEST Café can try our most notable dish - the pupusa – for breakfast, lunch, and dinner. It is the whole-grain flour tortilla stuffed with cheese and fried pork rinds. The distinct flavor _____ the chef's simple yet

           13 (A) reflects
            (B) reflected
            (C) have reflected
            (D) is reflected

high quality approach to Latin American cuisine. The BEST Café is located in the heart of Taipei City, across the street from Taipei Station. We are on the second floor of the Sun Plaza. Give the BEST Café a try next time when you are downtown.

1-10 Ans: 1.(D) 2.(A) 3.(C) 4.(B) 5.(D) 6.(D) 7.(B) 8.(B) 9.(C) 10.(B)

1. To supervise the new factory project, our president _____ visits our branches in Hsinchu.
   (A) frequence   (B) frequent   (C) frequency   (D) frequently

答案 D

眼球追蹤

❷ **看全句**
To supervise the new factory project, our | president _____ visits | our branches in Hsinchu.

❶ **看選項**
(A) frequence   (B) frequent   (C) frequency   ❸ (D) frequently

中譯 為了監督新廠計畫,我們總裁最近常去新竹分公司。

秒殺策略

❶ **判斷題型**

由選項得知,測驗點為「詞類變化」。

❷ **判斷空格需要何種詞類**

分析句子,To supervise, ...our president / visits /our branches in Hsinchu,主詞/動作皆完整敘述,空格又放**主詞後,動詞前**,立即聯想是「副詞」。

❸ **驗證答案**

選項唯一副詞字尾為 frequently,是**頻率副詞**。其位置為:**BE 動詞,助動詞後,一般動詞前**,符合本題要求。

檢查

(A) frequence,-ence 結尾,名詞(n)頻繁,屢次,刪除。

(B) frequent,-ent 結尾,形容詞(a)頻繁的,刪除。

(C) frequency,-cy 結尾,名詞(n)出現率,刪除。

(D) frequently,-ly 結尾,副詞(adv)頻繁地

故本題答案選 (D)

2. _____ the standard operating procedures, and all in the team can co-operate effectively and positively.

   (A) Follow   (B) Following   (C) Followed   (D) To follow

答案 A

眼球追蹤

❷ 看全句

_____ the standard operating procedures, and all in the team can cooperate effectively and positively.

❶ 看選項 ❸

 (A) Follow   (B) Following   (C) Followed   (D) To follow

中譯 按照標準作業程序進行，團隊中的每個人就能有效和積極地合作。

秒殺策略 👑

❶ 判斷題型

由選項得知，測驗點為「動詞用法」。

❷ 判斷空格需求

由 _____ the standard operating procedures / and / all in the team /can cooperate ...，得知有連接詞 and，可見前面亦為句子。但無主詞與動詞，立即聯想是「祈使句」。

❸ 驗證「祈使句」句型

搭配祈使句型，故選原形動詞 Follow。 👑

公式驗證：「**祈使句，and S + V**」的句型表「做…, 那麼…就會」。

檢查

(A) follow，原形動詞 👑
(B) following，動名詞，刪除。
(C) followed，過去式或過去分詞，刪除。
(D) To follow，不定詞，刪除。
故本題答案選 (A)

3. According to the Home Electrical Fires report, leaking ceilings make the _____ of electrical fires higher.
(A) possible   (B) possibly   (C) possibility   (D) impossible

答案 C

眼球追蹤

According to the Home Electrical Fires report, leaking ceilings make the _____ ❷ of electrical fires higher.

❶ 看選項

(A) possible   (B) possibly   ❸ (C) possibility   (D) impossible

中譯   根據 Home Electrical Fires 報告，天花板漏水使電器火災發生可能性較高。

秒殺策略 👑

❶ 判斷題型

由選項得知，測驗點為「**詞類變化**」。

❷ 判斷空格需要何種詞類

由make the _____ of 得知，定冠詞 the 後，of 前，應搭配名詞。

❸ 驗證答案

選項唯一名詞字尾為 possibility。👑

檢查

(A) possible，-ible 結尾，形容詞，刪除。（a）可能的
(B) possibly，-ibly 結尾，副詞，刪除。（adv）可能地，也許
(C) possibility，-ity 結尾，名詞。（n）可能性 👑
(D) impossible，-ible 結尾，形容詞，刪除。（a）不可能的
故本題答案選 (C)

4. Pliable working hours make employees' schedules _____, but it's also highly risky.

(A) flex　　　　(B) flexible　　　　(C) flexibly　　　　(D) flexibility

答案 B

眼球追蹤

Pliable working hours │make employees' schedules _____,│but it's also highly risky.

❶ **看選項**

(A) flex　　　❸　(B) flexible　　　(C) flexibly　　　(D) flexibility

中譯 彈性的工作時間讓員工的時程安排有彈性的，但它也是高風險的。

秒殺策略 👑

❶ **判斷題型**

由選項得知，測驗點為**「詞類變化」**。

❷ **判斷空格需要何種詞類**

看到 make / employees' schedules，make 為關鍵字，立即聯想可能是 make + O + OC 之句型。

❸ **搭配句型與語意**

make 的受詞補語（OC），有可能是形容詞、名詞、動詞，故先刪除副詞選項。再搭配語意，選形容詞 flexible。👑

檢查

(A) flex，（v）屈曲；收縮。語意不合，刪除。

(B) flexible-ible，結尾，形容詞（a）有彈性的 👑

(C) flexibly-ibly，結尾，副詞（adv）有彈性地，刪除。

(D) flexibility，-ity，結尾，名詞（n）靈活性；彈性（指狀態，非事務）。語意不合，刪除。

故本題答案選 (B)

5. The statement details the documentation required and advance procedures needed for _____.

(A) reimburse
(B) reimbursed
(C) reimbursing
(D) reimbursement

答案 D

眼球追蹤

The statement details the documentation required and advance procedures

needed |for ❷_____ .

❶ 看選項

(A) reimburse　　(B) reimbursed　　(C) reimbursing　　(D) reimbursement

中譯 　該敘述有詳細說明報銷時所需要的文件和事先程序。

秒殺策略 👑

❶ **判斷題型**

由選項得知，測驗點為「**詞類變化**」。

❷ **判斷空格需要何種詞類**

看到 for _____，關鍵字為介係詞for，立即聯想是「名詞」。

❸ **搭配句型與語意**

reimburse (v) 償還；歸還；補貼。用法：reimburse sb for sth，則動名詞 Ving 選項不合文法。reimbursement (n) 補貼，符合詞類與語意。👑

檢查

(A) reimburse，（v）償還；歸還；補貼詞性不合，刪除。

(B) reimbursed，動詞過去式或過去分詞詞性不合，刪除。

(C) reimbursing，動名詞詞性不合，刪除。

(D) reimbursement，（n）償還；歸還；補貼 👑

故本題答案選 (D)

6. To adjust workforce, many workers are transferred to China; _____, their family still choose to stay in Taiwan.
   (A) despite   (B) but   (C) although   (D) however

答案   D

眼球追蹤

❷ 看全句

To adjust workforce, many workers are transferred to China; _____, their family still choose to stay in Taiwan.

❶ 看選項

(A) despite   (B) but   (C) although   (D) however

中譯 為了調整勞動力，很多人被轉調到中國工作；然而，他們的家人仍留在台灣。

秒殺策略

❶ 判斷題型

由選項得知，測驗點為「**連接詞與轉承詞分辨**」。

❷ 判斷空格需要何種詞類

分析全句，由 many are transferred to China 與 their family remain in Taiwan 兩句為完整句。空格前，**有分號**，空格後，**有逗點**，立即聯想是「**轉承副詞**」。

❸ 搭配語意與文字使用

選項唯一轉承副詞為 however，亦符合語意。

檢查

(A) despite（prep），雖然，刪除。

(B) but（conj），但是，but 當對等連接詞，需要連接兩個對等的字詞片語或句子，刪除。

(C) although（conj），雖然，從屬連接詞，後面需要加從屬子句，刪除。

(D) however（adv），然而

故本題答案選 (D)

7. The proposal about an exclusive agency they would like to offer
_____ Linda a lot.

 (A) tempt   (B) tempted   (C) is tempted   (D) to tempt

答案   B

眼球追蹤

❷ 看全句

The proposal about an exclusive agency they would like to offer _____ Linda
a lot.

❶ 看選項

 (A) tempt   ❸ (B) tempted   (C) is tempted   (D) to tempt

中譯   對於他們希望提供獨家代理權的提議很吸引 Linda。

秒殺策略 👑

❶ 判斷題型

 由選項得知，測驗點為「**動詞變化**」。

❷ 判斷空格需求

 分析全句，由The proposal / about an exclusive agency they would like
to offer /_____ Linda a lot，得知主詞 the proposal，空格應找「主要動
詞」。

❸ 搭配語意與文字使用

 主詞 the proposal 為第三人稱單數，搭配時態要注意，第三人稱單數要加-s。
the proposal / tempt / Linda，依本句文意，用主動語態。👑

檢查

(A) 現在簡單主動，但第三人稱單數要加-s，刪除。

(B) 過去簡單主動 👑

(C) 現在簡單被動，語態不合，刪除。

(D) 不定詞，表目的，不為動詞，刪除。

故本題答案選 (B)

8. It is rumored that the NEXT is _____ to merge with BEST Publisher next month.
   (A) like   (B) likely   (C) likes   (D) likeness

答案 B

眼球追蹤

❷

It is rumored that the NEXT | is _____ to | merge with BEST Publisher next month.

❶ 看選項 ❸
(A) like   (B) likely   (C) likes   (D) likeness

中譯 傳言，NEXT 公司很可能與 BEST 出版社在下個月進行合併。

秒殺策略 👑

❶ **判斷題型**

由選項得知，測驗點為「**詞類變化**」。

❷ **判斷空格需要何種詞類**

由 the NEXT / is _____ to merge....，空格前有 BE 動詞，後面搭配 toV，空格應為「形容詞」。

❸ **搭配公式與語意**

be likely to V，符合語意。👑

檢查

(A) like，（v）喜歡；（prep）像，兩者語意與詞性搭配皆不合，刪除。
(B) likely，（adj）很可能的，多搭配 be likely to V/ that 子句 的句型 👑
(C) likes，主詞第三人稱單數，現在簡單式動詞，語意與詞性皆不合，刪除。
(D) likeness，（n）相像，語意與詞性皆不合，刪除。
故本題答案選(B)

9. Highly ＿＿＿＿＿ people always know their priorities and are clear on their direction.

(A) produce   (B) production   (C) productive   (D) productively

答案 C

眼球追蹤

Highly ＿＿＿＿＿ people ❷ always know their priorities and are clear on their direction.

❶ 看選項

(A) produce   (B) production   ❸ (C) productive   (D) productively

中譯 高生產力的人總是知道自己的優先事項，並明確自己的方向。

秒殺策略 👑

❶ 判斷題型

由選項得知，測驗點為「詞類變化」。

❷ 判斷空格需要何種詞類

由Highly ＿＿＿＿＿ people always know their priorities... 得知，空格前為副詞，空格後為名詞，立即聯想是「形容詞」。

❸ 搭配語意

highly productive 表「有高度生產力的」，修飾後方 people，符合語意。👑

檢查

(A) produce，-duce 結尾，動詞，刪除。（v）生產

(B) production，-tion 結尾，名詞，刪除。（n）生產

(C) productive，-tive 結尾，形容詞（a）有生產力的 👑

(D) productively，-ly 結尾，副詞，刪除。（adv）有結果地

故本題答案選 (C)

10. Mr. Arnault has been strategizing to increase LVMH's reve-nue _____.

(A) late (B) lately (C) latter (D) later

答案 B

眼球追蹤

❷ 看全句

Mr. Arnault has been strategizing to increase LVMH's revenue _____.

❶ 看選項

(A) late **❸** (B) lately (C) latter (D) later

中譯 Arnault 先生近來已經持續策略性的增加 LVMH 的收入。

秒殺策略

❶ 判斷題型

由選項得知，測驗點為「late 字群變化用法」。

❷ 判斷空格需要何種詞類

分析全句，Mr. Arnault ／has been strategizing ／to increase LVMH's revenue _____，主詞/動作皆完整敘述，

立即聯想是「副詞」，修飾全句。考慮(A)(B)(D)可為副詞的選項。

❸ 搭配語意，用時態驗證

(A)(B)(D)選項逐一驗證後，選(B)。lately (adv) 近來地，用在句中當時間標記，會搭配現在完成（完成進行）式，正符合 has been strategizing 的用法。

檢查

(A) late，（a）晚的；（adv）遲地，語意不合，刪除。

(B) lately，（adv）近來地

(C) latter，（adj）最近的，後者的詞性與語意不符，刪除。

(D) later，（a）較晚的；（adv）後來，語意不符，刪除。

故本題答案選 (B)

1 詞類

2 特殊動詞

3 時態

4 主詞與動詞的一致性

5 被動語態

11-13 請參閱下列一則廣告

中譯

　　BEST 咖啡館是家休閒的有拉丁美洲所有風味的咖啡館。我們提供各式各樣的拉美美食，像熱帶馬鈴薯沙拉，充滿餡料的玉米餅，淋上墨西哥奶酪的馬鈴薯煎餅，與撒上肉桂的甜蕉。此外，所有供應的食物都是有機和對你的健康有最好。

　　來 BEST 咖啡館，可以嘗試我們最招牌的菜 – pupusa 厚玉米餅 – 早餐，午餐和晚餐都有提供。它是用全麥麵粉做的玉米餅，包奶酪餡與炸豬皮。此獨特的風味反射出我們廚師簡單但高品質來做拉丁美洲菜餚的方法。

　　BEST 咖啡館位於台北市的中心，台北車站對面。我們是在 Sun Plaza 的二樓。下一次當你在市中心時，試一下 BEST 咖啡館。

秒殺策略

11. 答案　**(D) variety**
　　　We offer a **variety** of Latin American cuisines.
　　解題　a variety of 各式各樣的。由 a 與 of 得知，需要名詞。

12. 答案　**(C) Moreover**
　　　Moreover, all food served is organic and good for your health.
　　解題　moreover 為承接上下語意的副詞，修飾後面全句。
　　　(A) And (conj)，且 （不可放句首）(B) Beside (prep) 在...旁邊
　　　(C) Moreover (adv) 此外 (D) Instead of (prep) 反而不

13. 答案　**(A) reflects**
　　　The distinct flavor **reflects** our chef's simple yet high quality approach to Latin American cuisine.
　　解題　reflect (v) 顯示，反映出。flavor /reflect our chef's simple yet high quality approach 為主動關係，且用現在簡單式描述事實即可，第三人稱單數要加 s。

成為多益勝利組的字彙練功區

文法講解區	Mini Test 限時 5 分練習區
mutual funds **n.** 共同基金	supervise [`supə‚vaɪz] **v.** 監督
return policy **n.** 退貨政策	branch [bræntʃ] **n.** 分公司；分店
invoice [`ɪnvɔɪs] **n.** 發票	standard operating procedures (SOP) 標準作業程序
reference [`rɛfərəns] **n.** 參考	cooperate [ko`ɑpə‚ret] **v.** 合作
agent [`edʒənt] **n.** 代理者；代理商	pliable working hours **n.** 彈性工作時間
nominee [‚nɑmə`ni] **n.** 被提名者	flexible [`flɛksəbḷ] **a.** 彈性的
representative [rɛprɪ`zɛntətɪv] **n.** 代表	risky [`rɪskɪ] **a.** 高風險的
implement [`ɪmpləmənt] **v.** 執行	reimburse [‚riɪm`bɝs] **v.** 償還；退款報銷
cost down **v.** 降低成本	workforce [`wɝk‚fɔrs] **n.** 勞動力
ship [ʃɪp] **v.** 運送，裝運	transfer [træns`fɚ] **v.** 轉調；調職
penalty [`pɛnḷtɪ] **n.** 罰款	exclusive agency **n.** 獨家代理權
inventory [`ɪnvən‚torɪ] **n.** 存貨(清單)	proposal [prə`pozl] **n.** 提議
diminish [də`mɪnɪʃ] **v.** 減少	merge [mɝdʒ] **v.** 合併
fluctuate [`flʌktʃʊ‚et] **v.** 波動	highly productive **a.** 有高度生產力的
warehouse [`wɛr‚haʊs] **n.** 倉庫	strategize [strə`tidʒaɪz] **v.** 制訂策略
attendance record **n.** 缺席紀錄	revenue [`rɛvə‚nju] **n.** 收入；收益
eligible [`ɛlɪdʒəbḷ] **a.** 有資格的	variety [və`raɪətɪ] **n.** 多樣性
economic [‚ikə`namɪk] **a.** 經濟的	cuisine [kwɪ`zin] **n.** 烹飪；菜餚
essential [ɪ`sɛnʃəl] **a.** 必要的	distinct [dɪ`stɪŋkt] **a.** 獨特的
administrative assistant **n.** 行政助理	approach [ə`protʃ] **n.** 方法；途徑
unemployment [‚ʌnɪm`plɔɪmənt] **n.** 失業	high quality [haɪ`kwɑlətɪ]] **n.** 高品質
qualified [`kwɑlə‚faɪd] **a.** 合格的；勝任的	
sales department **n.** 銷售部門	
innovatively [`ɪno‚vetɪvlɪ] **adv.** 創新地	

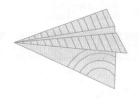

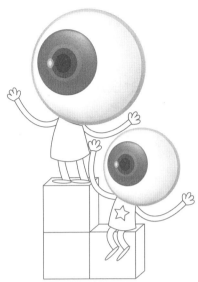

2
動詞 (Verbs)

文法講解區

❷ 動詞 (Verbs)

▋ 簡單看

　　動詞即描述主詞的「動作」和「狀態」之詞語。英文與中文不同，處理動詞時，要注意時態、情態、語態與主詞的人稱變化。動詞可以視為一個句子的心臟與靈魂，句中主要動詞若與第二個動詞結合時，可用不定詞、動名詞、對等連接詞、從屬連接詞等方式，在後面幾章會陸續講解。

　　英文句子的句型決定於動詞的特性，因此本章會根據五大句型的模式，來分類 TOEIC 常見的特殊動詞。

▋ 秒殺策略

（1）判斷動詞種類
（2）分析動詞搭配用法

1 五大句型簡介

不及物動詞類

1. S + Vi（主詞＋不及物動詞）

〉本類動詞本身意思清楚，可完整表達句子。後不須接「受詞」或「補語」。

〉不及物動詞沒有直接受詞，所以如果後面有受詞時，要先加上介系詞。

EX All employees must <u>conform</u> to the policy on the use of office supplies.

（所有員工必須遵守辦公文具的使用政策。）→ conform 搭配 to 才加受詞

2. S + Vi + SC（主詞＋BE 動詞與連綴動詞＋主詞補語）

〉本類動詞意思不完全清楚，要補充字詞（即「補語」)協助。

EX Oil prices have <u>remained</u> <u>stable</u> under government control for years.

（油價在政府數年的控制下維持平穩。）→ remain 後加形容詞 stable 當補語

及物動詞類

3. S + Vt + O（主詞＋及物動詞＋受詞）

〉本類動詞必加受詞，但不需補語，即能表示完整句意。

EX The manager held lots of workshops to <u>enhance</u> our production capabilities.

（經理舉辦很多專題討論會來增加我們的產能。）→ enhance 直接加受詞

4. S + Vt + IO + DO（主詞＋授與動詞＋間接受詞＋直接受詞）
S + Vt + DO + 介詞 + IO（主詞＋授與動詞＋直接受詞＋介詞＋間接受詞）

〉本類動詞需要兩個受詞，間接受詞（多用來表示人）通常在前，直接受詞（多用來表示物）通常在後。

〉兩受詞位置對調時，有固定搭配的介係詞。

EX Mr. Huber requested that the president <u>grant</u> <u>him</u> an interview.

（Huber 先生請求總裁給他會面的機會。）→ him 與 interview 都是 grant 的受詞

5. S + Vt + O + OC（主詞＋及物動詞＋受詞＋受詞補語）

〉本類動詞加受詞後，需要補語協助說明受詞才能表示完整句意。

EX The topic of the lecture is about how to get <u>our priorities</u> <u>straight</u>.

（本次演講主題是有關如何分清楚事情的輕重緩急。）→ our priorities 後加形容詞 straight 當其補語

2 不及物動詞 + 介係詞 + 受詞

新多益常出現組合字			
act for	代理	go for	襲擊；力爭
allow for	斟酌	go over	複習；視察
apply for	申請	go with	連同；與…搭配
apply to	適用	interfere with	干涉
amount to	相當於	live through	熬過
answer for	負責	look into	調查
appeal to	訴諸於；吸引	make for	走向；使成
associate with	結交；聯想	narrow down	減少
attribute to	歸因於	pass for	被誤認為
bargain with	討價還價	preside over	管理；領導
call for	要求	prevent from	預防
coincide with	同時；一致	prohibit from	禁止
collaborate with	與…合作	qualify for	具…資格
compensate for	賠償	react to	對…起反應
comply with	遵守	respond to	回覆；回應
consist of	由…組成	restrict to	僅限於
contribute to	貢獻；捐助	see about	安排；考慮
deal with	處理；交易	see to	注意；照料
dispense with	省卻；無需	stand for	代表；忍受
dispose of	處理；除去	sympathize with	同情
enroll for	報名上課	take for	誤認為
fall to	開始	take to	喜歡；開始從事
fill in / out	填寫	transfer to	轉移到

EX The staff in Four Seasons Hotels are calling for a raise in pay.
（四季酒店員工正要求加薪。）

EX Ms. Paglia speaks Japanese well enough to pass for a native speaker.
（Paglia 女士日語說地好到被誤認為是日本人。）

3 不完全不及物動詞（**BE** 動詞或連綴動詞）**+ 主詞補語**

〉連綴動詞包括

〔似乎〕 類	seem, appear
〔保持〕 類	remain, stay, keep, continue, hold
〔感覺〕 類	look, sound, smell, sound, taste, feel
〔變成〕 類	become, come, go, get, grow, turn, fall, run

〉主詞補語可為形容詞、名詞或介係詞片語

EX Our production process is <u>fully compliant with the industry standard.</u>

（我們的生產製造流程完全遵照業界標準。）→ is 後加形容詞 compliant 當主詞補語

EX US health care industry is reported to have become <u>a giant money making scam.</u>

（根據報導，美國醫療保健行業，已成為一個巨大的詐騙集團。）

→ become 後加 a...scam 名詞當主詞補語

EX One victim sent to the hospital remained <u>in serious condition.</u>

（被送往醫院的患者仍然病情嚴重。）

→ remain 後加介系詞片語 in serious condition 當主詞補語

4 及物動詞 **+ 特定介係詞**

搭配 for

exchange A for B	compensate A for B	substitute A for B
把 A 換成 B	向 A 賠償 B	用 A 替 B

搭配 of

convince A of B	notify/inform A of B	remind A of B
使 A 相信 B	通知 A B	提醒 A 關於 B

搭配 with

accommodate A with B	provide/supply A with B	replace A with B
向 A 提供 B	向 A 提供 B	用 B 代替 A

搭配 from

eliminate A from B	prohibit A from B	distinguish/tell A from B
使 A 從 B 淘汰／消除	禁止 A 去做 B	分辨 A 與 B

搭配 into

talk / persuade A into B	convert A into B	translate A into B
說服 A 去做 B	把 A 兌換成 B	把 A 翻譯成 B

5 及物動詞 + 兩個受詞

這邊的及物動詞即是授與動詞，相對的介係詞如下，請用力背。

授與動詞	DO（直接受詞）	介係詞	IO（間接受詞）
award, bring, give, grant, hand, lend, mail, offer, pass, send, offer, show, tell, write	sth	to	sb
buy, choose, make, order, save		for	
ask, demand		of	

EX The Awards committees awarded Barack Obama the Nobel Peace Prize for 2009.

＝The Awards committees awarded the Nobel Peace Prize for 2009 to Barack Obama.

（獎勵委員會授予 Barack Obama 2009 年的諾貝爾和平獎。）

6 及物動詞 + 受詞 + 受詞補語

〉使役動詞

(1) have/ make + O	原 V（主動）	不論主動或被動，受詞後面加的，皆為使役動詞之受詞補語。
	Vpp（被動）	
(2) let+ O	原 V（主動）	
	BE + Vpp（被動）	
(3) get+ O	to V（主動）	
	Vpp（被動）	

make/ have/ let/ get + O + adj.（形容詞當受詞補語）

> **EX** The CEO had the assistant <u>send</u> a copy of this notice to you.
> ＝The CEO had a copy of this notice <u>sent</u> to you.
> （執行長請助理發送此通知的副本給你。）

〉感官動詞

感官動詞 + O +	原 V / Ving （主動）
	Vpp （被動）

感官動詞包括：see, watch, look at, hear, listen to, feel, notice, observe

> **EX** The CFO has noticed the company's revenue decrease slightly.
> （財務長已經注意到公司營收有稍微地下滑。）
> 註：CFO＝chief financial officer

〉【視為、定義、指派】動詞

regard, see, view, take, see		把 A 視為 B
look upon, think of, refer to	A as B	
designate		把 A 指派為 B
define		把 A 定義成 B
consider AB 把 A 視為 B		

> **EX** Hong Kong has been regarded as a commercial hub for Southeast Asia for centuries.
> （幾世紀以來，香港一直被視為東南亞地區的商業中心。）

〉**find, keep, leave + O + OC (adj / Ving / Vpp)**

> **EX** Providing high-quality service keeps your customers coming back.
> （提供高品質服務會讓您的顧客再次光顧。）

Mini Test 練習區　限時 5 分

1. The digital media has drastically affected publishing in their never ending quest to stay _____.

   (A) profit　　　(B) profitable　　　(C) profitably　　　(D) profitability

2. To protect personal privacy, landlords are usually not allowed to _____ tenants' marital status.

   (A) ask for　　　(B) direct at　　　(C) inquire about　　　(D) preside over

3. Mr. Krumholz had the travel agent _____ his itinerary for the business trip to the UK.

   (A) plan　　　(B) planning　　　(C) planned　　　(D) to plan

4. To boost tourism, the local government _____ special buses for the tourists so that they have easy access to all tourist attractions.

   (A) offers　　　(B) gives　　　(C) provides　　　(D) supplies

5. After the president announced his resignation, Mr. Smith was _____ as the successor and assumed presidential powers.

   (A) considered　　　(B) referred　　　(C) defined　　　(D) designated

6. The fluency in German with which he could discuss commercial law made him _____ for the position.

   (A) perfect　　　(B) perfectly　　　(C) perfection　　　(D) perfectionism

7. Many doctors suggest that we _____ vegetable oil for butter in daily cooking.

   (A) replace　　　(B) exchange　　　(C) convert　　　(D) substitute

8. For tax deductions, most small businesses are willing to _____ some portion of their profits to charitable organizations each year.

   (A) attribute　　　(B) compensate　　　(C) contribute　　　(D) apply

9. The more government interference in the economy _____ a worsening of economic growth.

   (A) applied to　　　(B) called for　　　(C) coincided with　　　(D) disposed of

10. Once your visa has already expired, you must _____ a new one overseas before re-entering the U.S.

    (A) allow for　　　(B) apply for　　　(C) go for　　　(D) pass for

Question 11-13 refer to the following memo

To: All Personal
From: Henry Rollins, Officer Manager
Subject: New Rules for Office Supplies

Dear All,

Office supplies have been be a major expense recently in our company. Therefore, a new policy concerning the office supplies will be issued next week. Ms. Hallowell will be in charge of thesupply closet and she will keep it _____. Anyone requiring supplies needs to have the new request form

11 (A) lock
   (B) locking
   (C) locked
   (D) to lock

_____ out and hands it to her. The form is available in her office.

12 (A) fill
   (B) filling
   (C) filled
   (D) to fill

Once everyone can _____ the new regulation corporately, it will help to

   13 (A) abide by
      (B) dispense with
      (C) enroll for
      (D) take to

ensure better quality and the resources management in our company.

Thanks for your cooperation.

1-10 Ans: 1.(B) 2.(C) 3.(A) 4.(C) 5.(D) 6.(A) 7.(D) 8.(C) 9.(C) 10.(B)

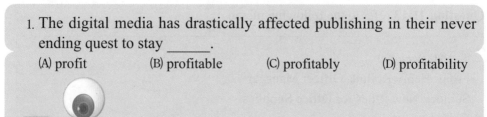

1. The digital media has drastically affected publishing in their never ending quest to stay _____.
(A) profit　　　(B) profitable　　　(C) profitably　　　(D) profitability

答案 B

眼球追蹤

The digital media has drastically affected publishing in their never ending

quest to ❷ stay _____.

❶ 看選項

(A) profit　　❸ (B) profitable　　(C) profitably　　(D) profitability

中譯 數位媒體極大地影響了出版業，並使他們永無止境的需要追求保持盈利。

秒殺策略 👑

❶ 判斷題型

由選項得知，測驗點為「詞類變化」。

❷ 判斷空格需要何種詞類

由空格前關鍵字 stay 得知，測驗「連綴動詞」觀念。

❸ 驗證答案

連綴動詞後面搭配形容詞，-able 結尾為形容詞，故選 profitable。👑

檢查

(A) profit（n）盈利；收益（v）得益；獲益刪除。

(B) profitable（a）有營利的 👑

(C) profitably（adv）有利地；有益地刪除。

(D) profitability（n）收益性；利益率刪除。

故本題答案選 (B)

2. To protect personal privacy, landlords are usually not allowed to
_____ tenants' marital status.
(A) ask for   (B) direct at   (C) inquire about   (D) preside over

答案 C

眼球追蹤

To protect personal privacy, landlords are usually not allowed to _____ ten-ants' marital status.

❶ 看選項

(A) ask for   (B) direct at   ❷ (C) inquire about   (D) preside over

中譯 為了保護個人隱私，房東通常不被允許打聽房客的婚姻狀況。

秒殺策略 👑

❶ 判斷題型

由選項得知，「片語搭配題型」。將選項帶進題目即可。

❷ 依語意個別判斷

依語意個別判斷，選 inquire about (v) 詢問（問題）。👑

檢查

(A) ask for （v）請求，要求語意不符，刪除。
(B) direct at （v）針對語意不符，刪除。
(C) inquire about （v）詢問（問題）👑
(D) preside over （v）管理；領導語意不符，刪除。
故本題答案選 (C)

3. Mr. Krumholz had the travel agent _____ his itinerary for the business trip to the UK.

(A) plan   (B) planning   (C) planned   (D) to plan

答案 **A**

眼球追蹤

❷　　　　　　　　　　　❸
Mr. Krumholz | had | the travel agent _____ | his itinerary for the business trip to the UK.

❶ 看選項

(A) plan   (B) planning   (C) planned   (D) to plan

中譯　Mr. Krumholz 讓旅行社安排他到英國出差的行程。

秒殺策略

❶ 判斷題型

由選項得知，測驗「**動詞變化**」題型。

❷ 找關鍵字

由關鍵字 had 得知，測驗「**使役動詞**」觀念。

❸ 判斷動詞種類，分析搭配方法

使役動詞搭配方式為：have / make + O + 原 V 或 Vpp，

由於 the travel agent / plan 是主動關係，故選 plan。

檢查

(A) plan 原形動詞

(B) planning 現在分詞使役動詞無此搭配法，刪除。

(C) planned 過去分詞為被動，刪除。

(D) to plan 不定詞使役動詞 have/make 無此搭配法，刪除。

故本題答案選 (A)

4. To boost tourism, the local government _____ special buses for the tourists so that they have easy access to all tourist attractions.

(A) offers   (B) gives   (C) provides   (D) supplies

答案　C

眼球追蹤

To boost tourism, the local government _____ special buses │for│ the tourists so that they have easy access to all tourist attractions.

❶ 看選項

(A) offers   (B) gives   ❸ (C) provides   (D) supplies

中譯　為了刺激旅遊業，地方政府提供遊客方便到達觀光景點的特殊交通車。

秒殺策略 👑

❶ 判斷題型

由選項得知，「授與、提供類動詞」題型。

❷ 找關鍵字

由關鍵字詞 for 得知。

❸ 分析搭配方法

見 for，即聯想到 provide sth for sb 的搭配，故選 provide。👑

註：本題若將兩受詞對調，則為 provide （或 supply 亦可） the tourists with special buses。

檢查

(A) offer（v）提供 offer sth to sb，刪除。

(B) give（v）給予 give sth to sb，刪除。

(C) provide（v）提供 provide sth for sb 👑

(D) supply（v）供給 supply sth to sb，刪除。

故本題答案選 (C)

5. After the president announced his resignation, Mr. Smith was
＿＿＿ as the successor and assumed presidential powers.

(A) considered　　(B) referred　　(C) defined　　(D) designated

答案  D

眼球追蹤

After the president announced his resignation, Mr. Smith was ＿＿＿ | as | the
successor and assumed presidential powers. ❷

❶ 看選項

(A) considered　　(B) referred　　(C) defined　　❸(D) designated

中譯　總裁宣布辭職之後，Smith 先生被指定為接班人，並掌握總裁權力。

秒殺策略

❶ **判斷題型**

由選項得知，測驗「動詞」題型。

❷ **找關鍵字**

由語意及**關鍵字 as** 得知，測驗「**視為、定義、指派**」觀念。

❸ **分析搭配方法**

A be designated as B，將 A 指派為 B，符合語意及用法。

檢查

(A) consider（v）視為 A be considered（to be）B 將 A 視為 B，不搭配 as，刪除。

(B) refer（v）提及 A be referred to as B 將 A 視為 B，需要搭配 refer to，刪除。

(C) define（v）定義語意不符，刪除。

(D) designate（v）指派

故本題答案選 (D)

6. The fluency in German with which he could discuss commercial law made him _____ for the position.
   (A) perfect
   (B) perfectly
   (C) perfection
   (D) perfectionism

答案 A

眼球追蹤

The fluency in German with which he could discuss commercial law | made | ❷

❸ | him _____ | for the position.

❶ 看選項
   (A) perfect　　　　(B) perfectly　　　　(C) perfection　　　　(D) perfectionism

中譯 可用德語流暢地討論商法使他很適合此職位。

秒殺策略 👑

❶ **判斷題型**

由選項得知，「詞類變化」題型。

❷ **找關鍵字**

由**關鍵字 make** 得知，測驗「make+ O+ OC」觀念。

❸ **分析搭配方法**

公式：make+ O+ OC，受詞為 him，受詞補語可以為原 V、過去分詞 Vpp 與形容詞，故選 perfect (a) 適合的。👑

檢查

(A) perfect（a）適合的 👑
(B) perfectly（adv）詞性不符刪除。
(C) perfection（n）詞性不符刪除。
(D) perfectionism（n）完美主義詞性及語意不符，刪除。
故本題答案選 (A)

67

7. Many doctors suggest that we _____ vegetable oil for butter in daily cooking.

(A) replace   (B) exchange   (C) convert   (D) substitute

答案 D

眼球追蹤

Many doctors suggest that we _____ vegetable oil |for| butter in daily cooking.

❶ **看選項**

(A) replace   (B) exchange   ❸ (C) convert   (D) substitute

中譯 很多醫生建議我們在日常烹飪用植物油代替奶油。

秒殺策略

❶ **判斷題型**

　　由選項得知，測驗「動詞」題型。

❷ **找關鍵字**

　　由語意及**關鍵字** for 得知，測驗「**substitute**」觀念。

❸ **分析搭配方法**

　　公式：substitute A for B 用 A 替 B，故選 substitute。

　　註：本題亦可寫成 replace butter with vegetable oil

檢查

(A) replace（v）取代，replace A with B 用 B 取代 A，用法不符，刪除。

(B) exchange（v）交換；調換，exchange A for B，語意不符，刪除。

(C) convert（v）轉變，變換 convert A into B, 語意及用法不符，刪除。

(D) substitute（v）代替

故本題答案選 (D)

8. For tax deductions, most small businesses are willing to _____ some portion of their profits to charitable organizations each year.
(A) attribute　　　　(B) compensate　　　(C) contribute　　　(D) apply

答案 C

眼球追蹤

For tax deductions, most small businesses are willing to _____ some portion

of their profits **❷**|to|charitable organizations each year.

❶ 看選項
| (A) attribute | (B) compensate | **❷** (C) contribute | (D) apply |

中譯　由於可減稅,多數小企業都願意每年捐助慈善機構部分利潤。

秒殺策略 ♛

❶ 判斷題型

由選項得知,「動詞搭配題型」。將選項帶進題目即可。

❷ 依語意個別判斷

依語意個別判斷與**關鍵字** to 判斷,選 contribute A to B 捐助 A 給 B 表「捐助A 給 B」。♛

檢查

(A) attribute A to B 將 A 歸因於 B 語意不符,刪除。

(B) compensate A for B 因 B 補償 A 語意及用法不符,刪除。

(C) contribute A to B,捐助 A 給 B ♛

(D) apply A to B 應用 A 於 B 語意與用法不符,刪除。

故本題答案選 (C)

9. The more government interference in the economy _____ a worsening of economic growth.
   (A) applied to   (B) called for   (C) coincided with   (D) disposed of

答案 C

眼球追蹤

The more government interference in the economy _____ a worsening of economic growth.

❶ 看選項

 (A) applied to   (B) called for   **❷**(C) coincided with   (D) disposed of

中譯 政府對經濟干預愈多，經濟狀況就愈差。

秒殺策略 👑

❶ 判斷題型

由選項得知，「片語搭配題型」。將選項帶進題目即可。

❷ 依語意個別判斷

依語意個別判斷，選 coincided with (v) 同時；一致。👑

檢查

(A) apply to 應用語意不符，刪除。
(B) call for 請求語意不符，刪除。
(C) coincided with 同時；一致 👑
(D) dispose of 處理，除去語意不符，刪除。
故本題答案選 (C)

10. Once your visa has already expired, you must _____ a new one overseas before re-entering the U.S.
    (A) allow for　　　(B) apply for　　　(C) go for　　　(D) pass for

答案 B

眼球追蹤

Once your visa has already expired, you must _____ a new one overseas before re-entering the U.S.

❶ **看選項**
　(A) allow for　❷　(B) apply for　　　(C) go for　　　(D) pass for

中譯　一旦你的簽證已經過期，重新進入美國之前，則必須在海外申請新的。

秒殺策略 ♛

❶ **判斷題型**
　由選項得知，「片語搭配題型」。將選項帶進題目即可。

❷ **依語意個別判斷**
　依語意個別判斷，選 apply for 申請。♛

檢查

(A) allow for 斟酌語意不符，刪除。

(B) apply for 申請♛

(C) go for 襲擊；力爭語意不符，刪除。

(D) pass for 被誤認為語意不符，刪除。

故本題答案選 (B)

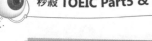

11-13 請參閱下列一則便箋

中譯

　　收件人：所有員工

　　寄件人：辦公室經理 Henry Rollins

　　主旨：　辦公室用品新規定

　　各位同仁：

　　辦公用品最近在我們公司一直都是很大的開銷。因此，下週將發布一個關於辦公用品的新政策。**Ms. Hallowell** 女士將負責供應櫃，她會將櫃子上鎖。任何需要用品的人需要填寫新的申請表，並遞交給她。表格可在她的辦公室拿取。

　　一旦每個人都可合作地遵守新規定，則有助於確保我們的公司有更好的質量和資源管理。

　　感謝您的合作。

秒殺策略 👑

11. 答案　**(C) locked**

　　　　Ms. Hallowell will be in charge of the supply closet and she will keep it **locked**.

　解題　keep + O + OC 受詞補語可以是形容詞、現在分詞與過去分詞。由於 the supply closet 是被鎖，所以用 locked。👑

12. 答案　**(C) filled**

　　　　Anyone requiring supplies needs to have the new request form **filled** out and hands it to her.

　解題　公式：have / make + O + OC (pp)。have /the new request form /filled out 的 have 當使役動詞，受格接受動作時，用過去分詞修飾，表格為人所填寫，所以用 filled。👑

13. 答案　**(A) abide by**

　　　　Once everyone can **abide by** new regulations corporately, ...

　解題　(A) abide by 遵守 👑　　　　　　　(B) dispense with 免除

　　　　(C) enroll for 報名參加　　　　　　(D) take to 喜歡；開始從事

成為多益勝利組的字彙練功區

文法講解區	Mini Test 限時 5 分練習區
conform [kən`fɔrm] **v.** 遵守	drastically [`dræstɪkəli] **adv.** 徹底地
office supply **n.** 文具	landlord [`lænd͵lɔrd] **n.** 房東；地主
production capability **n.** 產能	tenant [`tɛnənt] **n.** 房客；住戶
grant [grænt] **v.** 給予，授予	travel agent **n.** 旅行社代辦
lecture [`lɛktʃə] **n.** **v.** 演講	boost [bust] **v.** 推動；促進
priority [praɪ`ɔrətɪ] **n.** 優先考慮的事	tourism [`tʊrɪzəm] **n.** 旅遊業，觀光業
native speaker **n.** 母語	access [`æksɛs] **n.** 接近的機會；通道
compliant [kəm`plaɪənt] **a.** 遵照的	tourist attraction **n.** 旅遊景點
health care **n.** 醫療保健	resignation [͵rɛzɪg`neʃən] **n.** 辭呈
scam [`skæm] **n.** 詐騙集團	commercial law **n.** 商法
award [ə`wɔrd] **v.** 授予...獎	tax deduction [tæks dɪ`dʌkʃən] **n.** 減稅
assistant [ə`sɪstənt] **n.** 助理	charitable [`tʃærətəbḷ] **a.** 慈善的
chief financial officer **n.** 財務長	interference [͵ɪntə`fɪrəns] **n.** 介入
revenue [`rɛvə͵nju] **n.** 營收	expire [ɪk`spaɪr] **v.** （期限）終止
CEO (Chief Executive Officer) **n.** 執行長	personnel [͵pɝsṇ`ɛl] **n.** （總稱）人員
notice [`notɪs] **n.** **v.** 通知	issue [`ɪʃʊ] **v.** 核發
commercial hub [kə`mɚʃəl hʌb] **n.** 商業中心	in charge of **prep.** 負責
	request form [rɪ`kwɛst fɔrm] **n.** 申請表
	available [ə`veləbḷ] **a.** 可得的
	regulation [͵rɛgjə`leʃən] **n.** 條例
	resources management **n.** 資源管理

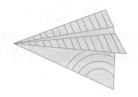

FAQ in TOEIC

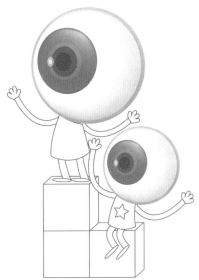

3

時態 (Tenses)

文法講解區

③ 時態 (Tenses)

簡單看

在英文句子中，我們可由動詞的變化，得知動作發生的時間點；反之亦然，我們亦可由時間點（時間標記）來推論出動詞的時態表現。

英語動詞時態：
以「時間」來歸類，分為：現在式、過去式、未來式
以「狀態」來歸類，分為：簡單式、進行式、完成式、完成進行式
以兩者交叉搭配組合起來，共有十二種時態。

簡單說，英語時態分三時四式 （三時：現在、過去、未來；四式：簡單、進行、完成、完成進行），而我們本單元介紹下列 9 式，而其中「完成進行式」的概念與「完成式」概念相仿，只是多了進行的意味，不詳加敘述。

秒殺策略

（1）搜尋「時間標記」（time marker）
（2）無時間標記時，即根據前後句或上下文的語意或時態來判斷

1 現在簡單式使用時機與時間標記

〉 使用時機

・現在的事實與狀態

Locals and tourists <u>usually</u> patronize the restaurant because of its quality food and nice service.

（因為優質的食物和周到的服務，當地人和遊客經常光顧這家餐廳。）

・習慣性、反覆性或週期的行為或狀態

The Edinburgh International Festival takes place in Scotland <u>every August</u>.

（愛丁堡國際藝術節在蘇格蘭每年八月舉行。）

・不變的真理或格言諺語

A rolling stone gathers no moss.

（滾石不生苔；轉業不聚財。）

〉 時間標記

✓ often/ usually/ always/ sometimes/ seldom/ never...

✓ every + morning/ night/ day/ week/ month/ year...

✓ from time to time/ once in a while/ at times

〉 主詞是第三人稱單數時，動詞要加 (e)s

Our food contain<u>s</u> no artificial additives, and it's good for consumers' health.

（我們的食品不加人工添加物，且有益消費者健康。）

生命加值室

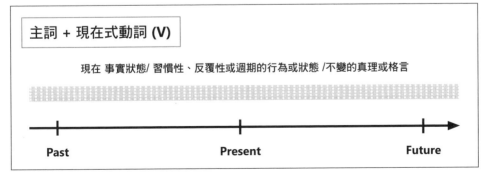

主詞 + 現在式動詞 (V)

現在 事實狀態/ 習慣性、反覆性或週期的行為或狀態 /不變的真理或格言

Past   Present   Future

② 過去簡單式使用時機與時間標記

〉 使用時機

• **過去的事實或狀態**

The president's response didn't satisfy each stockholder at the meeting <u>yesterday</u>.

（總裁昨天在會議上的回應似乎沒有滿足每個股東。）

• **過去的習慣**

Ted <u>used to</u> bury himself in his work all day, but now he spends more time on leisure activities.

（Ted 以前習慣整天埋首工作，但他現在花較多時間於休閒活動。）

〉 時間標記

- ✓ 時間 + ago （如：two days ago/ one year ago）
- ✓ last + morning / night / day / week / month / year
- ✓ in + 過去年份 （如：in 1980/ in the 18th century）
- ✓ when + 過去式子句
- ✓ once, yesterday, this morning, one day, the other day

生命加值室

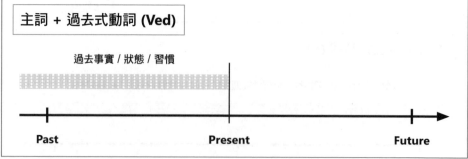

1 詞類

2 特殊動詞

3 時態

4 主詞與動詞的一致性

5 被動語態

❸ 未來簡單式使用時機與時間標記

〉使用時機

・**未來將發生的動作或狀態**

The office new policy will take effect <u>next month</u>.

（公司新政策將會在下月實施。）

The registered mail will be returned <u>if there is something wrong with recipient's information</u>.

（若收件人資料有誤，掛號信將會被退回。）

〉時間標記

✓ tomorrow + morning / afternoon / evening / night

✓ next + time / week / month / year

✓ in + 一段時間（如：in two days/ in five minutes）

✓ later, soon, in the future, tonight, as of +未來時間

✓ when / if / unless / until / before / after / as soon as + 現在式子句

〉表時間／條件的副詞子句，動詞用現在式／現在完成式代替未來式，主要子句用未來式或祈使句。

The manager <u>will retire</u> when his wife <u>finishes</u> her project next year.

（經理會在他太太明年完成專案時退休。）

生命加值室

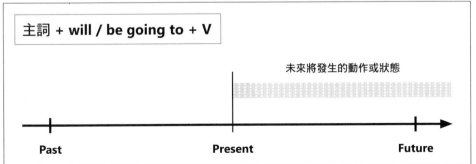

主詞 + will / be going to + V

未來將發生的動作或狀態

Past　　　　　Present　　　　　Future

④ 現在進行式使用時機與時間標記

〉使用時機

• **正在進行的動作，強調動作進行的狀態**

The board is <u>now</u> seriously considering laying off the CEO for the wrong decision.

（董事會正嚴重考慮要辭退執行長，由於他錯誤的決定。）

• **計畫性的未來動作** （多為來去動詞 *go, come, start, leave, arrive...*）

Josh is <u>arriving</u> in London <u>tomorrow morning</u>.

（Josh 明早將抵達倫敦。）

• **表一直重覆或習慣性之動作。亦可表達說話人的讚揚、厭惡、或不滿等情感。**

The biggest challenge we are <u>always</u> facing is the failure to keep the prices low.

（我們一直面對的最大挑戰就是無法讓價錢持續壓低。）

〉時間標記

 ✓ now, right now, at present, at the moment, for the time being, currently,
 ✓ Look!, Listen!
 ✓ this week / today / tomorrow / soon...
 ✓ always, constantly, forever, repeatedly...

生命加值室

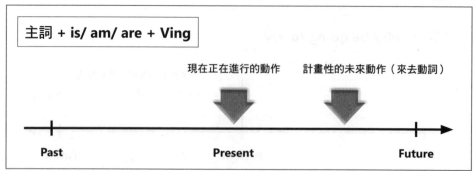

5 過去進行式使用時機與時間標記

〉使用時機

・**過去某個確定時間中進行的動作**

Last night at nine o'clock, Josh was still working in the office.

（昨晚 9 點，Josh 正在公司工作。）

・**過去某較短動作發生時，另一個動作仍在持續進行中**

Kathy was bargaining with a street vendor over the price when a police-man appeared in the market.

（當有一警察出現在市場時，Kathy 與小販正在議價。）

・**過去兩動作同時發生，並持續進行中**

While the ball handler was dribbling, he was also looking for his open teammate.

（當持球者運球時，他也一直在尋找他有空檔的隊友。）

〉時間標記

✓ at + 數字 + o'clock last night, at the time of ～

✓ when/ while + 過去式子句

生命加值室

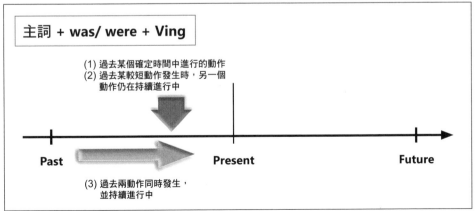

右欄目錄標籤：
1 詞類
2 特殊動詞
3 時態
4 主詞與動詞的一致性
5 被動語態

6 未來進行式使用時機與時間標記

〉使用時機

・未來某個確定時間點

Because of heavy fog, the bus will be departing <u>at 3 pm</u>, nearly two hours behind schedule.

（由於濃霧，公車將會在三點起程，幾乎比原定晚兩小時。）

・未來某期間將進行的動作

The economic situation will be getting better <u>when the employment rate starts rising this year</u>.

（當就業率今年開始上升，經濟狀況就會越來越好。）

〉時間標記

✓ at + this time / ～o'clock +未來時間
✓ all + morning / afternoon / day +未來時間
✓ when + 現在式子句

生命加值室

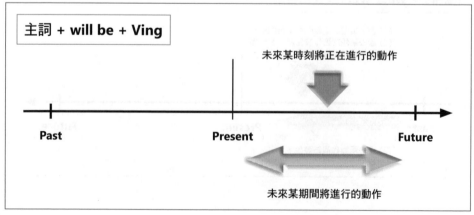

7 現在完成式使用時機與時間標記

〉使用時機

• 表「完成」：到現在已經完成的動作

The meeting has been cancelled and will be rescheduled for a later date.

（會議已經取消且將會擇期重開。）

• 表「繼續」：從過去繼續到現在的動作或狀態

Domestic rail fares have shot up <u>since this June</u> as result of soaring gas prices.

（由於飆漲的油價，自今年六月份，國內鐵路的票價已漲至歷史最高。）

• 表「經驗」：到目前為止的經驗

This is my first time to travel abroad; I've <u>never</u> applied for a visa <u>before</u>.

（這是我第一次出國旅遊；我以前還未申請過簽證。）

〉時間標記

　✓ just, yet, already, not yet...

　✓ since+ 過去某一點時間

　✓ for + 一段時間（如：two weeks）

　✓ these + 一段時間（如：days / weeks /...）

　✓ so far, recently, lately, since + 過去式子句

　✓ ever, never, many times, once, before...

生命加值室

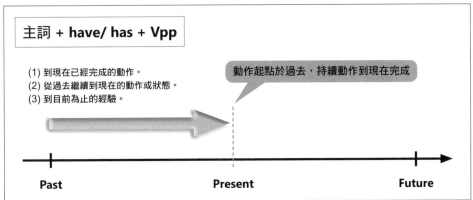

主詞 + have/ has + Vpp

(1) 到現在已經完成的動作。
(2) 從過去繼續到現在的動作或狀態。
(3) 到目前為止的經驗。

動作起點於過去，持續動作到現在完成

Past　　　Present　　　Future

1 詞類

2 特殊動詞

3 時態

4 主詞與動詞的一致性

5 被動語態

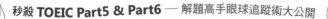
8 過去完成式使用時機與時間標記

〉使用時機

・**在過去某動作或某時之前就完成的動作或狀況**

Before the product launch this morning, the manager had taken care of all the details.

（早在產品今早推出前，經理已確定過所有的細節。）

・**兩個過去發生的動作有先後順序時，先發生用過去完成式，後發生用過去簡單式**

All my friends had already left when I arrived very late at the party,

（當我在很晚才到宴會時，我所有的朋友早已離開了。）

〉時間標記

✓ by the time / before / when + 過去時間 / 過去式子句

生命加值室

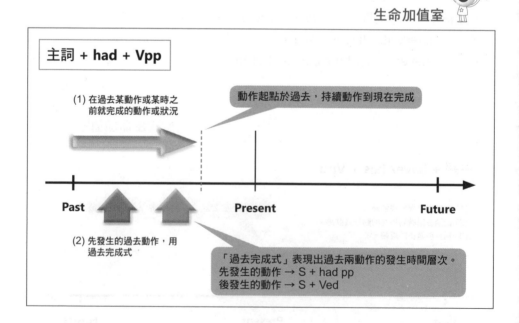

9 未來完成式使用時機與時間標記

〉使用時機

• **到未來某時為止會完成的動作。**

E-commerce will have expanded significantly <u>by the next decade.</u>

（電子商務會在未來十年內將會明顯擴張。）

• **到未來某時的經驗或狀態**

We'll have dominated the phone industry <u>when we get the exclusive distribution rights next year.</u>

（我們明年拿到的獨家經銷權時，我們將會佔據了手機行業。）

注意：時間副詞子句的動詞要用現在式

〉時間標記

　✓ for + 一段時間；by + 未來時間

　✓ by the time / when + 現在式子句

生命加值室

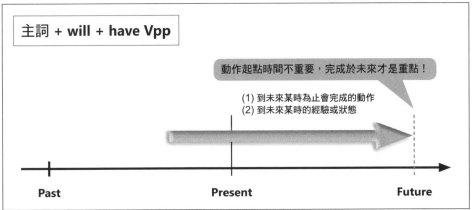

主詞 + will + have Vpp

動作起點時間不重要，完成於未來才是重點！

(1) 到未來某時為止會完成的動作
(2) 到未來某時的經驗或狀態

Past　　　Present　　　Future

Mini Test 練習區 限時 5 分 ⏱

1. Most travel guides _____ this tourist attraction a high rating so that plenty of visitors kept flooding in.
   (A) give   (B) gave   (C) will give   (D) has given

2. To avoid cavities, my family always _____ our dentist regularly, at least every six months.
   (A) visit   (B) visited   (C) will visit   (D) have visited

3. I _____ the annual company sale meeting at this time tomorrow.
   (A) am hosting   (B) will host   (C) have hosted   (D) will be hosting

4. The company _____ a large amount of money before it was acquired by another giant in 2012.
   (A) invested   (B) would invest   (C) had invested   (D) was investing

5. Sophie _____ a potluck at her house when I called her last evening.
   (A) had   (B) was having   (C) had had   (D) would have

6. Kathy's health _____ dramatically since she had enough sleep and a balanced diet.
   (A) improves   (B) improved   (C) was improving   (D) has improved

7. The price _____ to products ordered as of publication of the new price next month.
   (A) applies   (B) is applying   (C) has applied   (D) will apply

8. Currently, many forms of infrastructure are failing and _____ a negative impact on ecosystems.
   (A) made   (B) make   (C) are making   (D) have made

9. By next month, the two sides _____ a compromise.
   (A) reach   (B) will reach
   (C) will be reaching   (D) will have reached

10. The authority concerned will take an immediate action after the police _____ a complete investigation about the attack.
    (A) receive   (B) will receive   (C) has received   (D) are receiving

Question 11-13 refer to the following letter

Dear Mr. Derrick,

I am writing you to remind there ＿＿＿＿ something wrong with the machines

    11 (A) is
       (B) was
       (C) will be
       (D) has been

on the assembly line for the past few weeks. High temperature ＿＿＿＿ in

      12 (A) results
        (B) resulted
        (C) has resulted
        (D) has been resulting

excessive expansion and last week the machines broke down from time to time. To avoid potential danger, the technicians in the maintenance department will repair on the machinery this afternoon.All the production on the assembly line has to stop now and will resume after they ＿＿＿＿ repairs.

      13 (A) finishes
        (B) will finish
        (C) have finished
        (D) will have finished

Please notify to all personnel concerned on the assembly lines. Many thanks for your assistance.

1-10 Ans:　1.(B)　2.(A)　3.(D)　4.(C)　5.(B)　6.(D)　7.(D)　8.(C)　9.(D)　10.(A)

1. Most travel guides _____ this tourist attraction such a high rating that plenty of visitors kept flooding in.

   (A) give   (B) gave   (C) will give   (D) has given

答案 **B**

眼球追蹤

❸ 看全句語意

Most travel guides _____ this tourist attraction such a high rating that ❷

plenty of visitors kept flooding in.

❶ 看選項

  (A) give   (B) gave   (C) will give   (D) has given

中譯 多數旅遊指南給了這觀光景點如此高的評價以致於大量遊客持續湧入。

秒殺策略 👑

❶ 判斷題型

由選項得知，測驗點為「**時態變化**」。

❷ 找時間標記

由 plenty of visitors kept flooding in 可知，前句 most travel guides...應亦為**過去式**的時態。

❸ 搭配語意，驗證答案

本句是由 such…that 所連接串起，that 子句後為結果句，結果句使用過去式 kept，代表前句引起原因的動作亦發生在過去時間，give 用「**過去簡單式**」。

👑 註：若本題有「過去完成式」表示比 kept 發生的更早的選項，亦可選擇。

檢查

(A) 現在簡單式刪除。

(B) 過去簡單式表示過去的事實或習慣 👑

(C) 未來簡單式刪除。

(D) 現在完成式主詞第三人稱單數刪除。

故本題答案選 (B)

2. To avoid cavities, my family always _____ our dentist regularly, at least every six months.

(A) visit　　　　(B) visited　　　　(C) will visit　　　　(D) have visited

答案  A

眼球追蹤

To avoid cavities, my family ❷|always| _____ our dentist regularly,❸ at least ❷|every six months.|

❶ 看選項

(A) visit　　　　(B) visited　　　　(C) will visit　　　　(D) have visited

中譯 為避免蛀牙，我家人總是至少每六個月規律地去看牙醫一趟。

秒殺策略 ♛

❶ 判斷題型

由選項得知，測驗點為「**時態變化**」。

❷ 找時間標記

頻率副詞 always 出現，用「簡單式」或「進行式」。

再加上 every six months，拉出時間是落在「現在」。

❸ 搭配語意，驗證答案

表 visit our dentist regularly 是習慣性的動作，搭配時間標記，故選擇「**現在簡單式**」無誤。♛

檢查

(A) 現在簡單式 ♛

(B) 過去簡單式，刪除。

(C) 未來簡單式，刪除。

(D) 現在完成式，刪除。

故本題答案選 (A)

3. I _____ the annual company sale meeting at this time tomorrow.
   (A) am hosting　　　　　　　　(B) will host
   (C) have hosted　　　　　　　　(D) will be hosting

答案　D

眼球追蹤

I _____ the annual company sale meeting ❷ at this time tomorrow.

❶ 看選項

(A) am hosting　　　(B) will host　　　(C) have hosted　　❸ (D) will be hosting

中譯　明天這時候我將正在主持公司銷售年度會議。

秒殺策略

❶ **判斷題型**

由選項得知，測驗點為「**時態變化**」。

❷ **找時間標記**

由時間標記 at this time tomorrow 得知，代表動作是發生在「未來的某一時刻」，故動詞 host 應用「**未來進行式**」呈現。

❸ **驗證答案**

host 可用進行式，will be hosting 為「未來進行式」。

檢查

(A) 現在進行式，刪除。

(B) 未來簡單式，刪除。

(C) 現在完成式，刪除。

(D) 未來進行式，表示「未來某個確定時間中」將進行的動作

故本題答案選 (D)

4. The company _____ a large amount of money before it was acquired by another giant in 2012.
   (A) invested
   (B) would invest
   (C) had invested
   (D) was investing

答案　C

眼球追蹤

❸ 看全句語意

The company _____ a large amount of money │before it was acquired by another giant in 2012.│　②

❶ 看選項

(A) invested　　(B) would invest　　(C) had invested　　(D) was investing

中譯　在 2012 被另一家巨頭所併購之前，這家公司早已投入大量資金。

秒殺策略 👑

❶ 判斷題型

　由選項得知，測驗點為「**時態變化**」。

❷ 找時間標記

　時間標記為副詞子句 before it was acquired by a giant in 2012。

❸ 驗證答案

　由語意與時間標記得知，主要句中的動作 invest，發生於較 2012 之前更早的時間，故動詞應用「**過去完成式**」呈現。👑

檢查

(A) 過去簡單式，刪除。

(B) would + 原 V，「過去常常」、「過去時間的未來狀況」或「假設語氣」，刪除。

(C) 過去完成式，表示在過去某動作或某時之前就完成的動作或狀況👑

(D) 過去進行式，刪除。

故本題答案選 (C)

1 詞類

2 特殊動詞

3 時態

4 主詞與動詞的一致性

5 被動語態

5. Sophie _____ a potluck at her house when I called her last evening.
  (A) had   (B) was having   (C) had had   (D) would have

答案 B

眼球追蹤

❸ 看全句語意   **❷**
Sophie _____ a potluck at her house | when I called her last evening.

❶ 看選項
  (A) had   (B) was having   (C) had had   (D) would have

中譯   當我昨傍晚打電話給 Sophie 時，她正在舉辦聚餐。

秒殺策略 👑

❶ 判斷題型

由選項得知，測驗點為「**時態變化**」。

❷ 找時間標記

時間標記為副詞子句 when I called her last evening。

❸ 驗證答案

當過去有兩個動作並列進行，「剎那間」或「持續較短」的動作用**過去簡單**，「持續較長」的動作用**過去進行**。由全句 Sophie _____ a potluck at her house / when I called her last evening 得知，主要句中的 have a potluck 又為「持續比較長的動作」，故動詞時態應用「**過去進行式**」。👑

檢查

(A) 過去簡單式，刪除。
(B) 過去進行式，表示過去某動作發生時，原正在進行的另一個動作持續進行中 👑
(C) 過去完成式，刪除。
(D) would + 原 V，表「過去常常」、「過去時間的未來狀況」或「假設語氣」，刪除。
故本題答案選 (B)

6. Kathy's health _____ dramatically since she had enough sleep and a balanced diet.
   (A) improves   (B) improved   (C) was improving   (D) has improved

答案 D

眼球追蹤

Kathy's health _____ dramatically ❷ since she had enough sleep and a balanced diet.

❶ 看選項

(A) improves   (B) improved   (C) was improving ❸ (D) has improved

中譯 自從 Kathy 有足夠的睡眠與均衡的飲食後，她的健康有很大地改善。

秒殺策略 ♛

❶ **判斷題型**

由選項得知，測驗點為「**時態變化**」。

❷ **找時間標記**

時間標記為副詞子句 since she had enough sleep and a balanced diet。

❸ **驗證答案**

當「since + 過去時間點／過去式子句」引導時間副詞子句時，主要句時態多用「**現在完成式**」。♛

檢查

(A) 現在簡單式，刪除。
(B) 過去簡單式，刪除。
(C) 過去進行式，刪除。
(D) 現在完成式，表示「從過去繼續到現在的動作或狀態」。♛
故本題答案選 (D)

7. The price _____ to products ordered as of publication of the new price next month.

   (A) applies   (B) is applying   (C) has applied   (D) will apply

答案 D

眼球追蹤

The price _____ to products ordered | ❷ as of publication of the new price next

month.

❶ 看選項

   (A) applies   (B) is applying   (C) has applied   ❸ (D) will apply

中譯 該價格將適用於下個月最新價格公告後訂購的產品。

秒殺策略

❶ **判斷題型**

由選項得知，測驗點為「**時態變化**」。

❷ **找時間標記**

時間標記為 as of 為自(…時間) 起，next month 提供未來時間點的線索。

❸ **驗證答案**

因此判斷時間為「自下個月最新價格公告後」，時態應選擇「**未來簡單式**」，用來表示未來將發生的事實或狀態。

檢查

(A) 現在簡單式，刪除。

(B) 現在進行式，刪除。

(C) 現在完成式，刪除。

(D) 未來簡單式，表示未來將發生的動作或狀態。

故本題答案選 (D)

1 詞類

8. Currently, many forms of infrastructure are failing and _____ a negative impact on ecosystems.
   (A) made   (B) make   (C) are making   (D) have made

答案 C

2 特殊動詞

眼球追蹤

Currently, ❷ | many forms of infrastructure | ❸ are failing | and ❷ | _____ a negative impact on ecosystems.

❶ **看選項**
   (A) made   (B) make   (C) are making   (D) have made

中譯 當前，許多基礎設施功能不斷在退化，正對生態系統產生負面影響。

3 時態

秒殺策略 ♛

❶ **判斷題型**

由選項得知，測驗點為「**時態變化**」。

❷ **找時間標記**

時間標記 currently 表示當下正在發生的時間點，連接詞 and 前後連接的時態應一致。

❸ **驗證答案**

由 are failing 與 and 可推知，空格為「現在進行式」，make a negative impact 搭配「**現在進行式**」。♛

4 主詞與動詞的一致性

檢查

(A) 過去簡單式，刪除。
(B) 現在簡單式，刪除。
(C) 現在進行式，表示現在當下正在進行的動作，或強調動作進行的狀態 ♛
(D) 現在完成式，刪除。
故本題答案選 (C)

5 被動語態

9. By next month, the two sides _____ a compromise.
  (A) reach
  (B) will reach
  (C) will be reaching
  (D) will have reached

答案 D

眼球追蹤

❷
| By next month, | the two sides _____ a compromise. |

❶ **看選項**
(A) reach   (B) will reach
(C) will be reaching   ❸ (D) will have reached

中譯 到下個月之前，雙方將已經達成妥協。

秒殺策略

❶ **判斷題型**

由選項得知，測驗點為「**時態變化**」。

❷ **找時間標記**

時間標記為 by next month。

❸ **驗證答案**

當「by + 未來時間點」引導時間副詞子句時，主要句時態多用「**未來完成式**」，搭配語意無誤。👑

檢查

(A) 現在簡單式，刪除

(B) 未來簡單式，刪除

(C) 未來進行式，刪除

(D) 未來完成式，表示到未來某時為止會完成的動作👑

故本題答案選 (D)

10. The authority concerned will take an immediate action after the police _____ a complete investigation about the attack.
(A) receive　　(B) will receive　　(C) has received　　(D) are receiving

答案 A

眼球追蹤

The authority concerned │will take│ an immediate action │after the police _____ a

complete investigation about the attack.

❶ 看選項

(A) receive　　(B) will receive　　(C) has received　　(D) are receiving

中譯　在警察得到完整的偵查後，有關當局將會採取立即措施。

秒殺策略 ♛

❶ 判斷題型

由選項得知，測驗點為「**時態變化**」。

❷ 找時間標記

由主要句 will take an immediate action，可推知時間標記應為「**未來式**」。

❸ 驗證答案

時間標記為從屬時間連接詞 after 所帶的副詞子句，要用「**現在簡單式**」代替
未來式。♛

檢查

(A) 現在簡單式 ♛
(B) 未來簡單式，刪除。
(C) 現在完成式，刪除。
(D) 現在進行式，刪除。
故本題答案選 (A)

1 詞類

2 特殊動詞

3 時態

4 主詞與動詞的一致性

5 被動語態

11-13 參考下列信件

中譯

親愛的 Derrick 先生：

我在此寫信提醒您過去幾周生產線上的機器有些問題，高溫導致過度膨脹且上週機器偶發故障。 為避免潛在危險，維修部們的技術人員將會在今天下午進行維修。所有生產線上的生產必須現在停止，且在他們完成維修後重新開始。請通知生產線上相關人員。

感謝您的協助。

秒殺策略

11. 答案　**(D) has been**

　　to remind there **has been** something wrong...line for the past few weeks.

　解題　由 for the past few weeks 推知，需搭配現在完成式。👑

12. 答案　**(D) has been**

　　High temperature **resulted** in excessive expansion and last week the machines broke down

　解題　由...and last week the machines broke down from time to time
　　　依照語意，and 應連接兩個時態對等子句→搭配過去簡單式。👑

13. 答案　**(C) have finished**

　　and will resume after they **have finished** repairs

　解題　after 所帶的時間副詞子句，表示未來時間時，需用現在簡單式或現在完成式代替。👑

成為多益勝利組的字彙練功區

文法講解區	Mini Test 限時 5 分練習區
patronize [`petrənˌaɪz] v. 光顧	travel guide n. 旅遊手冊
artificial additive n. 人工添加物	flood in v. 湧進
consumer [kənˋsjumɚ] n. 消費者	cavity [`kævətɪ] n. 蛀牙
stockholder [`stakˌholdɚ] n. 股東	annual [`ænjʊəl] a. 年度的
take effect v. 實施	host [host] v. 主持
registered mail n. 掛號信	acquire [əˋkwaɪr] v. 併購
recipient [rɪˋsɪpɪənt] n. 收件人	giant [`dʒaɪənt] n. 商業巨擘
board [bord] n. 董事會	potluck [`patˌlʌk] n. 百樂餐
lay off v. 解雇	（參加聚餐者每人各帶菜餚共享的餐會）
bargain [`bargɪn] v. 議價	dramatically [drəˋmætɪklɪ] adv. 顯著地
drib [drɪb] v. 運球	balanced diet n. 均衡飲食
depart [dɪˋpart] v. 起程	apply to v. 適用於
behind schedule adv. 比預定時間晚	as of prep. 自(...時間)起
employment rate n. 就業率	infrastructure [`ɪnfrəˌstrʌktʃɚ] n. 基礎設施
domestic [dəˋmɛstɪk] a. 國內的	ecosystem [`ɛkoˌsɪstəm] n. 生態系統
fare [fɛr] n.（交通工具的）票價	reach a compromise v. 達成協議
soar [sor] v. 暴漲	authority concerned n. 有關當局
apply for v. 申請	take an action v. 採取行動
launch [lɔntʃ] v. 將...推行於市場	investigation [ɪnˌvɛstəˋgeʃən] n. 調查
E-commerce [iˋkamɚs] n. 電子商務	assembly line n. 生產線
significantly [sɪgˋnɪfəkəntlɪ] adv. 明顯地	maintenance [`mentənəns] n. 維修
dominate [`daməˌnet] v. 支配，統治	notify [`notəˌfaɪ] v. 通知；通報
exclusive distribution right n. 獨家經銷權	

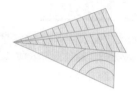

FAQ in TOEIC

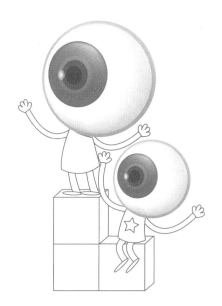

4

主詞與動詞的一致性
(Subject-Verb Agreement)

文法講解區

❹ 主詞與動詞的一致性 (Subject-Verb Agreement)

簡單看

　　英文句子中的動詞變化，除了時態外，便取決於主詞的人稱和單複數。主詞為單數，動詞則用單數形；若主詞為第三人稱、現在式時，動詞字尾加-s/-es 或去 y 加-ies。同理，主詞為複數，動詞則搭配複數形。

　　常考的主詞與動詞一致性題型有三種：
(1) 主詞與主動詞分離時，判斷主要動詞的單複數
(2) 連接詞連接兩主詞、主詞部分呈現、動名詞或不定詞當主詞時，主動詞單複數的判斷
(3) 關係子句中動詞的單複數判斷

秒殺策略

（1）判斷真正的主詞
　　　思考方向：「穿插的片語或子句」、「連接詞片語類型」、「動名詞與不定詞」
（2）判斷主詞的單複數
（3）判斷時態與主被動

> 主詞後面跟著的片語與子句是用來修飾這主詞，不影響主動詞的單複數形。

❶ 主詞和動詞分開的題型

〉主詞後帶有修飾的介系詞片語／不定詞片語／分詞片語

EX The results of the previous year's training surveys are available on-line.

（前一年訓練測試結果可以在網路上取得。）

EX The best way to improve relationships between two sides is to resume talks.

（改善兩方之間關係的最好方式就是恢復會談。）

EX The short fictions written by Stephen King have been adapted into feature films.

（Stephen King 的短篇小說已經被改編成劇情片。）

〉主詞後帶有修飾的子句

EX Initial reports which were collected by the institute show that cancer is a leading cause of death in the world.

（由此機構所蒐集的最初報告顯示癌症是全球主要死因。）

❷ 主詞部分呈現的題型

all		
some		
most		
part	限定詞	+ 單數名詞 → 單數動詞
the rest	(the／所有格)	+ 複數名詞 → 複數動詞
half		
分數／幾分之幾		
percent/percentage		

表示一部分時，動詞的單、複數形由 of 後面的名詞來決定

EX A small percentage of each purchase goes toward a charity of customers' choice.

（每次購買的少部分由顧客選擇作為慈善捐獻。）

EX About four out of five <u>employees</u> in the company <u>are</u> willing to take the internal promotion test next month.

（公司約五分之四的員工願意參加下個月的內部升遷考試。）

③ 連接詞片語連接兩主詞題型

(Either) A or B	A 或 **B**	
Neither A nor B	既非 A 亦非 **B**	
Not only A but also B	不止 A，**B** 也是	
Not A but B	不是 A 而是 **B**	+ V（動詞單複數看 B）
B as well as A B along with A B together with A	不止 A，**B** 也是 （強調 B，A 只是附帶）	
Both A and B	**A** 與 **B** 兩者都	+ 複數 V

EX Not only the fans but also <u>the critic</u> <u>was</u> impressed by the album that the band released this year.

（不但歌迷連評論家都對這樂團今年所推出的專輯感到印象深刻。）

EX <u>The colleagues</u> as well as the manager <u>are</u> complimentary about May's work.

（不只是經理連同事對於 May 的工作表現讚譽有加。）

④ 其他

1. 動名詞或不定詞當主詞時，動詞要用單數型。

EX <u>To analyze marketing strategies</u> <u>is</u> Lin's main job in the company.

（分析行銷策略是 Lin 在公司的主要工作。）

EX <u>Arguing with the referee</u> <u>has</u> made a penalty of 4 points deducted from the team.

（和裁判爭論已經使此隊失去四分。）

2. There is + 單數名詞

There are + 複數名詞

EX There <u>is</u> <u>a chance</u> for Kim to get the position as a management consultant at the multinational company.

（Kim 有機會可以在這家跨國公司擔任管理顧問。）

EX There <u>are</u> <u>three versions</u> of the gossip about the president's love affair.

（對於總裁婚外情的八卦有三種版本。）

3. Each / Every +單數名詞 + 單數動詞

Each of the + 複數名詞 + 單數動詞

EX Every ride in the amusement park <u>is</u> very safe.

（在這遊樂園中的每項遊樂設施都很安全。）

EX <u>Each</u> of the investors in the stock market <u>is</u> hoping that the economic can recover soon.

（股市中的每一投資者希望經濟可以盡快恢復。）

4. a number of + 複數名詞 + 複數動詞 （一些的…）

the number of + 複數名詞 + 單數動詞 （…的數目是…）

EX A number of stockholders <u>were</u> absent during the shareholder's meeting yesterday.

（昨天股東會議有些股東缺席。）

EX The number of visiting tourists <u>is</u> on the increase this year.

（這旅遊景點的遊客數量今年有增加。）

5. 關係子句中動詞的單複數

單數名詞 + 【 **who/which** +單數動詞 】……

複數名詞 + 【 **who/which** +複數動詞 】……

EX The <u>bistro</u> which <u>provides</u> good service is usually patronized by locals.

（當地人經常光顧那家提供很好服務的小酒館。）

EX <u>People</u> who <u>are</u> diligent and humble are highly respected.

（勤奮且謙卑的人很受尊重。）

Mini Test 練習區 限時5分 ⏱

1. The important clause arranged in the Legislative Yuan, for the shortage of time, _____ not reviewed as expected.
   (A) be   (B) was   (C) were   (D) have been

2. In this season, neither the sales nor profit _____ on the decrease due to the new marketing strategy.
   (A) was   (B) had   (C) were   (D) have

3. Two thirds of the furniture in the cities _____ completely submerged in flood waters by the unexpected disaster.
   (A) be   (B) was   (C) being   (D) were

4. Porsche with an awe-inspiring wider rear wheel arches _____ to release on the market next month.
   (A) is   (B) has   (C) are   (D) be

5. The procedures of requesting leaves workers have to follow _____ from company to company.
   (A) differ   (B) is differ   (C) are differing   (D) has differed

6. All candidates who _____ participated in the debate have to prepare a speech。
   (A) is   (B) are   (C) has   (D) have

7. A number of qualified workers _____ required to join the training program next year.
   (A) is   (B) are   (C) will   (D) X

8. The guidebook translated into plenty of different languages _____ popular among backpackers.
   (A) is   (B) are   (C) be   (D) been

9. Purchasing machine and supplies through the Internet _____ a trend in manufacturing industry recently.
   (A) becomes   (B) become   (C) has become   (D) have become

10. The number of engineers in hi-tech industries who want to quit and start their own business _____ on the increase.
    (A) is   (B) are   (C) be   (D) X

Question 11-13 refer to the following email

To: Mike Chen
From: Fredrick
Subject: renovations of multi-media conference room

Hi Mike,
Is there any possible way for you to postpone the renovations of multi-media
conference room which _____ planned to undertake next Wednesday? My

11 (A) is
(B) are
(C) has
(D) have

department has a presentation scheduled right on that day. We can't change
the place because some specific media devices are required during the pre-
sentation.Besides, one fifth of buyers _____ supposed to join from Japan,

12 (A) is
(B) are
(C) has
(D) have

so it is also difficult to reschedule the presentation for flights.I know that
making some modifications _____ a pain, but I have no choice but to use

13 (A) is
(B) are
(C) has
(D) have

this conference room.I hope you will understand my situation and I really
appreciate your help.

Fredrick

1-10 Ans: 1.(B) 2.(A) 3.(B) 4.(A) 5.(A) 6.(D) 7.(B) 8.(A) 9.(C) 10.(A)

1. That important clause arranged in the Legislative Yuan, for the shortage of time, _____ not reviewed as expected.

(A) be   (B) was   (C) were   (D) have been

答案 B

眼球追蹤

❷ **看全句** ❷

That important | clause | arranged in the Legislative Yuan, for the shortage of

time, _____ not reviewed as expected.

❶ **看選項** ❸

(A) be   (B) was   (C) were   (D) have been

中譯 那在立法院安排的重要條文,由於時間短缺,所以沒有如期審查。

秒殺策略

❶ **判斷題型**

由選項得知,測驗點為「**動詞變化**」。

❷ **判斷空格需求**

由 That important clause /arranged....for the shortage of time/ _____ not reviewed as expected 得知,That important clause 為真正主詞,空格需要主要動詞。

❸ **判斷主詞的單複數與主要動詞的一致性**

clause 為單數,was 為唯一單數動詞選項。

檢查

(A) 原形動詞,刪除。

(B) 過去式單數

(C) 過去式複數,刪除。

(D) 現在完成式複數,刪除。

故本題答案選 (B)

2. In the fourth quarter, neither the sales nor profit _____ on the decrease due to the new marketing strategy.

(A) was　　　(B) had　　　(C) were　　　(D) have

答案 A

眼球追蹤

❷ 看全句

In the fourth quarter, | neither the sales nor profit | _____ on the decrease | due to

the new marketing strategy.

❶ 看選項

(A) was　　　(B) had　　　(C) were　　　(D) have

中譯 在第四季，由於新的行銷策略，銷售與盈利皆沒有往下降了。

秒殺策略 👑

❶ **判斷題型**

由選項得知，測驗點為「**動詞**」。

❷ **判斷空格需求**

由 neither the sales nor profit /_____ on the decrease/due to …得知，the sales 與 profit 為真正主詞，由 neither...nor...所連接，**空格需要主要動詞**。

❸ **判斷主詞的單複數**

neither A nor B，動詞看 B，profit 單數。

❹ **搭配語意與用法**

be on the decrease，空格需要搭配 BE 動詞，故選「**單數 BE 動詞**」。👑

檢查

(A) BE 動詞過去式單數 👑

(B) have 過去簡單式，非 BE 動詞，刪除。

(C) BE 動詞過去式複數，刪除。

(D) have 現在簡單式，非 BE 動詞，刪除。

故本題答案選 (A)

109

3. Two thirds of the furniture in the cities _____ completely submerged in flood waters and damaged by the unexpected disaster.

(A) be   (B) was   (C) being   (D) were

答案 B

眼球追蹤

❷ 看全句 ❸ ❹

Two thirds of│the furniture│in the cities _____ completely submerged│in flood

waters and damaged by the unexpected disaster.

❶ 看選項

(A) be   (B) was   (C) being   (D) were

中譯 城市裡有三分之二家具被無預警的災害,完全被洪水淹沒與破壞。

秒殺策略

❶ **判斷題型**

由選項得知,測驗點為「**BE 動詞變化**」。

❷ **判斷空格需求**

分析句子得知,two thirds of the furniture 為真正主詞,空格搭配主要動詞。

❸ **判斷主詞的單複數**

the furniture 不可數,因此主詞為單數,搭配**單數動詞**。

❹ **搭配語意與用法**

依選項提供得知,空格要 BE 動詞,故選「**單數 BE 動詞**」。

檢查

(A) BE 動詞原形,刪除。

(B) BE 動詞過去式單數

(C) BE 動詞的進行式,刪除。

(D) BE 動詞過去式複數,刪除。

故本題答案選 (B)

4. Porsche with an awe-inspiring wider rear wheel arches _____ to release on the market next month.
(A) is　　　　　(B) has　　　　　(C) are　　　　　(D) be

答案 A

眼球追蹤

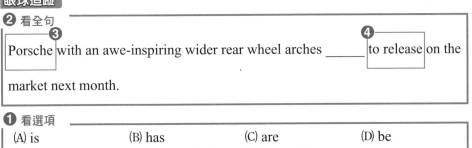

❷ 看全句

Porsche with an awe-inspiring wider rear wheel arches _____ to release on the market next month.

❶ 看選項
(A) is　　　　　(B) has　　　　　(C) are　　　　　(D) be

中譯 保時捷令人驚嘆的較寬大後輪拱門將預計在下個月登場發表。

秒殺策略

❶ **判斷題型**

由選項得知,測驗點為「**動詞**」。

❷ **判斷空格需求**

分析句子得知,Porsche 為主詞,with... arches 為介系詞片語修飾語,**空格需要主要動詞**。

❸ **判斷主詞的單複數**

Porsche 為單數,搭配**單數動詞**。

❹ **搭配語意與用法**

be to V「表示正式的計畫或安排」,需要 BE 動詞搭配。

檢查

(A) BE 動詞現在式單數 ♛

(B) has 現在式單數,刪除。

(C) BE 動詞現在式複數,刪除。

(D) BE 動詞原形,刪除。

111

故本題答案選 (A)

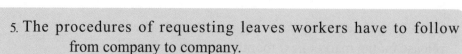

5. The procedures of requesting leaves workers have to follow
   ＿＿＿＿ from company to company.

   (A) differ   (B) is differ   (C) are differing   (D) has differed

答案 **A**

眼球追蹤

② 看全句

The procedures ③ of requesting leaves workers have to follow ＿＿＿＿ from company to company.

① 看選項

(A) differ ④   (B) is differ   (C) are differing   (D) has differed

中譯 員工必須遵守的請假程序依各家公司而不同。

秒殺策略 👑

❶ 判斷題型

由選項得知，測驗點為「**動詞 differ 變化**」。

❷ 判斷空格需求

分析句子得知，the procedures 為主詞，**空格需要主要動詞**。

❸ 判斷主詞的單複數

the procedures 為複數，搭配**複數動詞**，考慮(A)與(C)。

❹ 驗證答案

本句為表達一般常態現象，不用進行式，用「**現在簡單式**」表達即可。👑

檢查

(A)現在簡單式複數 👑

(B) 無此用法，刪除。

(C) 現在進行式複數，刪除。

(D) 現在完成式單數，刪除。

故本題答案選 (A)

6. All candidates who ＿＿＿ participated in the debate need to prepare a speech.

(A) is   (B) are   (C) has   (D) have

答案 D

眼球追蹤

❸ | ❷
All candidates | who ＿＿＿ participated in | the debate have to prepare a speech.

❶ 看選項
(A) is   (B) are   (C) has   ❹ (D) have

中譯 已參加辯論的所有候選人必須準備一則演講。

秒殺策略

❶ **判斷題型**

由選項得知，測驗點為「**BE 動詞與 have 用法**」。

❷ **判斷空格需求**

who 為關代，**空格要搭配 participated in**。

❸ **判斷主詞的單複數**

who 代的是主詞 all candidates，為複數，搭配**複數動詞**，考慮(B)與(D)。

❹ **驗證答案**

participate 為過去分詞狀態，若搭配 BE 動詞，為被動，不合邏輯，故選(D)。

檢查

(A) BE 動詞現在式單數，搭配分詞，不合語意與單複數，刪除。

(B) BE 動詞現在式複數，搭配分詞，不合語意，刪除。

(C) has 現在完成式助動詞單數，單複數不符，刪除。

(D) have 現在完成式助動詞複數

故本題答案選 (D)

7. A number of qualified workers _____ required to join the training program next year.

(A) is   (B) are   (C) will   (D) X

答案 **B**

眼球追蹤

❷ 看全句

❸

A number of qualified workers _____ required to join the training program next year.

❶ 看選項

(A) is   ❹ (B) are   (C) will   (D) X

中譯 一些合格的員工被要求參與明年的訓練計劃。

秒殺策略

❶ **判斷題型**

由選項得知，測驗點為「BE 動詞或助動詞 will」。

❷ **判斷空格需求**

A number of qualified workers 為主詞，_____ required 為主要動詞。

❸ **判斷主詞的單複數**

a number of + 複數 N + 複數 V，搭配**複數動詞**，考慮(B)與(C)選項。

❹ **驗證答案**

但(C)will 助動詞後仍缺 BE 動詞，不合文法，得(B)。👑

檢查

(A) BE 動詞現在式單數，刪除。

(B) BE 動詞現在複數 👑

(C) 未來式助動詞，少原 BE 動詞，刪除。

(D) 需要搭配 BE 動詞，刪除。

114 故本題答案選 (B)

8. The guidebook translated into plenty of different languages _____ popular among backpackers.

   (A) is   (B) are   (C) be   (D) been

答案 A

眼球追蹤

❷ 看全句

❸

The guidebook │ translated into plenty of different languages _____ popular among backpackers.

❶ 看選項

❹

(A) is   (B) are   (C) be   (D) been

中譯 這本被翻譯成很多不同的旅遊指南很受到背包客的歡迎。

秒殺策略

❶ **判斷題型**

   由選項得知，測驗點為「**BE 動詞或助動詞 will**」。

❷ **判斷空格需求**

   the guidebook 為主詞，**空格為主要動詞**。

❸ **判斷主詞的單複數**

   the guidebook 為單數，搭配**單數動詞**。

❹ **驗證答案**

   唯一單數選項 is，用刪去法即得答案。

檢查

(A) BE 動詞現在式單數

(B) BE 動詞現在式複數，刪除。

(C) BE 動詞原形，刪除。

(D) BE 動詞過去分詞，刪除。

故本題答案選 (A)

9. Purchasing machine and supplies through the Internet _____ a trend in manufacturing industry recently.

   (A) becomes   (B) become   (C) has become   (D) have become

答案 C

眼球追蹤

❷ 看全句

Purchasing machine and supplies through the Internet ❸ _____ a trend in manufacturing industry ❹ recently.

❶ 看選項

   (A) becomes   (B) become   (C) has become   (D) have become

中譯　透過網路購買機器與供應品近來已成為製造業的趨勢。

秒殺策略 👑

❶ 判斷題型

由選項得知，測驗點為「**動詞**」。

❷ 判斷空格需求

主詞為動名詞 purchasing... the Internet，空格為主要動詞。

❸ 判斷主詞的單複數

動名詞當主詞，視為第三人稱單數，搭配**單數動詞**，考慮(A)與(C)。

❹ 驗證答案

時間標記 recently，指示時態使用完成式，故選(C)。👑

檢查

(A) 現在簡單式單數，刪除。   (B) 現在簡單式複數，刪除。

(C) 現在完成式單數 👑   (D) 現在完成式複數，刪除。

故本題答案選 (C)

10. The number of engineers in hi-tech industries who want to quit and start their own business _____ on the increase.

(A) is   (B) are   (C) be   (D) X

答案 **A**

眼球追蹤

❷ 看全句

❸

The number of engineers in hi-tech industries who want to quit and start their own business _____ on the increase.

❹

❶ 看選項

(A) is   (B) are   (C) be   (D) X

中譯 在高科技產業裡，想要辭職開始創業的工程師的數目正在增加之中。

秒殺策略

❶ **判斷題型**

由選項得知，測驗點為「**BE 動詞變化**」。

❷ **判斷空格需求**

the number of engineers 為主詞，**空格為主要動詞**。

❸ **判斷主詞的單複數**

the number of + 複數 N + 單數 V，搭配**單數動詞**。

❹ **驗證答案**

be on the increase 需要 BE 動詞搭配，故選「**單數 BE 動詞**」。

檢查

(A) BE 動詞現在簡單式單數   (B) BE 動詞現在簡單式複數，刪除。

(C) BE 動詞原形，刪除。   (D) 句中需要 BE 動詞搭配，刪除。

故本題答案選 (A)

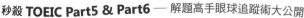

11-13

中譯

收件人: Mike Chen
寄件人: Fredrick
主題: 關於多媒體會議室的整修

嗨，Mike

　　你是否有可能延後預計下周三計劃要動工的整修呢? 我的部門正好將一個展示安排在那一天。我們無法改變地方因為在展示中，需要用到有些特定的多媒體裝置。此外，有五分之一的買家應該是從日本來參加的，由於班機，所以要重新安排展示時間也是困難的。我知道要做調整是痛苦的，但我沒有辦法不使用到這間會議室。我希望你了解我的處境，我真的感謝您的幫忙。

　　Fredrick

秒殺策略

11. 答案　**(B) are**

解題　to postpone the renovations ...which **are** planned to undertake
由...planned to undertake 得知，which 所代的是 renovations，而非 conference room，故選(B)。👑

12. 答案　**(B) are**

解題　one fifth of buyers **are** supposed to join from Japan
one fifth of buyers 為複數，故選(B)或(D)，be supposed to 為慣用法，故選(B)。👑

13. 答案　**(A) is**

解題　that making some modifications **is** a pain, but I...
that 子句中，真正主詞是動名詞 making some modifications，視為單數，故選(A)。👑

成為多益勝利組的字彙練功區

文法講解區	Mini Test 限時 5 分練習區
resume [rɪˋzjum] **v.** 恢復	clause [klɔz] **n.** 條款
adapt [əˋdæpt] **v.** 改編	review [rɪˋvju] **v.** 審查
feature film **n.** 劇情片	submerge [səbˋmɝdʒ] **v.** 淹沒
charity [ˋtʃærətɪ] **n.** 慈善	rear wheel **n.** 後輪
internal promotion test **n.** 內部升遷考試	request leaves **v.** 請假
critic [ˋkrɪtɪk] **n.** 評論家	candidate [ˋkændədet] **n.** 候選人
release [rɪˋlis] **v.** 發行（書、電影、音樂專輯）	qualified [ˋkwɑləˌfaɪd] **a.** 合格的
complimentary [ˌkɑmpləˋmɛntərɪ] **a.** 讚譽的	guidebook [ˋgaɪdˌbʊk] **n.** 旅行指南；手冊
referee [ˌrɛfəˋri] **n.** 裁判	backpacker [ˋbækˌpækɚ] **n.** 背包客
penalty [ˋpɛnḷtɪ] **n.** 犯規的處罰；罰球	manufacturing industry **n.** 製造業
deduct [dɪˋdʌkt] **v.** 扣除	renovation [ˌrɛnəˋveʃən] **n.** 裝修
position [pəˋzɪʃən] **n.** 職位；職務	multi-media [mʌltɪˋmidɪə] **a.** 多媒體的
consultant [kənˋsʌltənt] **n.** 顧問	conference room **n.** 會議室
multinational company **n.** 跨國公司	postpone [postˋpon] **v.** 使延期
version [ˋvɝʒən] **n.** 版本	undertake [ˌʌndɚˋtek] **v.** 進行
gossip [ˋgɑsəp] **n.** 八卦	device [dɪˋvaɪs] **n.** 設備
love affair **n.** 婚外情	modification [ˌmɑdəfəˋkeʃən] **n.** 修正
ride [raɪd] **n.** 遊樂設施	have no choice but to + V 不得不
recover [rɪˋkʌvɚ] **v.** 恢復	
absent [ˋæbsnt] **a.** 缺席的	
bistro [ˋbistro] **n.** 小酒館	

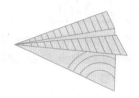

FAQ in TOEIC

5

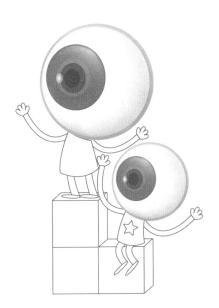

被動語態 (Passive Voice)

文法講解區

⑤ 被動語態 (Passive Voice)

簡單看

　　一般敘述中，我們都是習慣用主動語態來描述事情或狀態，即「主詞對某一對象（即受詞）做了什麼行為（即動詞）」。但若有下列情況，我們可將句子改成「被動語態」：

(1) 強調動作接受者

Citizens over 60 years old are admitted into the gallery free of charge.

（超過 60 歲以上的公民可以免費進入畫廊參觀。）

(2) 強調動作或是事實：

Lucky customers will be given discount coupons available on the web.

（幸運的顧客可以在網路上得到折價券。）

(3) 表達客觀立場：

Mike is said to have the best chance to be promoted to manager.

(Mike 據說最有機會升遷到經理。)

　　英文的被動語態有固定的句型與用法，基本形式是「BE +Vpp」；根據不同的時態，BE 動詞會有變化。TOEIC 的 Part 5 和 Part 6 常出現的考題包括：「授與動詞的被動語態」、「有受詞補語句型的被動語態」與「特殊被動語態的動詞片語」。再者，動詞當然還要搭配時態觀念才能輕鬆解題。

秒殺策略

（1）判斷「主被動」

（2）分辨「被動語態」類型

（3）搭配「時態觀念」解題

1 基本句型：只要有受詞的句型，就可以改寫成被動語態。

> 英文五大句型，以下列三句型都有受詞，後兩者為 *TOEIC* 常考句型。

〉**S + V + O**

EX

主動　Everyone discussed the new marketing strategy for the low sales last month.

被動　The new marketing strategy was discussed for the low sales last month.

（每個人在為上個月銷售不佳，討論新的行銷策略。）

〉**S + 授與 V + 間接受詞（IO）+ 直接受詞（DO）**或
　S + 授與 V + 直接受詞（DO）+ 介系詞 + 間接受詞（IO）

• **授與動詞的間接受詞（IO）與直接受詞（DO）對調時，**

(1) 接 **to** 的動詞：award, bring, give, grant, hand, lend, mail, offer, send, show, tell , write

(2) 接 **for** 的動詞：buy, choose, make, order, save, get, leave, find

(3) 接 **of** 的動詞：ask, demand, beg, inquire, rob

EX

主動　The manager offered the president many institutional innovations.

語態　= The manager offered many institutional innovations to the president.

　　　• IO 當主詞：

被動　The president was offered many institutional innovations by the manager.

語態　• DO 當主詞：

　　　Many institutional innovations were offered to the president by the manager.

（經理提供總裁很多制度創新的想法。）

　　注意：五個「提供類」動詞： give, offer, provide, supply, present，其中 provide, supply 與 present 由於用法不同於 give 與 offer，在形成被動時，請注意介係詞部分。

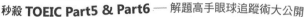
- **provide / supply / present+ 間接受詞 +with+ 直接受詞**
  → **間接受詞 + be provided / supplied / presented+with+ 直接受詞**

  EX The restaurant will provide the first 50 customers with free desserts on Mother's Day.
  → The first 50 customers <u>will be provided with</u> free desserts on Mother's Day.

  （在母親節，餐廳免費提供前 50 位顧客免費的甜點。）

〉**S＋V＋O＋O C**（受詞補語）

· **以名詞（片語）為受詞補語的動詞：**

  (1)【任命、命名】類：appoint, elect, name, label, choose, call
  (2)【使⋯變成某狀態】類：make
  (3)【認為】類：consider

  EX The members of committee elected <u>Thomas the MVP of the Year</u>.
  → Thomas was elected the MVP of the Year (by the members of committee).

  （委員會會員選 Thomas 為年度最有價值球員。）

> 情緒動詞：會使某一個人
> 對某事，或是某事引起某
> 人情緒上的反應。

· **以「（代）名詞 + to V」為受詞補語的動詞：**

  ask / advise / allow / convince / enable / encourage / expect / forbid / force / invite / need /order / persuade / permit / prompt / remind / require / tell / want / warn...

  EX Unions will require <u>management to increase wages</u> next year.
  → Management will be required to increase wages (by unions) next year.

  （工會將會在明年要求資方調升薪資）

② **特殊被動語態的動詞片語**

　　英文的動詞中，有一類動詞常被定義為「使⋯⋯」的意思，其用法常用被動語態來使用，以【 BE＋ Vpp ＋介係詞 】呈現，且都有自己獨特的搭配介係詞。此類動詞，我們可以分類為「情緒動詞」與「非情緒動詞」。

〉情緒動詞

表正面情緒：		表負面情緒：	
be satisfied with	對…感到滿意的	be worried about	對…擔憂的
be amused at	對…感到好笑的	be frightened	對…感到驚嚇的
be pleased with	對…感到喜悅	be tired of	對…感到厭煩的
be delighted with	對…感到滿意的	be disappointed at	對…感到失望的
be interested in	對…感到有興趣的	be annoyed at	對…感到惱怒的
be excited about	對…感到興奮的	be disgusted with	對…感到噁心的
be fascinated with	對…感到著迷的	be frustrated with	對…感到沮喪的
be enchanted with	對…感到著迷的	be upset about	對…感到沮喪的
be touched by	對…感到感動的	be embarrased about	對…感到尷尬的
be encouraged by	受到…感到鼓勵的	be alarmed at / by	對…感到恐慌/擔憂的

EX If customers <u>are not satisfied with</u> the service, they can file a complaint with our corporation.

（如果客戶不滿意的服務，他們可以對我們公司提出投訴。）

EX Sam <u>was very delighted to learn</u> that his proposal was accepted by the president.

（Sam 很高興地得知他的建議被總裁接受。）

〉非情緒動詞：

此類動詞雖是使用被動語態，但用法不一定全然是被動意味，多是為慣用。

與 with 搭配		與 to 搭配	
be associated with	與…有關聯	be opposed to	反對
be faced with	裝滿	be exposed to	暴露於
be equipped with	配備了	be related to	與…有關係
be crowded with	擠滿了…	be devoted to	致力於
be covered with	用…蓋著	be committed to	承諾、委託
be occupied with/in	忙於	be known to	為（人）所知

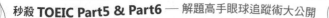

其他			
be concerned about	擔心…	be based on	為基礎
be convinced of	確信	be composed of	由…組成
be engaged in...	從事	be absorbed in	專注於
be skilled in/at	對…很熟練	be involved in	牽涉；與…有關

Our company <u>is always committed to</u> taking corporate social responsibility.
（本公司一向致力於承擔起企業社會責任。）

The CEO <u>is convinced of</u> the need to accelerate efforts to fully implement global marketing strategies
（執行長深信加速努力實行全球行銷策略的必要。）

3 其他

〉搭配情態助動詞：情態助動詞＋BE＋Vpp

EX If the consignee does not keep the goods for the moment, they <u>may simply be returned.</u>
（若此承銷人暫時不能保存貨品，貨品可能被退回。）

〉使役動詞 make 的被動態：BE made to＋V

EX The employees in the factory <u>are often made to work</u> overtime to meet deadlines.
（這工廠的員工常被迫加班以趕上出貨期限。）

〉不用被動式呈現的動詞（片語）：

· 發生：**take place, happen, occur**

· 連綴動詞：**look, feel, smell, taste, remain** 等

· 其他：**arrive**（到達），**exist**（存在），**miss**（失去），**belong to**（屬於），**consist of**（包含），**break out**（爆發）等

EX Clashes <u>broke out</u> between riot police officers and protesters on Thursday.
（週四時防暴警察和示威者之間爆發衝突。）

4 主被動搭配時態

基本加法公式過程	公式
	簡單式 被動語態：BE + Vpp

EX The organization was widely criticized for failing to give support in time.
（那組織遭各方批評未能及時給予支持。）

BE　+　Ving +)　　　　　BE　+ Vpp be　+　being + Vpp	進行式 被動語態：BE + being + Vpp

EX Our new product is being exhibited at the trade fair.
（我們新產品正在商展中展示著。）

have + Vpp +)　　　BE　+ Vpp have + been + Vpp	完成式 被動語態：have + been + Vpp

EX The businessman has been penalized for evading taxes on purpose.
（那商人因為故意逃稅而已受懲罰了。）

注意：依照不同時間，be 動詞與 have 做不同變化。原則上各主動語態都可以改成被動，但未來進行式與現在／過去／未來完成進行式較少以被動語態出現。

生命加值室

情態助動詞

又稱情態動詞，後面必須搭配原形動詞。此類助動詞本身表示「可能性、意願、能力、確定性、義務、許可」等意義。例如：may, will, can, shall, ought to, must 等。

Mini Test 練習區 限時 5 分

1. Much to the delight of the fans, they _____ to appearances of the new sports cars when automobile company launches the program for the 2015 season.
   (A) treat   (B) were treated   (C) are treating   (D) will be treated

2. A large sum _____ for compensation for civilian loss of life, injury, and property damage from unlawful attack.
   (A) allocated   (B) will allocate
   (C) has been allocated   (D) was to allocate

3. Morocco might face the risk of _____ a tax haven and sanctioned if it did not adopt the prevailing OECD standard.
   (A) labelling   (B) being labelled
   (C) having labelled   (D) having been labelling

4. A retiring pension shall _____ a government servant who retires, or is retired before attaining the age of superannuation.
   (A) grant to   (B) be granted to   (C) grant from   (D) be granted from

5. The board has been presented _____ the plan for emergent official approval.
   (A) with   (B) to   (C) for   (D) by

6. Each of our suites _____ with air conditioning, Wi-Fi Internet connection, 1 mini-bar, and 1 TV.
   (A) equips   (B) has equipped   (C) is equipping   (D) is equipped

7. The peace talk in Geneva will _____ next month and seven political leaders will be present.
   (A) hold   (B) held   (C) take place   (D) be taken place

8. James _____ at Linda's rejective attitude and then left without saying anything.
   (A) disappointed   (B) was disappointing
   (C) was disappointed   (D) has disappointed

9. Under some circumstances, females in particular experience multiple forms of discrimination and _____ verbal violence.
   (A) expose   (B) expose to
   (C) are exposed to   (D) exposed themselves to

10. The new committee _____ widely renowned experts with distinguished academic credentials and professional experience.

(A) is made of   (B) is consisted of   (C) is comprised by   (D) is composed of

Question 11-13 refer to the news article

Recently, it _____ that participating in more mental games can assist we

      11 (A) reported
          (B) was reported
          (C) has reported
          (D) has been reported

humans in warding off the symptoms of cognitive decline. An experiment which _____ by a group of the UK scientists proved the inference true. The

      12 (A) conducted
          (B) is conducted
          (C) was conducted
          (D) has conducted

experiment was involved 1000 testers. They were divided into 2 groups. Testers of one group _____ in many games designed to challenge their mental

      13 (A) was engaged
          (B) were engaged
          (C) has engaged
          (D) have engaged

abilities, while those of the other group were not encouraged to do so. Therefore, the scientists found the ones performing the activities significantly had better cognitive abilities.

1-10 Ans: 1.(D) 2.(C) 3.(B) 4.(B) 5.(A) 6.(D) 7.(C) 8.(C) 9.(C) 10.(D)

1. Much to the delight of the fans, they _____ to appearances of the new sports cars when automobile company launches the program for the 2015 season.

    (A) treat   (B) were treated   (C) are treating   (D) will be treated

答案 D

眼球追蹤

❷ 看全句

Much to the delight of the fans, they _____ to appearances of the new sports cars when automobile company 「launches」❸ the program for the 2015 season.

❶ 看選項

    (A) treat   (B) were treated   (C) are treating   (D) will be treated

中譯 令車迷高興的是，當汽車公司發表 2015 季計畫時，他們將被招待觀賞新跑車亮相。

秒殺策略

❶ 判斷題型

由選項得知，測驗點為「**動詞**」。

❷ 判斷空格需求

分析句子得知，they _____ 車迷是被招待，空格需要**被動語態的主要動詞**。

❸ 搭配時態，驗證答案

搭配副詞子句 when... launches ...時態，主要子句時態應為未來式。

故選「**未來被動式**」。

檢查

(A) 現在簡單主動式，刪除。
(B) 過去簡單被動式，刪除。
(C) 現在進行主動式，刪除。
(D) 未來簡單被動式

故本題答案選 (D)

2. A large sum _____ for compensation for civilian loss of life, injury, and property damage from unlawful attack.

(A) allocated   (B) will allocate

(C) has been allocated   (D) was to allocate

答案 C

眼球追蹤

❷ 看全句

A large sum _____ for compensation for civilian loss of life, injury, and property damage from unlawful attack.

❶ 看選項

(A) allocated   ❸   (B) will allocate

(C) has been allocated   (D) was to allocate

中譯 一大筆款項已撥給賠償平民生命損失，人身傷害，以及不受非法攻擊的財產損失。

秒殺策略

❶ 判斷題型

由選項得知，測驗點為「**動詞**」。

❷ 判斷空格需求

分析句子得知，主詞為 A large sum，**空格為主要動詞。**

依主詞與選項，sum / allocate，款項是被配置，空格需要**被動語態的主要動詞。**

❸ 驗證答案

選項中，只有(C)為被動語態。

檢查

(A) 過去式簡單主動或過去分詞，刪除。

(B) 未來簡單主動式，刪除。

(C) 現在完成被動式

(D) 過去簡單主動語態，為 be to V 的用法，表示「不久的將來幾乎肯定會發生的事件」或是「正式的計畫或安排」，但仍不是被動語態，刪除。故本題答案選 (C)

3. Morocco might face the risk of _____ a tax haven and sanctioned if it did not adopt the prevailing OECD standard.

(A) labelling　　　　　　　　　　(B) being labelled

(C) having labelled　　　　　　　(D) having been labelling

答案 B

眼球追蹤

❷ 看全句

Morocco might face the risk of _____ a tax haven and sanctioned if it did not adopt the prevailing OECD standard.

❶ 看選項

(A) labelling

❸ (B) being labelled

(C) having labelled

(D) having been labelling

中譯　摩洛哥若不採納現行經濟合作發展組織的標準，可能會被標籤為避稅天堂而受制裁。

秒殺策略 👑

❶ **判斷題型**

由選項得知，測驗點為「**動詞**」。

❷ **判斷空格需求**

分析句子得知，主詞為 Morocco，**空格為接介係詞 of 之後的動詞**。依主詞與選項，Morocco / label，摩洛哥應該被標籤為，空格需要**被動語態的動詞**。

❸ **驗證答案**

選項中，只有(B)為被動語態。👑

檢查

(A) 簡單主動式，刪除。

(B) 簡單被動式 👑

(C) 完成主動式，刪除。

(D) 完成進行主動式，刪除。

註：(1) 本句為與現在事實相反的假設語氣

　　(2) OECD（Organization for Economic Co-operation and Development）經濟合作暨發展組織

故本題答案選 (B)

4. A retiring pension shall _____ a government servant who retires, or is retired before attaining the age of superannuation.

   (A) grant to   (B) be granted to

   (C) grant from   (D) be granted from

答案 B

眼球追蹤

❷ 看全句

A retiring pension shall _____ a government servant who retires, or is retired before attaining the age of superannuation.

❶ 看選項

(A) grant to   (B) be granted to ❸   (C) grant from   (D) be granted from

中譯 對於在達到領養老金年紀前退休的政府公職人員，應給予退休金。

秒殺策略 ♛

❶ 判斷題型

由選項得知，測驗點為「**動詞 grant 變化與用法**」。

❷ 判斷空格需求

分析句子得知，主詞為 A retiring pension，**空格為接助動詞 shall 之後的主要動詞**。依主詞與選項，retiring pension / grant，退休金是被授予（給人），空格需要**被動語態的動詞**，考慮 (B) 與 (D)。

❸ 驗證答案

grant 為授與動詞，grant sb sth = grant sth to sb，故介係詞應搭配 to。♛

檢查

(A) 簡單主動式，刪除。

(B) 簡單被動式 ♛

(C) 簡單主動式，且介係詞搭配錯誤，刪除。

(D) 簡單被動式，但介係詞搭配錯誤，刪除。

故本題答案選 (B)

133

5. The board has been presented _____ the plan for emergent official approval.

   (A) with   (B) to   (C) for   (D) by

答案 A

眼球追蹤

❷ 看全句 ── ❸
The board has been | presented | _____ the plan for emergent official approval .

❶ 看選項
(A) with   (B) to   (C) for   (D) by

中譯 計畫已經呈交於董事會做緊急正式批准。

秒殺策略

❶ 判斷題型

由選項得知，測驗點為「**介係詞**」。

❷ 判斷空格需求

分析句子得知，主詞為 the board，主要動詞為 has been presented，故**空格為搭配 present 的介係詞用法**。

❸ 驗證答案

公式：present sb with sth = present sth to sb

the board 為 sb，the plan 為 sth，故搭配 present sb with sth 的用法。
被動語態為 sb be presented with sth，故搭配選項(A)。

檢查

故本題答案選 (A)

6. Each of our suites _____ with air conditioning, Wi-Fi Internet connection, 1 mini-bar, and 1 TV.
   (A) equips   (B) has equipped   (C) is equipping   (D) is equipped

答案 D

眼球追蹤

❷ 看全句   **❸**
Each of our suites _____ with air conditioning, Wi-Fi Internet connection, 1
mini-bar, and 1 TV.

❶ 看選項
  (A) equips   (B) has equipped   (C) is equipping   (D) is equipped

中譯 我們的每一套房內皆配有空調，無線網絡連接，一個迷你吧和一個電視。

秒殺策略 👑

❶ 判斷題型

由選項得知，測驗點為「**動詞 equip 變化與用法**」。

❷ 判斷空格需求

分析句子與選項得知，主詞為 each of our suites，**空格為 equip 動詞**。
依主詞與選項 Each of our suites / equip 套房是被給予裝備的，故採**被動語態**。

❸ 驗證答案

公式：be equipped with 表「（人/物）具有...的配備」，已成慣用搭配語，其中只有(D)為被動語態。 👑

檢查

(A) 簡單主動式，刪除。
(B) 完成主動式，刪除。
(C) 進行主動式，equip 鮮少用進行式，刪除。
(D) 簡單被動式 👑
故本題答案選 (D)

1 詞類　2 動詞　3 時態　4 主詞與動詞的一致性　5 被動語態

7. The peace talk in Geneva will _____ next month and seven political leaders will be present.

(A) hold　　　　　　　　　　(B) held

(C) take place　　　　　　　(D) be taken place

答案　C

眼球追蹤

❷ 看全句

The peace talk in Geneva will _____ next month and seven political leaders will be present.

❶ 看選項

(A) hold　　　　(B) held　　　❸(C) take place　　　(D) be taken place

中譯　日內瓦和平會談將在下個月舉行，有七個政治領袖將出席。

秒殺策略

❶ 判斷V題型

由選項得知，測驗點為「**動詞 hold 與 take place 變化與用法**」。

❷ 判斷空格需求

分析句子與選項得知，主詞為 the peace talk，**空格為主要動詞**。

hold (v)舉辦：人/組織單位 hold 活動 = 活動 + be held (by 人/組織單位)

take place (v)舉行，發生：活動 + take place，**不用被動式**。

❸ 驗證答案

the peace talk 為活動，後方搭配 **be held 的被動語態**或 **take place 的主動語態**。

檢查

(A) hold 主動語態，刪除。

(B) hold 過去分詞，放在 will 後，應再搭配原形，被動為 will be held 才符合文法，刪除。

(C) take place 的主動語態

(D) take place 的被動語態，但 take place 無被動，刪除。

136 故本題答案選 (C)

8. James _____ at Linda's rejective attitude and then left without saying anything.
   (A) disappointed
   (B) was disappointing
   (C) was disappointed
   (D) has disappointed

答案 C

眼球追蹤

❷ 看全句
James _____ at Linda's rejective attitude and then left without saying anything.

❶ 看選項
   (A) disappointed
   (B) was disappointing
   (C) was disappointed ❸
   (D) has disappointed

中譯　James3 對於 Linda 拒絕的態度很失望，之後就不發一語離開了。

秒殺策略 👑

❶ 判斷題型

由選項得知，測驗點為「disappoint 情緒動詞用法」。

❷ 判斷空格需求

分析句子與選項得知，主詞為 James，**空格為主要動詞**。

disappoint 慣用法為 人+be disappointed at sth with sb。由 James/disappoint/at Linda rejective attitude 得知，空格應用**被動語態**表示 James **所發出的情緒**。

❸ 驗證答案

唯有(C)可以表示被動語態的動作，故選(C)。👑

檢查

(A) 過去簡單主動式或是過去分詞，刪除。

(B) 過去進行主動式，刪除。

(C) 過去簡單被動式 👑

(D) 現在完成主動式，刪除。

故本題答案選 (C)

137

9. Under some circumstances, females in particular experience multiple forms of discrimination and _____ verbal violence.
   (A) expose
   (B) expose to
   (C) are exposed to
   (D) exposed themselves to

答案 C

眼球追蹤

❷ 看全句

Under some circumstances, females in particular experience multiple forms of discrimination and _____ verbal violence.

❶ 看選項

(A) expose
(B) expose to
(C) are exposed to ❸
(D) exposed themselves to

中譯　某些情況下，女性特 容易受到多種形式的歧視與受到語言暴力的侵害。

秒殺策略 👑

❶ 判斷題型

由選項得知，測驗點為「**expose 動詞變化與用法**」。

❷ 判斷空格需求

分析句子 females...experience ... /and /_____ verbal violence 得知，
主詞為 females，**空格為與 experience 時態一致的動詞**。
expose (v) 表「使接觸到」，用法為：人 expose oneself to Ving/N = 人 be exposed to Ving/N。依 expose 的用法，故可選(C)或(D)。

❸ 驗證答案

將時態納入考量，應，故選(C)。👑

檢查

(A) 應為 expose themselves to 或 are exposed to，刪除。

(B) 應為 expose themselves to 或 are exposed to，刪除。

(C) 現在式且符合 expose 用法 👑

(D) 應為 expose themselves to，刪除。

故本題答案選 (C)

10. The new committee _____ widely renowned experts with distinguished academic credentials and professionalexperience.
(A) is made of
(B) is consisted of
(C) is comprised by
(D) is composed of

答案 **D**

眼球追蹤

❷ 看全句

The new committee _____ widely renowned experts with distinguished academic credentials and professional experience.

❶ 看選項

(A) is made of　(B) is consisted of　(C) is comprised by　(D) is composed of

中譯 新的委員會是由傑出的學術成與專業經驗的知名專家所組成的。

秒殺策略 👑

❶ 判斷題型

由選項得知，測驗點為「**組成動詞的用法**」。

❷ 判斷空格需求

分析句子與選項，The new committee / _____ / widely renowned experts，主詞為 the new committee，**空格為表「組成」的主要動詞**，widely renowned experts 為組成的個體。

公式：A〔團體〕，B〔個體〕

A be made up of B = A be composed of B

= A consist of B = A comprise B

❸ 驗證答案

看題目判斷 committee（團體）/ experts（個體），用公式逐一檢視，故選 (D)。👑

檢查

(A) 應改為 is made up of，刪除。

(B) 應改為 consists of，主動語態，刪除。

(C) 應改為 comprise，主動語態，刪除。

(D) is composed of 選項為正確選項👑

故本題答案選 (D)

139

11-13 題參考下列新聞文章

中譯

　　近來，據報導，有參與更多的智力遊戲可以幫助我們人類防範知能退化的症狀。由一群英國科學家所做的實驗證實這推論是事實。實驗有一千名測試者。他們被分成兩組。一組測試者從試了許多被設計用來挑戰他們知能的遊戲，而另一組並沒被鼓勵如此做。因此，科學家發現有做活動的那組測試者明顯地有較好的知能能力。

秒殺策略

11. 答案　**(D) has been reported**
    Recently, it **has been reported** that ...
    解題　此為 it is/was reported that S+V 的句型。that 子句為真正主詞。(B)(D)選項為被動式，為可參考答案。接著由時態 recently 來判斷，本句應選完成式。故選(D)。

12. 答案　**(C) was conducted**
    An experiment which **was conducted** by...proved the inference true.
    解題　which 代表 experiment，做 which 關係子句的主詞，句中的動詞 conduct 與 experiment 的關係應用被動來呈現，故選(B)或(C)，主要子句的動詞為 proved 過去時態，因此答案選(C)。

13. 答案　**(B) were engaged**
    Testers of one group **were engaged** in many games designed to challenge their mental abilities...
    解題　本題選主要動詞，測驗使用被動語態的習慣搭配片語。be engaged in「從事…活動/事情」，故(A)(B)為可參考答案。本句主詞為 Testers of one group，複數，故選(B)。

成為多益勝利組的字彙練功區

文法講解區	Mini Test 限時 5 分練習區
admit [əd`mɪt] v. 准許進入	compensation [ˌkɑmpən`seʃən] n. 補償
discount coupon n. 折價券	allocate [`ælə͵ket] v. 分配
promote [prə`mot]] v. 升遷	property [`prɑpə·tɪ] n. 財產
marketing strategy n. 行銷策略	sanction [`sæŋkʃən] v. 制裁
innovation [ˌɪnə`veʃən] n. 創新	prevailing [prɪ`velɪŋ] a. 主要的
committee [kə`mɪtɪ] n. 委員會	label [`lebḷ] [v. 把...列為
union [`junjən] n. 工會	retiring pension n. 退休養老金
management [`mænɪdʒmənt] n. 資方	superannuation n. 老年退休
wage [wedʒ] n. 薪資	approval [ə`pruvḷ] n. 批准
file a complaint n. 提出投訴	suite [swit] n. 套房
corporation [ˌkɔrpə`reʃən] n. 公司	equip [ɪ`kwɪp] v. 裝備，配備
proposal [prə`pozḷ] n. 建議；提議	peace talk n. 和談
accelerate [æk`sɛlə͵ret] v. 加速	multiple [`mʌltəpḷ] a. 複合的；多樣的
implement [`ɪmpləmənt] v. 履行；實施	discrimination [dɪ͵skrɪmə`neʃən] n. 歧視
consignee [ˌkɑnsaɪ`ni] n. 承銷人	verbal violence n. 語言暴力
meet deadline v. 趕上期限	credential [krɪ`dɛnʃəl] n. 憑證
riot police officer n. 防暴警察	distinguished [dɪ`stɪŋgwɪʃt] a. 卓越的
protester [pro`tɛstə·] n. 示威者	renowned [rɪ`naʊnd] a. 有名的
criticize [`krɪtɪ͵saɪz] v. 批評	ward off v. 防止
exhibit [ɪg`zɪbɪt] v. 展示	symptom [`sɪmptəm] n. 症狀
trade fair n. 商展	cognitive [`kɑgnətɪv] a. 認知的
penalize [`pinḷ͵aɪz] v. 懲罰	inference [`ɪnfərəns] n. 推論
evade [ɪ`ved] v. 逃避	

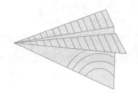

FAQ in TOEIC

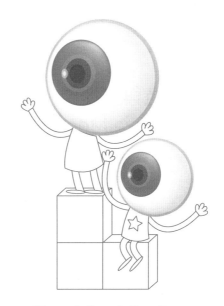

6

假設語氣與條件句

(Subjunctive Mood & Conditionals)

文法講解區

6 假設語氣與條件句
(Subjunctive Mood & Conditionals)

簡單看

本單元所指的條件句，都是包含if子句，用來描述某一動作的發生與否，觀念有二：

(1) **條件副詞子句**：表示**習慣或真理**的條件句
   使用時機：用在一般現在和未來時間中**可能發生**的事件或情況

(2) **假設條件句**：表示**假設語氣**的條件句
   使用時機：用來描述現在與過去時間**不可能發生**的事件或情況

秒殺策略

（1）判斷題型：測驗「條件副詞子句」還是「假設語氣（條件句）」
（2）測驗「條件副詞子句」→ 現在簡單式代替未來式
（3）測驗「假設語氣」
   → 空格在 if 子句中，用主要子句時態來推
   → 空格在主要子句中，用 if 子句時態來推
（4）以上都不是，則測驗「假設語氣的特殊句型」
   → 思考「混搭、should、替代、省略與倒裝」

1 條件副詞子句

此即「一般條件句」，表示不確定但**現在或將來可能發生**的條件狀態。if 條件副詞子句，時態會用現在式代替未來式，其結果子句可能為表習慣的現在式、語態助動詞加原形動詞，或祈使句。

條件句	結果子句	
If＋S1＋現在式 V,	**S2＋**	現在式 V （表示習慣）
		will / can / may / shall＋原 V
		祈使句

EX If he arrives in the office earlier, he often has a cup of brewed coffee first.

（若他提早到公司，他通常先來杯咖啡。）

EX If interest rates keep rising, the price of a bond will go down.

（若利率持續上升時，債券價格將下跌。）

EX If Mr. Chen comes back, please ask him to call me back.

（若陳先生回來，請他回撥給我。）

2 與現在事實相反的假設語氣

表達與現在事實不符的假定、想像與願望的敘述時，可用「與現在事實相反」的假設語氣。要注意的是，此 if 條件子句中，無論是第幾人稱(I, you, he)的 be 動詞一律用 were。

條件句		結果子句	
If＋S1	＋ **were** ＋ 過去式 V ＋ 過去式助動詞＋原形 V	**S2＋**	**would / should could / might** ＋原 V
（與現在事實相反之假設）		（與現在事實相反之假設）	

EX If my schedule were not so tight, I would take today off.

（要是我的行程沒如此緊湊，我今天一定休一天。）

EX If the client took the MRT, he might be present at our meeting now.

（要是這顧客有搭捷運，他或許現在就出席於我們的會議上。）

EX If the supervisor could have a video meeting with us, we might solve the problem right away.

（要是上司可以現在和我們視訊會議，我們或許可以立刻解決問題。）

❸ 與過去事實相反的假設語氣

表達與過去事實不符的假定、想像與願望的敘述時，可用「與過去事實相反」的假設語氣。

條件句	結果子句		
If＋S1＋had p.p.	**S2＋**	**would / should could / might**	**＋have p.p.**
（與過去事實相反之假設）	（與過去事實相反之假設）		

EX If we had received the order a week ago, we would have had time for material preparation then.

（若我們一周前提早收到訂單，我們當時就有時間準備材料。）

❹ 混合搭配的假設語氣

表達與過去事實不符的假定、想像與願望的敘述時，但結果是與現在事實不符的狀況時，可用「混合搭配」的假設語氣。

條件句	結果子句		
If＋S1＋had p.p.	**S2＋**	**would / should could / might**	**＋原 V**
（與過去事實相反之假設）	（與現在事實相反之假設）		

EX If the president had noticed the problem , our company wouldn't collapse for lack of support.

（若總裁有注意到問題，我們公司現在也不會因無力支持而倒閉。）

❺ 含有 should 的假設語氣

條件句	結果子句		
If＋S1＋should＋原 V	**S2＋**	**will/would shall/should can/could may/might**	**＋原 V**
（目前實現可能性小，且對未來的不確定,中文用「要是」或是「萬一」表示）			

146

EX If you should pay one million dollars deposit in advance, we can give you a 5% discount.

（要是你事先預付一百萬訂金，我們會給你 5%的折扣。）

6 if 替代語句

若非……；要不是……				
與現在事實相反的用法				
But for Without If it were not for	+N	S+	**would / should could / might**	+原 V
與過去事實相反的用法				
But for Without If it had not been for	+N	S+	**would / should could / might**	+have p.p.

EX Without your timely help, the whole work wouldn't be done now.

（要不是你及時幫忙，全部工作不可能現在完成的。）

EX But for the security guard, our apartment would have been broken into last weekend.

（要不是那警衛，我們公寓上周末就遭竊入了。）

7 if 省略與倒裝句型

原句（條件句）	▶	▲省略 if + 倒裝
If + S + were + adj / N If + S + had p.p. If + S + should + 原 V	進行倒裝	Were + S + adj / N Had + S + p.p. Should + S + 原 V

EX Were I younger, I would jump ship.

（要是我年輕點，我就會跳槽了。）

EX Had the equipment been purchased earlier, we could have demonstrated it in the meeting.

（要是有早點購買設備，我們就可以在會議上展示了。）

EX Should there not be enough tickets sold, the charity concert would be cancelled.

（萬一票賣得不好，慈善演唱會將會被取消。）

Mini Test 練習區 限時5分 ⏱

1. If immediate action _____ to prevent the accident, our workers mightn't have been hurt so seriously.

   (A) took   (B) were taken   (C) was taken   (D) had been taken

2. If a firm _____ to reduce labor costs, one possible way is to slash expenditures by laying off workers.

   (A) plans   (B) planned   (C) were planned   (D) had planned

3. If the company didn't achieve some level of production, its profits _____ so rapidly.

   (A) could increase   (B) couldn't increase

   (C) could have increased   (D) couldn't have increased

4. If it _____ for preparation in advance, the accounting firm couldn't have performed a full audit for our company.

   (A) was not   (B) were not   (C) had been   (D) had not been

5. If we _____ lower our prices, our competitors would feel obligated to do likewise.

   (A) will   (B) shall   (C) should   (D) were

6. The power outage could be avoided now if the maintenance team _____ the plant more closely last evening.

   (A) checked   (B) would check

   (C) had checked   (D) would have checked

7. _____ the poor hygiene conditions, tourism and urban development in Africa would be better.

   (A) With   (B) But   (C) But for   (D) Had it not been for

8. We _____ annual profit forecasts now if we had properly advertised for our products.

   (A) met   (B) have met   (C) could have met   (D) could meet

9. Had the young manager had a successful presentation, he _____ a new level of respect from his subordinates then.

   (A) attained   (B) were attained

   (C) should attain   (D) should have attain

10. If Lin _____ the manager, he might make the same decision now.
 (A) was (B) were (C) is (D) has been

Question 11-13 refer to the following advertisement

To Whom It May Concern,

Two weeks ago I took part in a trip organized by your travel agency. Unfortunately, I did not get almost anything of what I expected. If I _____ this

11 (A) write
 (B) wrote
 (C) didn't write
 (D) hadn't written

letter now, you wouldn't know how to train your tour guide.

Our guide did not have enough qualification. He did not follow the trip program, which made the trip behind schedule and caused lots of inconvenience. Besides, he was not familiar with the places he needed to introduce, so the whole trip was tedious. If he could provide us with accurate and amusing information on the tourist attractions, we _____ more fun during

12 (A) will have
 (B) would have
 (C) will have had
 (D) would have had

the trip.

My letter of complaint may not be the only one that you will receive.

If your company _____ to build customer loyalty, please try to come up

13 (A) tends
 (B) will tend
 (C) would tend
 (D) would have tended

with some remedies as soon as possible.

1-10 Ans: 1.(D) 2.(A) 3.(B) 4.(D) 5.(C) 6.(C) 7.(C) 8.(D) 9.(C) 10.(B)

1. If immediate action _____ to prevent the accident, our workers mightn't have been hurt so seriously.
   (A) took
   (B) were taken
   (C) was taken
   (D) had been taken

答案 D

眼球追蹤

❶ ❸ If | immediate action _____ | to prevent | the accident, our workers | ❷ mightn't have been hurt | so seriously.

❸ **看選項**
   (A) took   (B) were taken   (C) was taken   (D) had been taken

中譯 若是有採取立即行動去預防意外，我們員工就不會受傷如此嚴重。

秒殺策略 👑

❶ **判斷題型**

看到 if 與空格位置，立即聯想是條件副詞子句或是假設句型。

❷ **判斷何種假設句型**

由結果子句 mightn't have been hurt 得知，本題測驗「**與過去事實相反的假設語氣**」或「**混合句型**」觀念，搭配 if 條件句公式應為「If＋S1＋had Vpp」。

❸ **判斷主被動**

看主詞與選項，immediate action/take 為被動關係，故用**被動語態**，因此空格需要使用「**過去完成被動式**」。👑

檢查

(A) 過去簡單式主動，刪除。
(B) 過去簡單被動複數，刪除。
(C) 過去簡單被動單數，刪除。
(D) 過去完成被動式 👑

公式		套用公式
過去完成　had Vpp		had Vpp
＋被動　　　　　be　Vpp.	→	+)　　be taken
had been taken		**had been taken**

故本題答案選 (D)

6.假設語氣與條件句｜秒殺實戰區

6 假設語氣與條件句

7 不定詞與動名詞

8 分詞

9 比較句型

10 名詞與代名詞

2. If a firm _____ to reduce labor costs, one possible way is to slash expenditures by laying off workers.
(A) plans   (B) planned   (C) were planned   (D) had planned

答案 A

眼球追蹤

If a firm _____ to reduce labor costs, one possible way is to slash expenditures by laying off workers.

❸ **看選項**
(A) plans   (B) planned   (C) were planned   (D) had planned

中譯 如果公司計劃削減勞動力成本，一種可能的方式是通過裁員來削減開支。

秒殺策略

❶ **判斷題型**

看到 if 與空格位置，立即聯想是條件副詞子句或是假設句型。

❷ **if 條件句的時態**

由結果子句 one possible way is to slash 得知，為測驗「**條件副詞子句**」觀念。主要句時態為 is to slash，if 條件句公式應為「If＋S1＋現在式 Ｖ」。

❸ **判斷主被動**

看主詞與選項，a firm/plan 為主動關係，故應用**主動語態**，
因此空格需要「**現在簡單主動式**」，主詞第三人稱單數時，動詞加 s/es。

檢查

(A) 現在簡單主動單數
(B) 過去簡單主動，刪除。
(C) 過去簡單被動複數，刪除。
(D) 過去完成主動，刪除。
故本題答案選 (A)

3. If the company didn't achieve some level of production, its profits _____ so rapidly.

    (A) could increase   (B) couldn't increase

    (C) could have increased   (D) couldn't have increased

答案 B

眼球追蹤

❶❷

If | the company didn't achieve | some level of production, | its profits _____ so

rapidly.

    (A) could increase   ❸ (B) couldn't increase

    (C) could have increased   (D) couldn't have increased

中譯 公司沒有達到生產某種程度，利潤就不能增加得如此之快。

秒殺策略 👑

❶ **判斷題型**

看到 if 與空格位置，立即聯想是條件副詞子句或是假設句型。

❷ **判斷何種假設句型**

由條件句 the company didn't achieve 得知，本題測驗「**與現在事實相反的假設句型**」的觀念，結果子句公式應為「S2＋would/should/could/might＋原 V」。

❸ **判斷語意**

本題旨在測試時間（現在／過去）與語意，依題意，空格需要「**否定的／現在事實相反假設句型**」的結果句。👑

檢查

(A) 肯定／現在事實相反的假設，刪除。   (B) 否定／現在事實相反的假設 👑

(C) 肯定／過去事實相反的假設，刪除。   (D) 否定／過去事實相反的假設，刪除。

故本題答案選 (B)

4. If it _____ for preparation in advance, the accounting firm couldn't have performed a full audit for our company.

(A) was not　　(B) were not　　(C) had been　　(D) had not been

答案 D

眼球追蹤

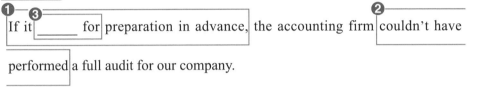

If it _____ for preparation in advance, the accounting firm couldn't have performed a full audit for our company.

(A) was not　　(B) were not　　(C) had been　　❸ (D) had not been

中譯 　若不事先準備，會計師事務所不可能為我們公司進行完整的審計。

秒殺策略 ♛

❶ 判斷題型

看到 if 與空格位置，立即聯想是條件副詞子句或是假設句型。

❷ 判斷何種假設句型

由結果子句 couldn't have performed 得知，本題測驗「**與過去事實相反的假設句型**」的觀念，條件子句公式應為「If＋S1＋had Vpp」。

❸ 判斷語意

依空格推測，本題測試點為「若非；要不是」的語。

依題意，空格需要「**否定的／過去事實相反假設句型**」的條件子句。♛

檢查

(A) 非假設語氣句型，刪除。

(B) 否定的／現在事實相反的假設，刪除。

(C) 肯定的／過去事實相反的假設，刪除。

(D) 否定的／過去事實相反假設 ♛

故本題答案選 (D)

5. If we _____ lower our prices, our competitors would feel obligated to do likewise.

   (A) will   (B) shall   (C) should   (D) were

答案 C

眼球追蹤

❶   **❷**

If we _____ lower our prices, | our competitors | should feel obligated | to do

likewise.

❸ 看選項

 (A) will   (B) shall   (C) should   (D) were

中譯 要是我們降低價格,我們的競爭對手會覺得有義務這樣做。

秒殺策略 👑

❶ 判斷題型

看到 if 與空格位置,立即聯想是條件副詞子句或是假設句型。

❷ 判斷條件句空格與選項

由結果子句 should feel obligated to do 得知,為測驗「**條件副詞子句**」或「**假設句型**」觀念。若是測試「**條件副詞子句**」,則 lower 動詞前無須搭配助動詞,得知,本題測試「**假設句型**」。

❸ 驗證答案

依選項判定,本題測試點是「**含有 should 的假設語氣**」,表示「要是;萬一」。公式為:If+S1+_should_+原 V,S2+shall/should+原 V。👑

檢查

(A) 條件句中不可能有未來式動詞,刪除。

(B) 用於第一人稱,表示「將,會」或是「徵求對方意見」,刪除。

(C) 「If+S1+should+原 V,...」,should 表示「萬一」👑

(D) lower 為動詞,無須搭配 Be 動詞,刪除。

故本題答案選 (C)

6. The power outage could be avoided now if the maintenance team ＿＿＿ the plant more closely last evening.
   (A) checked
   (B) would check
   (C) had checked
   (D) would have checked

答案  **C**

眼球追蹤

The power outage │could be avoided now│ if the maintenance team ＿＿＿ the

plant more closely │last evening│

   (A) checked
   (B) would check
   (C) had checked
   (D) would have checked

中譯　如果維修團隊昨晚可以更仔細檢查，那現在就可以避免停電了。

秒殺策略

❶ **判斷題型**

看到 if 與空格位置，立即聯想是條件副詞子句或是假設句型。

❷ **判斷何種假設句型**

由結果句 The power outage could be avoided now 得知，為測驗「**與現在事實相反的假設語氣**」或「**混合句型**」觀念。

❸ **驗證答案**

條件句中有 last evening，故測試點是「**混合句型**」。

混合句型公式：If＋S1＋had Vpp,S2＋would/should/could/might＋原 V

依題意與文法，空格為「**過去完成式**」，搭配與過去事實相反假設句型。👑

檢查

(A) 搭配與現在事實相反的條件子句，刪除。

(B) 搭配與現在事實相反的條件子句，刪除。

(C) 搭配與過去事實相反假設句型條件子句👑

(D) 假設語氣條件句中不可能有 would have pp，刪除。

故本題答案選 (C)　　　　　　　　　　　　　　　　　　　155

7. _____ the poor hygiene conditions, tourism and urban development in Africa would be better.

(A) With   (B) But

(C) But for   (D) Had it not been for

答案 C

眼球追蹤

_____ the poor hygiene conditions, tourism and urban development in Africa

❷

would be better.

❶ **看選項**

(A) With   (B) But

(C) But for ❸   (D) Had it not been for

中譯   要不是衛生環境不好，非洲的旅遊與城市發展現在應會更好。

秒殺策略 👑

❶ **判斷題型**

由選項，可猜測是測驗 if 替代語句型「若非；要不是」的假設句型。

❷ **判斷何種假設句型**

由主要句 would be better 得知，為測驗「**與現在事實相反的假設語氣**」。

❸ **驗證答案**

搭配「若非；要不是」與「**與現在事實相反**」的假設句型公式。依題意與文法，可選「but for/without/If it were not for/Were it not for」。👑

─────────────────────────────

檢查

(A) 不符合文法與語意，刪除。

(B) 不符合文法與語意，刪除。

(C)「**與現在事實相反**」的「若非；要不是」假設句型 👑

(D)「與過去事實相反」的「若非；要不是」句型，刪除。

故本題答案選 (C)

8. We _____ annual profit forecasts now if we had properly advertised for our products.

(A) met   (B) have met   (C) could have met   (D) could meet

答案 D

眼球追蹤

We _____ annual profit forecasts |now| if we |had properly advertised| for our products.

(A) met   (B) have met   (C) could have met   (D) could meet

中譯 如果之前我們有替產品作廣告，我們現在就可以達到年度預測的盈利值了。

秒殺策略

❶ **判斷題型**

見 if 與 had properly advertised，聯想是條件副詞子句或是假設句型。

❷ **判斷何種假設句型**

由條件句 had properly advertised，得知，為測驗「**與過去事實相反的假設語氣**」或「**混合句型**」觀念。

❸ **驗證答案**

結果子句中有 now，因此本題測試點是「**混合句型**」。本題是結果句放句首。
混合句型公式：If＋S1＋had Vpp,S2＋would/should/could/might＋原 V
依題意，空格需要符合與現在事實相反的結果子句。

檢查

(A) 不會置於假設語氣結果句內，刪除。
(B) 不會置於假設語氣結果句內，刪除。
(C) 用於與過去事實相反的結果子句，見 now，刪除。
(D) 與現在事實相反的結果子句
故本題答案選 (D)

9. Had the young manager had a successful presentation, he _____ a new level of respect from his subordinates then.

(A) attained　(B) were attained　(C) should attain　(D) should have attain

答案 C

眼球追蹤

❶ 看全句

❷

Had the young manager had a successful presentation, | he _____ | a new level of respect from his subordinates.

❸

❸ 看選項

(A) attained　(B) were attained　(C) should attain　(D) should have attain

中譯　若這年輕經理那時發表成功,他現在應該就會得下屬的另一新層次的尊重水平。

秒殺策略

❶ 判斷題型

看到 had 為句首,但後面為肯定句點,立即聯想到是假設句型的倒裝句。

❷ 判斷何種假設句型

由條件子句中 Had...had(由 If + S + had Vpp 倒裝)得知,條件句時間為「過去事實相反」時,結果句有可能為「現在或過去事實相反」的假設語氣。

❸ 驗證答案

由選項與主詞得知, he / attain a new level 為主動關係,依題意與文法,空格需要「主動/與現在或過去事實相反」的結果子句。

檢查

(A) 不會置於假設語氣結果句內,刪除。

(B) 被動,刪除。

(C) 與現在事實相反的結果子句

(D) have 後要加 Vpp,應改為 should have attained, 刪除。

故本題答案選 (C)

10. If Lin _____ the manager, he might make the same decision now.
    (A) was   (B) were   (C) is   (D) has been

答案 B

眼球追蹤

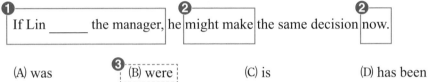

(A) was   ❸ (B) were   (C) is   (D) has been

中譯 若Lin是經理，他現在或許也會做同樣決定。

秒殺策略 👑

❶ 判斷題型

看到 if 與空格位置，立即聯想是條件句或是假設句型，依語意，為假設語氣。

❷ 判斷何種假設句型

由結果句 might make... now 得知，為測驗「**與現在事實相反**」或「**混合句型**」假設語氣觀念。

❸ 驗證答案

若為「**與現在事實相反的假設語氣**」，條件句動詞則用 were。

若為「**混合句型的假設語氣**」，條件句動詞則用 had been。👑

檢查

(A) 不適用於假設語氣，刪除。

(B) 與現在事實相反的假設語氣 👑

(C) 不適用於假設語氣，刪除。

(D) 不適用於假設語氣, 應改成 had been, 刪除。

故本題答案選 (B)   **159**

11-13 參考下列信件

中譯

敬啟者您好,

兩個星期前,我參加了貴旅行社所籌辦的旅行。不幸的是,我幾乎沒有得到我所期待的。若我現在不寫這封信,你會不知如何要如何訓練你的導遊。

我們的導遊沒有足夠的資格。他沒有按照行程計劃,這使得行程進度落後,也造成很多不便。此外,他對他需要介紹的地方不熟悉,所以整個行程是單調乏味的。如果他能為我們提供的旅遊景點準確和有趣的資訊,我們會在旅途中有更多的樂趣。

我的投訴信可能不是您將收到的唯一一封。如果貴公司想建立好客戶忠誠度,請盡快提出一些補救措施。

秒殺策略

11. 答案 **(C) didn't write**

If I **didn't write** this letter now, you wouldn't know ...

解題 依投訴者寫信當時時間點,故用「與現在事實相反的條件句」依語意,用否定。

12. 答案 **(D) would have had**

If he could provide us ..., we **would have had** more fun...

解題 由條件句中 could provide,與 during the trip 得知,應用「與過去事實相反的假設語氣」,搭配公式 would have p.p.,故選(D)。

13. 答案 **(A) tends**

If your company **tends** to build ..., please try to come up with...

解題 依...please try to come up with....,與上下文語意得知,if 所帶的為條件的副詞子句,your company 為第三人稱單數,故選(A)。

成為多益勝利組的字彙練功區

文法講解區	Mini Test 限時 5 分練習區
brewed coffee n. 過濾式咖啡	labor cost n. 勞動力成本
interest rate n. 利率	slash [slæʃ] v. 大幅度削減
bond [bɑnd] n. 債券	expenditure [ɪk`spɛndɪtʃə] n. 支出
take (a day) off v. 休假(一天)	rapidly [`ræpɪdlɪ] adv. 迅速地
supervisor [ˌsupə`vaɪzə] n. 上司	accounting firm n. 會計師事務所
present [`prɛznt] a. 出席的	audit [`ɔdɪt] n. v. 審計
collapse [kə`læps] v. 倒閉	obligated [`ɑblɪgetɪd] a. 有義務的
deposit [dɪ`pɑzɪt] n. 訂金	power outage n. 停電
in advance adv. 預先	maintenance team n. 維修小組
discount [`dɪskaʊnt] n. 折扣	hygiene [`haɪdʒin] n. 衛生
security guard n. 警衛	urban development n. 城市發展
break into v. 竊入	forecast [`for͵kæst] n. v. 預測
demonstrate [`dɛmən͵stret] v. 展示	subordinate [sə`bɔrdnɪt] n. 下屬
	to whom it may concern 敬啟者
	familiar [fə`mɪljə] a. 熟悉的
	amusing [ə`mjuzɪŋ] a. 有趣的
	remedy [`rɛmədɪ] n. v. 補救措施
	customer loyalty n. 客戶忠誠度

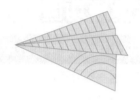

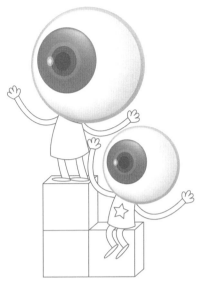

7

不定詞與動名詞
(Infinitives & Gerunds)

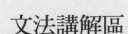
文法講解區

❼ 不定詞與動名詞 (Infinitives & Gerunds)

簡單看

　　不定詞（to V）具有**名詞、形容詞與副詞**的功能，在句中扮演非動詞的角色；因仍具有動詞的特徵，所以可以帶有受詞、補語或副詞，也可以用否定、進行式、完成式，甚至被動式，是個多方位的角色。

　　動名詞（Ving）**具有**名詞的性質。與不定詞相同，是可以有受詞、補語、副詞修飾語，及完成式時態、被動語態的用法，與真正名詞還是不同。

秒殺策略

（1）**判斷題**♕

　　　思考空格前後的動詞、名詞或形容詞等關鍵
字詞的型態

（2）**判斷相關用法**

　　　熟記「動名詞」與「不定詞」習慣搭配用語

1 不定詞（to V）的功能與時態

〉功能

• 當名詞：當句子的主詞、受詞、主詞補語或受詞補語

EX <u>To confirm receipt of taxes</u> is the purpose of his calling.

（確定稅務的收據是他來電的目的。）→ 當主詞

EX IBM decided <u>to lay off some of their employees</u> for the restructuring project.

（為了重建計劃，IBM 決定掉部分員工裁員。）→ 當受詞

EX The aim of the talk is <u>to welcome guests to our hotel</u>.

（此會談目的旨在歡迎嘉賓泛臨我們的飯店。）

EX The email reminded all the staff <u>to attend the meeting on time tomorrow</u>.

（這電子郵件提醒所有員工明日準時出席會議。）→ 當受詞補語

• 當形容詞：放在所要修飾的名詞後方

EX Each candidate will have the right <u>to attend the TV debate</u>.

（每個候選人將有權利參加電視辯論。）

> 表示目的不定詞，可放句首，用逗點與主要句分開。

• 當副詞：修飾形容詞或動詞，通常表示「原因、理由或目的」

EX <u>To realize her dream to be a super star,</u> Kathy went to every casting call and audition.

（Kathy 參加每一個演員甄選和試演的機會，為的是實現她成為大明星的夢想。）

〉時態：簡單式與完成式

• 簡單式：動作與主要動詞時態一致時

EX The police <u>intend</u> to recruit more officers this year.

（警察機關今年試圖招募更多新成員。）

• 完成式：動作比主要動詞時態更早發生

EX The authorities concerned <u>seemed</u> <u>to have found out</u> the truth.

（有關當局似乎當時在更早之前已經發現事實。）

② 將不定詞作為受詞的動詞：即 **S + V + to V**

ask（要求）、expect（期待）、intend（打算）、mean（打算）、plan（計畫）、offer（提議）、propose（提議）、tend（傾向）、promise（承諾）、seem（似乎）、appear（似乎）、decide（決定）、afford（負擔的起）、manage（設法做到）、desire（想要）、aim（意圖）、agree（同意）、wish（希望）、prefer（寧願）、fail（無法）、refuse（拒絕）、pretend（假裝）等。

EX The engineer <u>managed to retrieve</u> and analyze information to maximize efficiency in system.

（工程師設法有效地檢索與分析資料以提高系統效率。）

③ 將不定詞作為受詞補語的動詞：即 **S + V + O + to V**

ask（要求）、expect（期待）、encourage（鼓勵）、allow（允許）、advise（建議）、convince（說服）、enable（使能夠）、invite（邀請）、force（迫使）、prompt（引起）、remind（提醒）、require（要求）、permit（允許）、persuade（說服）、forbid（禁止）、warn（警告）、tell（告訴）、order（命令）等。

EX The fund will <u>enable employers to invest</u> in their own vocational training.

（此基金使得僱主得以投資自己業內的職業訓練。）

④ 後面常搭配不定詞的名詞：即 **N + to V**

ability（能力）、capacity（能力）、authority（權力）、effort（努力）、opportunity（機會）、plan（計畫）、 decision（決定）、way（方法）、right（權利）、claim（聲稱）等。

EX Whoever has worked in the company for three years has <u>the right to apply</u> for the training program.

（凡已經在公司工作三年的任何人皆有權利申請此訓練計畫。）

⑤ 後面常搭配不定詞的形容詞：即 **Adj + to V**

able（能夠的）、unable（不能夠的）、eligible（有資格的）、liable（易於，可能的）、likely（可能的）、unlikely（不太可能的）、ready（準備好

的）、willing（有意願的）、unwilling（不情願的）、reluctant（勉強，不情願的）、eager（熱切的）、anxious（急切的）等。

EX James was <u>anxious to know the result</u> after he was interviewed.

（在面談後，James 很急切想知道結果。）

6 以 it 當虛主詞或虛受詞代替不定詞的用法：

〉It 當虛主詞時：It 開頭的句子，真主詞（to + V）放在後面

It is / was + adj + for 人 to V

It is / was + adj + of 人 to V = 人 + be + adj + to V
（此類形容詞表示人的性格或能力）

EX It is illegal for the owner to supply alcohol to a minor.

（店家賣或提供酒類飲料給未成年是不合法的。）

EX It is stupid of the owner to supply alcohol to a minor.

＝The owner is stupid to supply alcohol to a minor.

（店家很愚蠢提供酒類飲料給未成年。）

〉It 當虛受詞時：放動詞之後，代替後面出現的真受詞（to + V）

S + V + it + adj + to V

S + V + it + N + to V

EX The flight delay made it impossible to reach our tourist destination on schedule.

（班機延誤造成要準時到達觀光景點是不可能。）

EX We make it a rule to check everything before shipment.

（在裝運前，我們習慣將每件事確定好。）

7 表示「結果」的句型

肯定	如此…以至於…	否定	太…而（某人）不能…
S + V	so + adj/adv + as to + V adj/adv + enough + to V	S + V	too + adj/adv + (for someone) + to V

EX The hall is <u>so</u> spacious <u>as to</u> accommodate up to 1,000 people.

（講堂是如此寬敞以至於可以容納一千人。）

EX The director is <u>too</u> picky <u>to</u> get along well with her colleagues.

（這主管太挑剔以至於無法和同事相處融洽。）

8 動名詞（Ving）的功能與時態

〉當名詞：當句子的主詞、受詞、主詞補語

EX <u>Cancelling appointment without advanced notice</u> is not appropriate.（當主詞）

（沒有事先取消約會是不適當的。）

EX The patrons will not consider <u>supporting the company financially next year</u> .（當受詞）

（贊助商明年將不考慮財務上贊助這家公司。）

EX The best chance to size up our rival is <u>going to the international trade fair</u>.（當主詞補語）

（估量我們的對手的最好機會就是參加這次的國際商展。）

〉時態：簡單式與完成式

　• 簡單式：動作與主要動詞時態一致時

EX The assistant <u>practices speaking</u> English everyday so that she can attend the training program.

（助理每天練習說英語為的是可以參加培訓計畫。）

　• 完成式：動作比主要動詞時態更早發生

EX He denied <u>having undergone</u> medical treatment in the US.

（他已否認更早之前曾在美國接受治療。）

9 將動名詞作為受詞的動詞：即 S + V + Ving

enjoy（喜歡）、mind（介意）、imagine（想像）、suggest（建議）、recommend（推薦）、avoid（避免）、admit（承認）、consider（認為）、postpone（延期）、practice（練習）、deny（拒絕）、quit（停止）、discuss（討論）等。

EX The counselor <u>recommended seeking</u> the debt assistance at a local bank.

（顧問建議在當地銀行尋求借貸協助。）

➓ 動名詞慣用語

片語後搭配動名詞的慣用語	
be capable of 有能力做	be aware of 意識到做了
be worth 值得做	be busy 忙於
be opposed to 反對	be devoted to 致力於
be committed to 致力於	be dedicated to 獻身於
be accustomed to 習慣	be used to 習慣
look forward to 期待	object to 反對
can't help Ving 不得不	do a lot of Ving 常做
feel like Ving 想要	go Ving 從事
It is no use Ving 做⋯沒有用	
There is no Ving 做⋯是不可能的	
have difficulty / trouble / a problem Ving 做⋯有困難	

EX We look forward to obtaining the necessary financial support from your company soon.

（我們期待得到貴公司在財務上的資助。）

➓ 動名詞與名詞的不同

名詞	動名詞
前面可加 a 或 the	前面可加 the，但不可以加 a
前面可加「形容詞」修飾	前面可加「副詞」或是「所有格」修飾。
後面不可接受詞	後面可接受詞

EX Diligently developing new projects is the key to increasing our sales figures this year.

（極力發展新企畫是今年增加我們銷售數據的關鍵。）

→ 動名詞前用副詞修飾，且後面可加受詞

Mini Test 練習區 限時5分

1. I always avoid _____ in the peak season because the traveling expenses at that time must be beyond my budget.
   (A) travel   (B) traveling   (C) to travel   (D) be traveling

2. Special efforts were made to meet the extremely tight timeframe in order to allow our team to _____ all work plans at the beginning of the new year.
   (A) valid   (B) validity   (C) validate   (D) validating

3. Lisa was very eager _____ this season's new lines from Paris.
   (A) buy   (B) buying   (C) bought   (D) to buy

4. The president was reluctant to face the fact and his pride forbade him _____ for help from other companies.
   (A) ask   (B) asking   (C) to ask   (D) having asked

5. This environmental issue is worth _____ on the agenda.
   (A) list   (B) listing   (C) to list   (D) being listing

6. _____ talking on your phone isn't only rude but also extremely annoying.
   (A) Loud   (B) Loudly   (C) Loudish   (D) Loudness

7. Getting the sole distribution rights for the US makes _____ a great chance to develop a profitable business.
   (A) it   (B) that   (C) you   (D) X

8. Not entitled to any severance pay, the employer decided _____ and maintained the status quo.
   (A) quit   (B) to quit   (C) quitting   (D) not to quit

9. Our company gets accustomed to _____ fees on the import price.
   (A) base   (B) basis   (C) based   (D) basing

10. The price of corn in this season is too erratic for wholesalers _____ accurately.
    (A) estimate   (B) estimating   (C) to estimate   (D) to be estimated

Question 11-13 refer to the following announcement

Diaz Motors today announced a plan _____ one state-of-the-art plant in

11 (A) to erect
(B) erecting
(C) erected
(D) to erection

Chengdu. When completed in 12 months, the factory will offer more than 150 new jobs for Chengdu area residents. The positions available _____

12 (A) expect to
(B) are expecting to
(C) are expected to
(D) have expected

cover various skills, from assembly line workers to research and development. Al Diaz, CEO of the company, said "We are dedicated to _____ and

13 (A) invest
(B) invested
(C) be invested
(D) investing

developing what we are good at.Our team look forward to you joining us. "

1-10 Ans: 1.(B) 2.(C) 3.(D) 4.(C) 5.(B) 6.(B) 7.(A) 8.(D) 9.(D) 10.(C)

1. I always avoid _____ in the peak season because the traveling expenses at that time must be beyond my budget.

    (A) travel   (B) traveling   (C) to travel   (D) be traveling

答案 B

眼球追蹤

I always |avoid ❶| _____ in the peak season because the traveling expenses at that

time must be beyond my budget.

❷ 看選項

    (A) travel   (B) traveling   (C) to travel   (D) be traveling

中譯 我總是避免在旺季旅遊因為在那時間的旅遊支出一定超出我的預算。

秒殺策略

❶ **判斷題型**

看題目，判斷題型，測驗動詞 avoid 後面的搭配用法。

❷ **確定動詞型態與使用方法**

avoid 是以「動名詞做為受詞」的動詞，後方加 Ving。♛

檢查

(A) 原形動詞，刪除。

(B) 動名詞 ♛

(C) 不定詞，刪除。

(D) BE 動詞+Ving，刪除。

故本題答案選 (B)

2. Special efforts were made to meet the extremely tight timeframe in order to allow our team to ＿＿＿ all work plans at the beginning of the new year.
(A) valid　　　(B) validity　　　(C) validate　　　(D) validating

答案  C

眼球追蹤

Special efforts were made to meet the extremely tight timeframe in order to

❷ ──────────────────

|allow our team to ＿＿＿ all work plans| at the beginning of the new year.

❶ 看選項 ──────────────────
(A) valid　　　(B) validity　　　(C) validate　　　(D) validating

中譯　為了要讓我方團隊在新年度開始的所有工作計畫可以批准生效，必須要特別努力以符 合緊迫的時間。

秒殺策略 👑

❶ **判斷題型**

看選項，判斷題型，測驗「詞類觀念」。

❷ **確定動詞型態與使用方法**

空格前關鍵字 allow，測驗動詞 allow 後面的搭配用法。allow 是習慣以「不定詞作為受詞補語的動詞」，即 S + V + O + <u>to V</u> 的動詞。👑

檢查

(A) 形容詞，刪除。
(B) 名詞，刪除。
(C) 原形動詞👑
(D) 動名詞，刪除。
故本題答案選 (C)

3. Lisa was very eager _____ this season's new lines from Paris.
(A) buy   (B) buying   (C) bought   (D) to buy

答案 D

眼球追蹤

❷
Lisa | was very eager _____ | this season'new lines from Paris.

❶ 看選項
(A) buy   (B) buying   (C) bought   (D) to buy

中譯   Lisa 非常渴望買到本季來自巴黎的的新款式。

秒殺策略 👑

❶ 判斷題型

看選項，測驗點「動詞變化」。

❷ 確定 be eager 使用方法

空格前關鍵字，eager 為「後面搭配**不定詞**的形容詞」，即 be + adj + <u>to V</u> 👑

檢查

(A) 原形動詞，刪除。
(B) 動名詞，刪除。
(C) 過去式動詞，刪除。
(D) 不定詞 👑
故本題答案選 (D)

4. The president was reluctant to face the fact and his pride forbade him
   _____ for help from other companies.

(A) ask   (B) asking   (C) to ask   (D) having asked

答案  C

眼球追蹤

The president was reluctant to face the fact and his pride ╔forbade him ＿＿＿＿ ②
for help from other companies.

❶ 看選項

(A) ask   (B) asking   (C) to ask   (D) having asked

中譯 總裁不願面對事實且他的自尊阻止他不願向其他公司求救。

秒殺策略 👑

❶ 判斷題型

看選項，測驗點「動詞變化」。

❷ 確定 forbid 使用方法

空格前關鍵字 forbid，為「不定詞作為受詞補語的動詞」，即 S + V + O + to
V 👑

檢查

(A) 原形動詞，刪除。

(B) 動名詞，刪除。

(C) 不定詞 👑

(D) 完成式（主動），刪除。

故本題答案選 (C)

5. This environmental issue is worth _____ on the agenda.
　(A) list 　　　　　 (B) listing 　　　　 (C) to list 　　　　 (D) being listing

答案　B

眼球追蹤

②

This environmental issue | is worth _____ | on the agenda.

❶ **看選項**
　(A) list 　　　　 (B) listing 　　　　 (C) to list 　　　　 (D) being listing

中譯　這環境議題值得放入議程討論裡。

秒殺策略

❶ **判斷題型**

看選項，測驗點「動詞變化」。

❷ **確定 be worth 使用方法**

空格前關鍵字 worth，be worth 習慣後面搭配「動名詞」用法，即 be worth +Ving，表示「值得做...」

注意：b.e worth + Ving 後方的動作已含有被動意味，無須再用被動語態。

檢查

(A) 選項為原形動詞/名詞，刪除。

(B) 選項為動名詞

(C) 選項為不定詞，刪除。

(D) 選項為動名詞（被動），刪除。

故本題答案選 (B)

6. _____ talking on your phone isn't only rude but also extremely annoying.
(A) Loud　　　　(B) Loudly　　　　(C) Loudish　　　　(D) Loudness

答案 **B**

眼球追蹤

❷ 看全句

_____ talking on your phone isn't only rude but also extremely annoying.
❸

❶ 看選項
(A) Loud　　　　(B) Loudly　　　　(C) Loudish　　　　(D) Loudness

中譯 大聲説電話不但魯莽且十分令人討厭。

秒殺策略

❶ 判斷題型

看選項，測驗點「詞類觀念」。

❷ 判斷空格需求

看全句 _____ talking on your phone/isn't/only rude but also extremely annoying 得知空格為修飾 talking on your phone 動名詞的詞類。

❸ 確定「動名詞」的修飾詞

「動名詞」的修飾詞，非形容詞，為副詞。👑

檢查

(A) 形容詞，刪除。

(B) 副詞 👑

(C) 形容詞（聲音稍高的），刪除。

(D) 名詞，刪除。

故本題答案選 (B)

7. Getting the sole distribution rights for the US makes _____ a great chance to develop a profitable business.

(A) it　　　　　　(B) that　　　　　　(C) you　　　　　　(D) X

答案 A

眼球追蹤

❶ 看全句

Getting the sole distribution rights for the US makes _____ a great chance to develop a profitable business.

❷ 看選項

(A) it　　　　　　(B) that　　　　　　(C) you　　　　　　(D) X

中譯 取得對美國專賣權是個發展有利事業的好機會。

秒殺策略

❶ 判斷題型

分析全句，Getting... for the US/makes/_____ /a great chance/to develop a profitable business 得知，測驗「S + V + it + N + to V」的觀念。

❷ 確定相關用法

用選項驗證，it 帶入。「S + V + it + N + to V」，it 當虛受詞，代替後方 to develop a profitable business 不定詞，a great chance 為受詞補語。it 無誤。

檢查

(A) it 虛受詞

(B) 不符合本題句型，刪除

(C) 不符合本題句型，刪除

(D) 不符合本題句型，刪除

故本題答案選 (A)

8. Not entitled to any severance pay, the employer decided _____ and maintained the status quo.

(A) quit   (B)) to quit   (C) quitting   (D) not to quit

答案 D

眼球追蹤

❸ 看全句

Not entitled to any severance pay, the employer |decided| _____ and maintained the status quo.

❷ 看選項

(A) quit   (B) to quit   (C) quitting   (D) not to quit

中譯 無法有權拿到任何遣散費,這員工決定不辭職且保持現狀。

秒殺策略

❶ 判斷題型

由空格前關鍵字得知,此題為測試「decide」搭配用法。

❷ 確定動詞型態與使用方法

decide是以「不定詞做為受詞」的動詞,後方加to V。

❸ 判斷語意

依照全句上下文語意,選否定的不定詞 not to V。

檢查

(A) 原形動詞,刪除

(B) 不定詞,語意不合,刪除

(C) 動名詞,刪除

(D) 否定不定詞

故本題答案選 (D)

9. Our company gets accustomed to ＿＿＿＿ fees on the import price.
　(A) base　　　　　(B) basis　　　　(C) based　　　　(D) basing

答案　D

眼球追蹤

Our company | gets accustomed to | ＿＿＿＿ fees on the import price.

❷ 看選項

　(A) base　　　　　(B) basis　　　　(C) based　　　　(D) basing

中譯　我們公司習慣於以進口價來做計算。

秒殺策略

❶ **判斷題型**

　由空格前關鍵字得知，此題為測試「be/get accustomed to」用法。

❷ **依語意個別判斷**

　base (v) 以...做為基礎；(n) 基，基部
　basis (n) 基礎；準則

　be/get accustomed to + Ving/N（習慣於），後方可加動名詞或名詞，考慮
　(A)、(B)與(D)，但空格後面還有受詞，只能搭配動名詞。

檢查

(A) 原形動詞或名詞 ，刪除
(B) 名詞，刪除
(C) 過去式動詞或過去分詞，刪除
(D) 動名詞
故本題答案選 (D)

10. The price of corn in this season is too erratic for wholesalers _____ accurately.

(A) estimate
(B) estimating
(C) to estimate
(D) to be estimated

答案　C

眼球追蹤

The price of corn in this season is |too| erratic |for wholesalers| _____ accurately.

❷ **看選項**

(A) estimate　　(B) estimating　　(C) to estimate　　(D) to be estimated

中譯　這季節的玉米價錢太不穩定以致於批發商無法精確估計。

秒殺策略 ♛

❶ **判斷題型**

由關鍵字 too 與空格猜測，此題為測試「too + adj/adv + (for someone) + to V」用法。

❷ **刪去法**

搭配句型，考慮(C)與(D)

❸ **確定相關用法**

for wholesalers 為發出動作者，為 estimate 動作的主詞，故用主動即可。 ♛

檢查

(A) 原形動詞，刪除
(B) 動名詞，刪除
(C) 不定詞 ♛
(D) 不定詞（被動），刪除
故本題答案選 (C)

11-13 題參考下列公告

中譯

　　迪亞茲汽車公司今日宣布要在成都市興建一座先進的廠辦計畫。預計要在 12 個月內完成，此廠將為成都地區的居民提供超過 150 個新的就業機會。預計可提供的職缺涵蓋了各種技術需求，從生產線工作人員到研究和開發人員都有。首席執行長阿爾。迪亞茲說：「我們致力於投資與發展我們所在行的。我們的團隊期待您加入。」

秒殺策略

11. 答案　**(A) to erect**

　　　...announced a plan **to erect** one state-of-the-art plant...

　　解題　plan 此名詞後方習慣搭配不定詞，故選(A)。

12. 答案　**(C) are expected to**

　　　The positions available **are expected to** cover various skills...

　　解題　以 position（職缺）當主詞，所以應用被動式，而 expect 後方搭配不定詞，故選(C)。

13. 答案　**(D) investing**

　　　We are dedicated to **investing** and developing what we are good at.

　　解題　動名詞慣用語 be dedicated to Ving（專心致力於...），後方 and developing 再次確認答案無誤。

成為多益勝利組的字彙練功區

文法講解區	Mini Test 限時 5 分練習區
confirm [kənˋfɝm] v. 確定	peak season n. 旺季
receipt [rɪˋsit] n. 收據	traveling expenses n. 旅遊；交通開支
casting call n. 角色甄選試鏡	beyond one's budget 超支
audition [ɔˋdɪʃən] n. 演員甄選	tight timeframe n. 緊湊的時間範圍
recruit [rɪˋkrut] v. 招募	line [laɪn] n. (貨物等的) 種類
retrieve [rɪˋtriv] v. 檢索	reluctant [rɪˋlʌktənt] a. 不情願的
efficiency [ɪˋfɪʃənsɪ] n. 效率	forbid [fɚˋbɪd] v. 禁止
vocational training n. 職業訓練	issue [ˋɪʃʊ] n. 問題；爭論
anxious [ˋæŋkʃəs] a. 急切的	agenda [əˋdʒɛndə] n. 議程
alcohol [ˋælkəˏhol] n. 酒類飲料	annoying [əˋnɔɪɪŋ] a. 令人討厭的
minor [ˋmaɪnɚ] n. 未成年人	distribution right n. 經銷權
flight delay n. 班機延誤	entitle [ɪnˋtaɪtl] v. 給……資格 (或權力)
make it a rule toV 習慣	severance pay n. 遣散費
shipment [ˋʃɪpmənt] n. 裝運	status quo n. 現狀
picky [ˋpɪkɪ] a. 挑剔	erratic [ɪˋrætɪk] a. 不穩定的
spacious [ˋspeʃəs] a. 寬敞	wholesaler [ˋholˏselɚ] n. 批發商
accommodate [əˋkɑməˏdet] v. 能容納	estimate [ˋɛstəˏmet] v. 估計
patron [ˋpetrən] n. 贊助商	dedicated [ˋdɛdəˏketɪd] a. 專注的；獻身的
financially [faɪˋnænʃəlɪ] adv. 財務上	research and development (R&D) 研究和開發
size up v. 估量	state-of-the-art a. 最先進的
trade fair n. 展場	
debt assistance n. 借貸協助	
look forward to+ Ving 期待	
obtain [əbˋten] v. 得到	
figure [ˋfɪgjɚ] n. 數據	

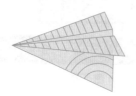

FAQ in TOEIC

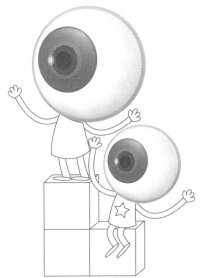

8

分詞 (Participles)

文法講解區

8 分詞 （Participles）

簡單看

　　分詞是由動詞變化而來的，可分成現在分詞（Ving）和過去分詞（Vpp），功能為形容詞，作為修飾名詞，或是作補語使用。所修飾的名詞若是具主動去做的能力，則搭配現在分詞修飾；若動作是被加諸在這名詞上，則使用過去分詞修飾。

秒殺策略

（1）判斷題型
　　　→ 是否缺乏主要動詞
（2）無動詞，即測驗「主要動詞」，思考
　　　→「詞彙」、「時態」、「主被動」
（3）有主要動詞，即測驗分詞概念
　　　→「詞彙用法」或「判斷主被動」
　　　→「現在分詞」或「過去分詞」

6 假設語氣與條件句

7 不定詞與動名詞

8 分詞

9 比較句型

10 名詞與代名詞

❶ 分詞的功能

〉當形容詞：可放名詞前面或後面修飾或是當補語修飾主詞或是受詞。

EX The donated supplies will be sent to victims in disaster areas.

（捐贈的補給品會儘快送給受災區民眾。）

→donated 修飾名詞 supplies

EX The workers were disappointed to learn their pay was docked by 20%.

（員工對於被減薪 20% 感到失望。）

→disappointed 當主詞補語，說明 the workers

〉當副詞（分詞構句）：來修飾主要動詞發生的時間、因果、條件、讓步……等關係。有時會和某些附屬連接詞（如：after/before/when/unless）一起出現

EX (After) hosting the important meeting, the manager felt exhausted, but relaxed.

（主持完會議後，經理感到精疲力竭但是很放鬆。）

→hosting the important meeting 說明後句的時間

生命加值室

〉分詞當補語

1. 五大句型中，其中兩句型：(1) S + V + SC　(2) S + V + O + OC
   句型(1)中，分詞可扮演 BE 動詞與連綴動詞後的主詞補語，說明主詞；
   句型(2)中，分詞可扮演受詞補語，來補充說明受詞。

2. 注意觀念，主詞或受詞與補語之間：
   主動關係，則用現在分詞；
   被動關係，則用過去分詞。

2 觀念加強區

		現在分詞 (Ving)	過去分詞 (Vpp)
含意		進行 / 主動	完成 / 被動
當形容詞	修飾名詞	a rolling stone 滾動的石頭（進行）	a lost chance 錯過的機會（完成）
		the shop offering a cordial atmosphere 提供熱情友好的氣氛 （主動）	tickets purchased in advance 事先購買的票券 （被動）
	當補語	Interacting with clients is challenging. 和顧客互動是有挑戰性的。 （主詞補語）	The players were excited to know the result. 球員興奮的想知道結果。 （主詞補語）
		The supervisor has caught the employee making personal calls 4 times during office hours. 主管已抓到此員工辦公時間撥打私人電話四次。 （受詞補語）	The secretary had the agenda amended before the meeting. 秘書已經在會議前將議程修正好。 （受詞補語）
當副詞		Applying for a mortgage, I put down 20% for a down payment. 在申請貸款前， 我已經付了百分二十的頭期款。 （表示時間副詞）	Forced to retire due to ill health, May decided to be a SOHO at home. 由於健康不好被迫退休， May 決定在家當 SOHO 族。 （表示原因副詞）

❸ 情緒動詞的分詞

　　由情緒動詞所衍生出的過去分詞是用來描述修飾者／物的自身感受，而現在分詞是描述修飾者／物所帶給外界的感受。

過去分詞：修飾者/物的自身感受		現在分詞：修飾者/物所帶給外界的感受	
satisfied	對…感到滿意的	satisfying	令人滿意的
amused	對…感到好笑的	amusing	令人感到好玩的
pleased	對…感到喜悅的	pleasing	令人感到喜悅的
interested	對…感到有興趣的	interesting	令人感到有趣的
excited	對…感到興奮的	exciting	令人感到刺激的
fascinated	對…感到著迷的	fascinating	令人著迷的
enchanted	對…感到著迷的	enchanting	令人著迷的
touched	對…感到感動的	touching	令人感動的
encouraged	對…感到鼓勵的	encouraging	令人鼓舞的
embarrassed	對…感到尷尬的	embarrassing	令人尷尬的
bored	對…感到無聊的	boring	令人無趣的
confused	對…感到困惑的	confusing	令人困惑的
puzzled	對…感到困惑的	puzzling	令人困惑的
perplexed	對…感到困惑的	perplexing	令人困惑的
worried	對…感到擔憂的	worrying	令人擔憂的
frightened	對…感到驚嚇的	frightening	令人恐懼的
tired	對…感到厭煩的	tiring	令人疲倦的
disappointed	對…感到失望的	disappointing	令人失望的
annoyed	對…感到惱怒的	annoying	令人惱怒的
disgusted	對…感到噁心的	disgusting	令人作嘔的
frustrated	對…感到沮喪的	frustrating	令人沮喪的
depressed	對…感到沮喪的	depressing	令人沮喪的
alarmed	對…感到恐慌的	alarming	令人恐慌的
stunned	對…感到訝異的	stunning	令人訝異的
surprised	對…感到意外的	surprising	令人意外的
shocked	對…感到震驚的	shocking	令人震驚的
amazed	對…感到驚奇的	amazing	令人驚奇的
astonished	對…感到驚愕的	astonishing	令人驚愕的

EX The perplexing new office policy made most employees perplexed.

（令人困惑的新政策使得多數的員工感到困惑的。）

❹ 慣用搭配語

demanding jobs	吃力的工作
demanding supervisors	要求高的主管
challenging / overwhelming tasks	有挑戰的 / 過重的任務
existing equipment / system	現存的設備 / 系統
opposing viewpoints / voices	相反的觀點 / 聲音
opening / closing remark	開幕 / 閉幕致詞
missing luggage	遺失的行李
mounting workload	增加的工作量
a letter inviting...	邀請…的信件
experienced / dedicated employees	有經驗的 / 勤勞的員工
qualified applicants	有資格的申請者
written documents / consent	書面檔案 / 同意
designated area	指定區域
required inspections / training	必需的檢查 / 訓練
detailed information	細部資訊
confirmed reservation	已確定的預約
items unclaimed	無人認領的物品

EX The new recruits need to submit relevant <u>required documents</u> before this Friday.

（新成員需要在這周五之前繳交相關文件。）

❺ 分詞片語的形成

　　「分詞片語」由形容詞子句（即關係子句）簡化而來的形容詞片語，放在名詞之後修飾該名詞。

〉名詞 + 分詞片語

• 主動含意：N+現在分詞 Ving 片語 （N 為動作的主事者）

EX The coordinator <u>overseeing all details of your wedding</u> will arrive here at 6：00 a.m. tomorrow morning.

（監督你婚禮所有細節的統籌人將會在明早六點到達這裡。）

- 被動含意：**N+過去分詞 Vpp** 片語 （**N** 為動作的接受者）

  EX The figures <u>shown in the meeting</u> demonstrated we would face large-scale financial problems.

  （會議上顯示的數據說明我們將面對大規模的經濟問題。）

〉【形容詞子句轉成分詞片語】變化步驟：

Step 1 形容詞子句（即關係子句）中，關代為主詞時，將其刪去

Step 2 判斷子句中，語態為主動還是被動

Step 3 動詞分詞化：

主動語態→將動詞轉成 Ving

被動語態→將動詞轉成 Vpp

- 現在分詞片語

  原句：The coordinator **who will oversee all details of your wedding** will arrive here at 6：00 a.m.

  (1) who 為主格，刪去。

  (2) will oversee all details of your wedding，為主動語態。

  (3) 將動詞改成 overseeing，形容詞子句即轉變成分詞片語

  overseeing all details of your wedding

  →The coordinator **overseeing all details of your wedding** will arrive here at 6: 00 a.m.

- 過去分詞片語

  原句：The figures **which were shown in the meeting** demonstrated we would face large-scale financial problems.

  (1) which 為主格，刪去。

  (2) which were shown in the meeting，為被動語態。

  (3) 將動詞改成 shown，形容詞子句即轉變成分詞片語 shown in the meeting

  →The figures **shown in the meeting** demonstrated we would face large-scale financial problems.

6 分詞構句的形成

「分詞構句」是由副詞子句／對等子句簡化而來，放在句子前或後修飾該句。

〉分詞構句, 主要子句

(1) 主動含意： 現在分詞 Ving 構句, S + V

EX <u>Turning to the left</u>, you won't miss the church you are searching for.

（向左轉，你就會看到你在找的教堂。）

(2) 被動含意： 過去分詞 Vpp 構句, S + V

EX <u>Used properly</u>, some gadgets prove clever and useful.

（使用得當，有些機械小工具是很精巧且有用的。）

〉**【副詞子句 / 對等子句轉成分詞構句】變化步驟：**

(1) 將連接詞刪去

(2) 判斷前句與後句主詞是否相同

主詞相同，省略其一；

主詞不同，皆保留（形成獨立分詞構句。題型較少，在此不討論）。

(3) 判斷刪去連接詞與主詞的子句中，語態為主動還是被動

(4) 動詞分詞化：

主動語態→將動詞轉成 Ving

被動語態→將動詞轉成 Vpp

• **現在分詞構句**

原句：**If you turn to the left,** you won't miss the church you are searching for.

(1) 刪除 If 連接詞。

(2) 主詞 you 相同，省略其一。

(3) turn to the left 是主動，將主要動詞簡化成 turning to the left

(4) If you turn to the left 副詞子句即轉變成分詞構句 turning to the left

➡ **Turning to the left**, you won't miss the church you are searching for.

• **過去分詞構句**

原句：**If some gadgets are used properly,** they prove clever and useful.

(1) 刪除 If 連接詞。

(2) some gadgets 與 they 相同，省略其一。

(3) some gadgets are used properly 是被動，將主要動詞簡化成 used properly

(4) If some gadgets are used properly 副詞子句即轉變成分詞構句 used properly

➡ **Used properly,** some gadgets prove clever and useful.

生命加值室

分詞構句進階觀念

　　由上述解說後，我們可以知道「分詞構句」就是副詞子句或對等子句簡化而來的副詞片語。簡化的目的就是使文句更簡潔、漂亮。分詞構句，除上述基本觀念外，還有下列進階觀念，要修練成文法達人的你，不可不知。

〉完成式分詞構句 → Having +Vpp：已經～（表時間相對較早之事件）

　EX Having handed in his resignation, James had no intention to stay even if getting a raise.

　　（早就提出辭呈，James 即使有被加薪也沒意願留著。）

〉否定分詞構句 → Not +Ving/Vpp；Not having + Vpp

　EX Not having raised enough funds, the enterprise failed to launch a takeover bid for another company.

　　（沒有籌募足夠資金，那家企業無法收購另一家公司。）

〉附屬連接詞＋S＋BE 動詞＋形容詞 → 可省略「S＋BE 動詞」

　EX If possible, just finish what you can, and then take the rest of the day off.

　　（如果有可能，把未了結的部分留著。今天下午請個病假回家休息。）

〉BE 動詞＋形容詞分詞構句 → (being) +形容詞

　EX Strange enough, the problems have existed for years though officials seem to deal with them.

　　（奇怪的很，雖然官員似乎多年來一直處理它們，但這些問題還是存在。）

Mini Test 練習區　限時5分

1. The modern skyscrapers _____ with steel and reinforced concrete can withstand the impacts of the weather and earthquakes.
   (A) build　　　(B) built　　　(C) building　　　(D) are built

2. The department store _____ in the hotspot of the Myeongdong's fashion district.
   (A) locate　　　(B) located　　　(C) is located　　　(D) is locating

3. The pretty state boasts plenty of _____ sites as well as delightful scenery.
   (A) fascinate　　　(B) fascinated　　　(C) fascinating　　　(D) fascination

4. You need to present an ID card and expired visa when _____ for extension.
   (A) apply　　　(B) applying　　　(C) applied　　　(D) you applying

5. If you don't know how to write an invitation letter, you can refer to this sample _____ a keynote speaker for a conference.
   (A) invite　　　(B) invited　　　(C) inviting　　　(D) to invite

6. People _____ in furniture should schedule a visit to the international furniture fair next month.
   (A) interest　　　(B) interested　　　(C) interesting　　　(D) are interested

7. _____ many significant contributions to our company, the engineer finally got promoted the other day.
   (A) Make　　　(B) Made　　　(C) To make　　　(D) Having made

8. The audience was _____ by the _____ performance.
   (A) amused, amusing　　　　　　(B) amusing, amused
   (C) was amused, amusing　　　　　(D) amused, was amusing

9. The director has had the statement _____ carefully before publication.
   (A) scrutinize　　　(B) scrutinized　　　(C) scrutinizing　　　(D) to scrutinize

10. Once _____ a patent, you can sell it and be guaranteed a quick payoff for your idea.
    (A) grant　　　(B) granted　　　(C) granting　　　(D) having granted

Question 11-13 refer to the following notice

Dear customers,

In the unlikely event of your items being lost when you shop in our store. Here's some information on making a claim.A claim for missing item can be initiated through the Internet or by telephone. Our office updates the _____

11 (A) unclaim
(B) unclaimed
(C) unclaiming
(D) unclaimingly

property records daily, and account information can be accessed at any time. Checking on the Internet isrecommended first; however, if it's a _____

12 (A) press
(B) pressed
(C) pressing
(D) pressingly

matter, you can contact us by telephone. The customer service representative (CSR) will ask you relevant personal information _____ to

13 (A) require
(B) required
(C) requiring
(D) be required

make further search on the Internet database.Taipei residents can call toll-free, at 886-2-12345678 between the hours of 8：00 AM and 5：00 PM, Monday through Friday (except holidays).The database and search instructions can be accessed on our web site, at http：//www.iloveshop.com.Click on "Unclaimed Property."

1-10 Ans: 1.(B) 2.(C) 3.(C) 4.(B) 5.(B) 6.(B) 7.(C) 8.(A) 9.(B) 10.(B)

1. The modern skyscrapers _____ with steel and reinforced concrete can withstand the impacts of the weather and earthquakes.
(A) build   (B) built   (C) building   (D) are built

答案 B

眼球追蹤

❷ 看全句 **❸**

The modern | skyscrapers _____ | with steel and reinforced concrete can withstand the impacts of the weather and earthquakes.

❶ 看選項

(A) build   (B) built   (C) building   (D) are built

中譯 這些全部由鋼鐵與鋼筋混凝土所建造成的現代摩登大樓可以承受天氣與地震的衝擊。

秒殺策略 ♕

❶ 判斷題型

由選項得知,測驗點為「動詞變化」。

❷ 判定空格需求

分析全句,判斷需要主要動詞還是分詞。主詞為 skyscrapers _____ with steel and reinforced concrete,**主要動詞 can withstand**,空格應為「分詞」。♕

❸ 判斷主被動

the modern skyscrapers/build 應為「受詞/動詞」關係,因此應用「過去分詞」built 來表示被動,修飾前方 skyscrapers。♕

檢查

(A) 原形動詞,刪除。
(B) 過去式動詞或是過去分詞 ♕
(C) 現在分詞,刪除。
(D) 現在簡單被動式,刪除。
故本題答案選 (B)

2. The department store _____ in the hotspot of the Myeongdong's fashion district.
   (A) locate   (B) located   (C) is located   (D) is locating

答案 C

眼球追蹤

❷ 看全句

The department store _____ in the hotspot of the Myeongdong's fashion district.

❶ 看選項

(A) locate   (B) located   ❸ (C) is located   (D) is locating

中譯 這百貨公司位於明洞流行街區的最熱鬧處。

秒殺策略

❶ 判斷題型

由選項得知，測驗點為「動詞變化」。

❷ 判定空格需求

分析全句，判斷需要主要動詞還是分詞。由…department store/_____ in the hotspot 得知，句子缺少主要動詞，空格為主要動詞。

❸ 判定選項變化

locate 意思為「使…座落於」，慣用被動式 be located in/on/at 表示「某物位於…」。♛

檢查

(A) 原形動詞，刪除。
(B) 過去式動詞或是過去分詞，刪除。
(C) 現在簡單被動式♛
(D) 現在進行式，刪除。
故本題答案選 (C)

3. The pretty state boasts plenty of _____ sites as well as delightful scenery.

   (A) fascinate   (B) fascinated   (C) fascinating   (D) fascination

答案 C

眼球追蹤

The pretty state boasts plenty | **②** of _____ sites as well as delightful scenery. |

① 看選項

  (A) fascinate   (B) fascinated   **③** (C) fascinating   (D) fascination

中譯　這美麗的州擁有很多迷人的景點與賞心 目的風景。

秒殺策略 👑

❶ 判斷題型

由選項得知，測驗點為「詞類觀念」。

❷ 判定空格需求

看空格前關鍵字 of 後的搭配 of/_____ sites/as well as/delightful scenery
空格應為分詞做形容詞修飾後方 sites。

❸ 確定情緒動詞衍生的分詞用法

fascinate 意思為「使……神魂顛倒、迷住」，為情緒動詞之一。「現在分詞」
為描述修飾者/物所帶給外界的感受，修飾 sites，要使用「**現在分詞**」，表
「迷人的」。👑

檢查

(A) 原形動詞，刪除。

(B) 過去式動詞或是過去分詞，刪除。

(C) 現在分詞 👑

(D) 名詞，刪除。

故本題答案選 (C)

4. You need to present an ID card and expired visa when _____ for extension.

(A) apply   (B) applying   (C) applied   (D) you applying

答案 B

眼球追蹤

❶ 看全句
You need to present an ID card and expired visa ❷ when _____ for extension.

❸ 看選項
(A) apply   (B) applying   (C) applied   (D) you applying

中譯 當在申請延期時，你必須出示身分證與到期的簽證。

秒殺策略

❶ 判斷題型

分析全句，由 You need to present…when _____ for extension 得知，句中有一個連接詞 when，因此左右兩邊應各為一完整句。

❷ 判定空格需求

when 所接的句子，空格中應該選擇的為「副詞子句」或是「分詞構句」的概念

❸ 判定選項變化

若是副詞子句，為 you apply，若是簡化成分詞構句，apply 應用主動觀念，故選現在分詞 applying

檢查

(A) 原形動詞，刪除。

(B) 現在分詞

(C) 過去式動詞或是過去分詞，刪除。

(D) 主詞+現在分詞，應改成 you apply，刪除。

故本題答案選 (B)

5. If you don't know how to write an invitation letter, you can refer to this sample _____ a keynote speaker for a conference.
   (A) invite　　　　(B) invited　　　　(C) inviting　　　　(D) to invite

答案 B

眼球追蹤

If you don't know how to write an invitation letter, you can refer to this ❷

❸ sample _____ a keynote speaker for a conference.

❶ **看選項**
(A) invite　　　　(B) invited　　　　(C) inviting　　　　(D) to invite

中譯　若你不知如何撰寫邀請函，可以參考這邀請主講嘉賓至會議的範文。

秒殺策略 👑

❶ **判斷題型**

由選項得知，測驗點為「動詞變化」。

❷ **判定空格需求**

分析主要子句，you can refer to this sample...是一完整句，有主要動詞 refer to，句子不缺主要動詞。空格選項考「分詞」的概念，修飾 sample。

❸ **判斷主被動**

由 sample/invite 推知，是主詞／動詞的關係，因此應用主動觀念，故選 現在分詞 inviting。👑

檢查

(A) 原形動詞，刪除。

(B) 過去式動詞或是過去分詞，刪除。

(C) 現在分詞 👑

(D) 不定詞，刪除。

故本題答案選 (C)

6. People _____ in furniture should schedule a visit to the international furniture fair next month.
(A) interest　　　(B) interested　　　(C) interesting　　　(D) are interested

答案　B

眼球追蹤

❷ 看全句 ❸

| People _____ in furniture should schedule a visit to the international furniture fair next month. |

❶ 看選項
(A) interest　　　(B) interested　　　(C) interesting　　　(D) are interested

中譯 對傢俱有興趣的民眾應安排下個月參觀國際傢俱展。

秒殺策略 ♛

❶ **判斷題型**
由選項得知，測驗點為「動詞變化」。

❷ **判定空格需求**
由全句與選項得知，判斷需要主要動詞還是分詞。分析全句…People _____ in furniture/should schedule/a visit to…得知，有**主要動詞 schedule**，空格選項考「**分詞**」的概念，修飾 people。

❸ **確定情緒動詞衍生的分詞用法**
interest 意思為「使…有興趣」，為情緒動詞之一。「過去分詞」為描述修飾者／物自身的感受，修飾 people，要使用「過去分詞」，中文為「對…感到有興趣的」。♛

檢查

(A) 原形動詞，刪除。
(B) 過去式動詞或是過去分詞 ♛
(C) 現在分詞，刪除。
(D) 簡單被動式，應刪去 are，刪除。
故本題答案選 (B)

201

7. _____ many significant contributions to our company, the engineer finally got promoted the other day.

   (A) Make   (B) Made   (C) To make   (D) Having made

答案 C

眼球追蹤

❷ 看全句

❸

_____ many significant contributions to our company, the engineer finally got promoted the other day.

❶ 看選項

   (A) Make   (B) Made   (C) To make   (D) Having made

中譯 已經對我們公司有許多重大貢獻，這工程師前些日子終於升遷了。

秒殺策略 👑

❶ 判斷題型

由選項得知，測驗點為「動詞變化」。

❷ 判定空格需求

分析全句，由逗號與無連接詞得知，逗點後為完整子句，逗點前不是。因此逗點前面一定是「副詞子句」或是表目的的「不定詞」來修飾後面全句。若搭配不定詞，表示目的，全句語意不通順。即確定考的觀念為「分詞構句」。

❸ 確定分詞構句用法

the engineer/make 的關係為「主詞／動詞」關係，因此用主動，選擇現在分詞。making 或是 having made 皆為正確答案，having made...代表發生時間比 got prompted 更早發生。👑

註：原句為 Because the engineer has made many significant contributions to our company, he finally got promoted the other day.

檢查

(A) 原形動詞，刪除。　　(B) 過去式動詞或是過去分詞，刪除。

(C) 不定詞，刪除。　　(D) 現在分詞完成式👑 故本題答案選 (D)

8. The audience was _____ by the _____ performance.
   (A) amused, amusing   (B) amusing, amused
   (C) was amused, amusing   (D) amused, was amusing

答案 Ⓐ

眼球追蹤

❷ 看全句 ─❸─❸──────❸
| The audience | was | _____ | by the | _____ | performance. |

❶ 看選項
   (A) amused, amusing   (B) amusing, amused
   (C) was amused, amusing   (D) amused, was amusing

中譯 觀眾被這好玩的表演逗笑了。

秒殺策略 👑

❶ **判斷題型**

由選項得知，本題為測試情緒動詞 amuse 所衍生的分詞用法。

❷ **判定空格需求**

分析全句，由 The audience/was _____ /by the _____ performance，得知，was _____ 為主要動詞，空格只需要搭配分詞，故只考慮(A)與(B)。

❸ **確定情緒動詞衍生的分詞用法**

第一空格應修飾 the audience，使用「過去分詞」描述修飾者/物的自身感受。第二空格應修飾 performance，使用「現在分詞」，描述修飾者/物所帶給外界的感受。👑

檢查

(A) 過去分詞，現在分詞 👑
(B) 現在分詞，過去分詞，刪除。
(C) 過去被動式，現在分詞，刪除。
(D) 過去分詞，現在進行，刪除。
故本題答案選 (A)

9. The director has had the statement _____ carefully before publication.

(A) scrutinize　　　(B) scrutinized　　　(C) scrutinizing　　　(D) to scrutinize

答案　B

眼球追蹤

❷ 看全句

The director has had the statement _____ carefully before publication.

❶ 看選項

(A) scrutinize　　　(B) scrutinized　　　(C) scrutinizing　　　(D) to scrutinize

中譯　　主任已經在聲明發布前詳細檢查過了。

秒殺策略

❶ 判斷題型

由選項得知,測驗點為「動詞變化」。

❷ 判定空格需求

分析全句,由 The director/has had /the statement _____ carefully/ efore
publication. 得知,有主要動詞 has had,關鍵字 had 提示本題測試重點為
「使役動詞」用法。

❸ 確定使役動詞用法

使役動詞 have 的用法,have + O + OC（原 V 或 Vpp)。the statement/
scrutinize 為「受詞/動詞」關係,意思為「使聲明（被）詳細檢查過」,因
此空格應選「過去分詞」表示被動以修飾前方 the statement。

註:此題為測驗分詞作「受詞補語」的概念

檢查

(A) 原形動詞,刪除。

(B) 過去式動詞或過去分詞

(C) 現在分詞,刪除。

(D) 不定詞,刪除。

故本題答案選 (B)

6 假設語氣與條件句

7 不定詞與動名詞

8 分詞

9 比較句型

10 名詞與代名詞

10. Once _____ a patent, you can sell it and be guaranteed a quick pay-off for your idea.

(A) grant   (B) granted   (C) granting   (D) having granted

答案 B

眼球追蹤

❷ 看全句 ❸

Once ____ a patent, you can sell it and be guaranteed a quick payoff for your idea.

❶ 看選項

(A) grant   (B) granted   (C) granting   (D) having granted

中譯 一旦取得專利權，你可以把它賣掉，並保證你的想法有快速的報酬。

秒殺策略

❶ 判斷題型

由選項得知，測驗點為「動詞變化」。

❷ 判定空格需求

分析全句，Once _____ a patent/you can sell it and be guaranteed...得知，空格應為「主詞＋動詞」的搭配，但由選項得知，並無主詞的搭配使用，即確定測驗子句簡化成「分詞構句」的概念。

❸ 確定分詞構句用法

由語意，主詞應為 you 才能簡化，所以應為 you/grant 的關係，表示「受詞／動詞」，因此用被動，故空格選擇「過去分詞」。 ♛

註 1：原句為 Once granted a patent, you can sell it and be guaranteed a quick payoff for your idea.

註 2：分詞構句，連接詞可以保留不省略

檢查

(A) 原形動詞，刪除。   (B) 過去式動詞或是過去分詞 ♛

(C) 現在分詞，刪除。   (D) 現在分詞完成式，刪除。

故本題答案選 (B)

11-13 請參閱下列公告

中譯

親愛的客戶，

萬一您的東西在我們的商店裡丟失，下面是關於提出招領的資訊。對遺失項目可先透由網路或是電話開始。我們公司會每日更新的無人認領失物記錄且帳戶信息可以在任何時候得取。建議您先上網確定訊息；但若是緊急事件，您可以通過電話與我們聯繫。客戶服務代表（CSR）為了進一步在網路資料庫裡做進一步搜尋，會詢問您必須的相關個人資訊。台北市民可在周一至週五（例假日除外）上午 8：00 到下午 5：00 之間，撥打免費電話 886-2-12345678。資料庫與搜索指示在我們的網站可以取得訊息。進入 http：//www.iloveshop.com，點擊「未認領物品」。

秒殺策略

11. 答案　**(B) unclaimed**

　　Our office updates the **unclaimed** property records daily...

　　解題　property 與 claim 為受詞與動詞的關係，所以應用 unclaimed 過去分詞來修飾 property。unclaimed 已轉變成「無人領取的」一形容詞習慣用法。

12. 答案　**(C) pressing**

　　..., if it's a **pressing** matter, you can contact us by telephone.

　　解題　press 此動詞有「催促、催逼」之意。
　　其現在分詞 pressing 已經變成「緊迫的，迫切的」的形容詞，與 urgent 同義。

13. 答案　**(B) required**

　　...(CSR) will ask you...information **required** to make...

　　解題　原句應為 relevant personal information which is required to...，
　　關係子句簡化的分詞片語，關代刪去，被動語態，留下「過去分詞」修飾前方名詞。

成為多益勝利組的字彙練功區

文法講解區	Mini Test 限時 5 分練習區
victim [ˋvɪktɪm] **n.** 受難者	skyscraper [ˋskaɪˌskrepɚ] **n.** 摩天大樓
disaster area **n.** 災區	reinforced [ˌriɪnˋfɔrsd] **a.** 強化的
dock [dɑk] **v.** 金錢的削減	hotspot [hɑt spɑt] **n.** 熱門景點
exhausted [ɪgˋzɔstɪd] **a.** 精疲力竭的	boast [bost] **v.** 以有 ... 而自豪；擁有
amend [əˋmɛnd] **v.** 修正	expired [ɪkˋspaɪrd] **a.** 過期的
mortgage [ˋmɔrgɪdʒ] **n.** 貸款	extension [ɪkˋstɛnʃən] **n.** 擴展
down payment **n.** 頭期款	refer to **v.** 參考
recruit [rɪˋkrut] **n.** 新成員；新兵 (手)	keynote speaker **n.** 主講嘉賓
submit [səbˋmɪt] **v.** 繳交	contribution [ˌkɑntrəˋbjuʃən] **n.** 貢獻
coordinator [koˋɔrdnˌetɚ] **n.** 統籌人	got promoted **v.** 升官
demonstrate [ˋdɛmənˌstret] **v.** 說明	scrutinize [ˋskrutnˌaɪz] **v.** 審議
large-scale **a.** 大規模的	patent [ˋpætnt] **n.** 專利
gadget [ˋgædʒɪt] **n.** 機械小工具	guarantee [ˌgærənˋti] **v.** 保證
clever [ˋklɛvɚ] **a.** 精巧的	payoff [ˋpeˌɔf] **n.** 收益
resignation [ˌrɛzɪgˋneʃən] **n.** 辭呈	claim [klem] **n.** **v.** 認領
getting a raise **v.** 加薪	initiate [ɪˋnɪʃɪɪt] **v.** 開始
raise [rez] **v.** 籌募	access [ˋæksɛs] **v.** 【電腦】取出（資料）
fund [fʌnd] **n.** 資金	database [ˋdetəˌbes] **n.** 資料庫
a takeover bid **n.** 收購投標	resident [ˋrɛzədənt] **n.** 居民
	toll-free **a.** 不用付電話費
	unclaimed property **n.** 未認領物品

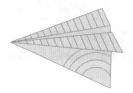

FAQ in TOEIC

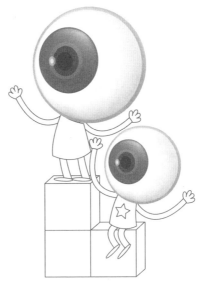

9

比較句型
(Patterns of Comparison)

文法講解區

❾ 比較句型 (Patterns of Comparison)

簡單看

　　簡單來說，不管是人與人，物與物或是事與事，都有互相比較的機會，在英語文法中，我們可以用原級、比較級和最高級的形容詞或副詞來比較二或多者以上的人、事、物甚至動作的性質、狀態或程度。

秒殺策略

（1）判斷題型，是否進行比較
（2）判斷搭配「原級」、「比較級」或是「最高級」何種句型

1 原級的比較句型

〉**as / so** ＋原級形容詞或副詞＋ **as**（像…一樣）

EX Many European businesses are <u>not so</u> competitive <u>as</u> they used to be.

（很多歐洲企業沒有像過去一般有競爭力。）

〉**as** ＋ **many / much / few / little** ＋名詞＋ **as**（…和…一樣多）

EX I've tried my best to think up <u>as</u> many practical ideas <u>as</u> possible for our proposal.

（我已經盡力替我們的企劃案想出可行的點子。）

〉**the same**（＋名詞）＋ **as**（與…相同）

EX The monthly average earnings this year are about <u>the same as</u> that in 2007.

（今年的月平均收入與 2007 年大致相同。）

〉修飾原級的程度副詞：**very, almost, nearly, just**

EX Best Hotel offers our customers <u>almost</u> as excellent service as five-star hotels do.

（Best 飯店提供與五星級飯店幾乎優等的服務給我們的顧客。）

生命加值室

如何搭配形容詞或是副詞

　　在第一個公式中，as / so ＋ 原級形容詞或副詞 ＋ as（像…一樣），很多人不思其解何時應搭配形容詞還是副詞。其實很簡單，只要看前方的主要動詞是「BE 動詞／連綴動詞」還是「一般動詞」即可。

〉BE 動詞 / 連綴動詞 ＋ as ＋ 形容詞原級 ＋ as

EX The weather is not so humid in the UK as (it is) in Taiwan.

（英國天氣不像台灣那麼潮濕。）

〉一般動詞 ＋ as ＋ 副詞原級 ＋ as

EX With proper maintenance, the old computer still works as quickly as the new model.

（有適當的維護，這舊電腦運作的和新款機一樣地快。）

211

➋ 比較級的比較句型

〉比較級形容詞或副詞 + **than**

EX The present system is more efficient than the old one.

（現在的系統比舊的要來的有效率。）

〉**more / fewer / less** + 名詞 + **than**

EX More companies than last year participated in the Angus Business Trade Show.

（跟去年相較，較多公司參加了 Angus 商業展會。）

〉**the** 比較級 + **of the two** + 名詞

EX Miss Christina is the better qualified of the two shortlisted candidates.

(Christina 小姐是兩名候選人中較具資格者。)

〉**The** 比較級 + 主詞 + 動詞，**the** 比較級 + 主詞 + 動詞 （越…就越…）

EX The more we discussed about the tender offer, the more suspicious we found it.

（關於招標，我們討論越多，我們越發覺更多疑點。）

〉本身即帶有比較意義的形容詞：**superior, inferior, senior, junior, prior** + **to**

EX Brain considers himself superior to most of his colleagues.

（Brian 認為自己比其他同事要來的優越。 ）

〉其他關於 **than** 的片語：

no later than	不可晚於	more than	非常、甚為
other than	除了、不同於	rather than	而不

EX No one is eligible for taking over the company other than Amanda.

（除了 Amanda 之外，無人有資格接掌公司。 ）

〉修飾比較級的程度副詞：**much, far, even, still, rather, a lot, a little, a bit**

EX It's rumored that the coming supervisor is much tougher than Mr. Kim.

（據說即將到來的上司比 Kim 先生要來的強悍。 ）

3 最高級的比較句型

〉**the** 最高級形容詞或副詞 + 指定範圍

EX The high operating costs are the most difficult problem <u>in the company</u>.

（高營運成本是公司最大的問題。）

〉**the** 最高級形容詞或副詞 + 關係子句（現在完成式）／不定詞

EX The new marketing manager is the most creative person <u>that I've worked with</u>.

（新任行銷經理是我共事過最有創意的人。）

〉修飾最高級的程度副詞：**much, by far, quite**

EX Cindy is <u>by far</u> the most accommodating assistant in our department.

（Cindy 是我們部門最樂於助人的助手。）

生命加值室

最高級的公式中，「the 最高級形容詞或副詞 + 指定範圍」，其中「指定範圍」包括：

〉in + 場所

EX The landmark is the most-visited tourist spot in Tokyo.

（這地標是東京受到最多參觀的旅遊景點。）

〉of + the + 群體

EX Of the five, Mr. Lin is the less eligible to work in our company.

（五個人之中，林先生是最沒資格在我們公司工作。）

〉of all

EX On the list of Top 10 Best tour guides, Wu is the most experienced and trustworthy one of all.

（在最佳 10 位導遊名單中，吳是所有之中最有經驗與可靠的導遊。）

---

6 假設語氣與條件句

7 不定詞與動名詞

8 分詞

9 比較句型

10 名詞與代名詞

Mini Test 練習區　限時5分

1. The new diet we are trying now can't eliminate toxins from the body as _____ as the previous one.
   (A) effect　　　　(B) effective　　　(C) effectively　　　(D) more effective

2. An interesting study shows that overweight doctors are often seen as _____ credible and professional than normal weight doctors, and patients are less likely to follow their medical advice.
   (A) more　　　　(B) less　　　　(C) most　　　　(D) least

3. The charity is coordinating its effort to distribute _____ possible to the distress area.
   (A) as much as　　(B) as soon as　　(C) as food as　　(D) as much food as

4. All applicants are required to submit CV and supporting documents to our personnel department _____ July 31th.
   (A) no more than　　(B) no sooner than　　(C) no other than　　(D) no later than

5. The earlier you start saving for retirement, the _____ it will be to afford.
   (A) easy　　　　(B) easier　　　　(C) easily　　　　(D) more easily

6. Coco Chanel is the most legendary female fashion designer that I _____.
   (A) hear　　　　(B) heard　　　　(C) have heard　　　　(D) am hearing

7. Carpooling is seen as a _____ more environmentally friendly and sustainable way to travel.
   (A) just　　　　(B) very　　　　(C) much　　　　(D) almost

8. Compared with the service provided by Elite PR Group, ours is not _____ theirs.
   (A) junior to　　(B) junior than　　(C) inferior than　　(D) inferior to

9. In terms of commuting costs, cycling is _____ the cheapest mean of transportation next to walking.
   (A) quite　　　　(B) very　　　　(C) nearly　　　　(D) almost

10. _____ compete with A & M, our board of directors decided to cooperate with it.
    (A) Instead　　　(B) Except　　　(C) More than　　　(D) Rather than

9.比較句型│迷你練習區

6 假設語氣與條件句

7 不定詞與動名詞

8 分詞

9 比較句型

10 名詞與代名詞

Question 11-13 refer to the following announcement

In today's business news, Mr. Michael Hunter, president of the BEST Ltd., has announced his retirement next year.Mr. Michael Hunter, who excels at public relations and corporate connections and helps to build the BEST Ltd into a large business, is viewed as one of the _____ influential entrepreneurs

11 (A) most
(B) more
(C) best
(D) very

in Taiwan.

Over the last few years, BEST has increased yields _____ dramatically than

12 (A) eminent
(B) eminently
(C) eminency
(D) more eminent

it did

before.BEST executives revealed that Jim Hunter, Mr. Michael Hunter's son, is presumed the designated successor. Qualified and experienced in the business, he is expected to lead the BEST Ltd. as _____ as his father.

13 (A) a lot
(B) a lot more
(C) the most
(D) much most

1-10 Ans: 1.(C) 2.(B) 3.(D) 4.(D) 5.(B) 6.(C) 7.(C) 8.(D) 9.(B) 10.(D)

1. The new diet we are trying now can't eliminate toxins from the body
   as _____ as the previous one.
   (A) effect
   (B) effective
   (C) effectively
   (D) more effective

答案 C

眼球追蹤

The new diet we are trying now can't |eliminate| toxins from the body |as

_____ as| the previous one.

(A) effect　　　(B) effective　　　❸(C) effectively　　　(D) more effective

中譯 我們現在試的新的飲食習慣無法像之前的一樣，將體內毒素有效地消除。

秒殺策略

❶ **判斷題型**

由關鍵字 **as...as** 得知，測驗點為「**原級**」的比較句型。

❷ **判斷空格搭配的詞類**

前方主要動詞 eliminate 需要「**副詞**」修飾。

❸ **驗證答案**

空格需要「**原級的副詞**」。

檢查

(A) 名詞，刪除。

(B) 形容詞，原級，刪除。

(C) 副詞，原級

(D) 形容詞，比較級，刪除。

故本題答案選 (C)

2. An interesting study shows that overweight doctors are often seen as
   _____ credible and professional than normal weight doctors, and patients are less likely to follow their medical advice.
   (A) more   (B) less   (C) most   (D) least

答案 B

眼球追蹤

An interesting study shows that overweight doctors are often seen as

_____ credible and professional |than| normal weight doctors, |and patients are

less likely to follow their medical advice.

(A) more   (B) less   (C) most   (D) least

中譯 一項有趣的研究表明，比起正常體重的醫生，過重的醫生往往被視為不太
可信和專業的，患者就不太可能接受他們的醫療建議。

秒殺策略

❶ 判斷題型

由關鍵字 than 得知，測驗點為「**比較級**」的比較句型。

❷ 搭配語意，驗證答案

已有形容詞，無須判斷詞性。但需要看語意。依語意，需要「**劣勢比較級**」。

檢查

(A) 形成比較級形容詞，不符合語意，刪除。
(B) 形成劣勢比較級
(C) 形成最高級，刪除。
(D) 形成劣勢最高級，刪除。
故本題答案選 (B)

6 假設語氣與條件句
7 不定詞與動名詞
8 分詞
9 比較句型
10 名詞與代名詞

3. The charity is coordinating its effort to distribute _____ possible to the distress area.

  (A) as much as   (B) as soon as

  (C) as food as   (D) as much food as

答案 D

原來是這樣

The charity is coordinating its effort to ③ distribute ② _____ possible to the distress area.

❶ 看選項

| (A) as much as | (B) as soon as | (C) as food as | (D) as much food as |

中譯 該慈善組織正盡努力協調將盡可能多的食物分配到災區。

秒殺策略 👑

❶ 判斷題型

看選項得知，測驗點為「as...as 的比較句型」。

❷ 判斷空格

判斷要使用「as / so + 原級形容詞或副詞 + as（像...一樣）」，
還是「as + many / much / few / little + 名詞 + as」。

❸ 判斷動詞，驗證答案

distribute 為及物動詞，需搭配受詞，故選擇「as + many / much / few / little + 名詞 + as」句型。👑

檢查

(A) 無法提供受詞給 distribute，刪除。

(B) 無法提供受詞給 distribute，刪除。

(C) 無 as+名詞+as 句型，刪除。

(D) as much food as possible 盡可能多的食物 👑

故本題答案選 (D)

4. All applicants are required to submit CV and supporting documents to our personnel department _____ July 31th.
(A) no more than　(B) no sooner than　(C) no other than　(D) no later than

答案 D

原來是這樣

❷ 看全句

All applicants are required to submit CV and supporting documents to our personnel department _____ July 31th.

❶ 看選項

(A) no more than　(B) no sooner than　(C) no other than　(D) no later than

中譯 所有申請人最晚於 7 月 31 日前，將簡歷及有關證明文件送至我們的人事部門。

秒殺策略

❶ 判斷題型

看選項得知，測驗點為「其他關於 than 的片語」。

❷ 搭配語意，驗證答案

逐一判斷每個選項的語意與用法，帶入句子。

(A) no more than 不超過；只是（=merely）

(B) no sooner than 必須改成為 no sooner...than... 一…就…

(C) no other than 只有；正是；就是（=nothing but）

(D) no later than 不可晚於 ♛

檢查

(A) 語意不合，刪除。

(B) 語意、文法不合，刪除。

(C) 語意不合，刪除。

(D) no later than 不可晚於 ♛

故本題答案選 (D)

5. The earlier you start saving for retirement, the ＿＿＿ it will be to afford.

(A) easy　　　　(B) easier　　　(C) easily　　　(D) more easily

答案 **B**

原來是這樣

❶ 看全句　　　　　　　　　　　　　　　　　　**❷**
The earlier you start saving for retirement, the ＿＿＿ it will be to afford.

❸
(A) easy　　　　(B) easier　　　(C) easily　　　(D) more easily

中譯　你越早開始為退休儲蓄，就越容易負擔得起。

秒殺策略

❶ 判斷題型

分析全句，由「The earlier..., the ＿＿＿...」得知，

測驗點為「**雙重比較**」the 比較級＋ S＋ V, the 比較級＋ V 的比較句型。

❷ 判斷空格搭配的詞類

先還原 the ＿＿＿ it will be to afford，應為 it will be ＿＿＿ to afford，故應搭配形容詞而非副詞。

❸ 驗證答案

空格需要「**比較級的形容詞**」。

檢查

(A) 形容詞，原級，刪除。

(B) 形容詞，比較級

(C) 副詞，原級，刪除。

(D) 副詞，比較級，刪除。

故本題答案選 (B)

6. Coco Chanel is the most legendary female fashion designer that I _____.

(A) hear   (B) heard   (C) have heard   (D) am hearing

答案 C

原來是這樣

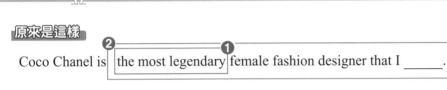

Coco Chanel is | the most legendary | female fashion designer that I _____.

(A) hear   (B) heard   ❸ (C) have heard   (D) am hearing

中譯 Coco Chanel 是我聽過的最富有傳奇色彩的女時裝設計師。

秒殺策略 ♛

❶ **判斷題型**

由「**the most legendary**」得知，測驗點為「**最高級**」的比較句型。

❷ **判斷空格需求**

由 the most legendary female fashion designer / that... 得知是，本題為「最高級形容詞或副詞 + 關係子句（現在完成式）/ 不定詞」的句型。

❸ **驗證答案**

空格需要「**現在完成式（have/has p.p.）**」的動詞。♛

檢查

(A) 現在簡單式 刪除。

(B) 過去簡單式 刪除。

(C) 現在完成式 ♛

(D) 現在進行式，刪除。

故本題答案選 (C)

221

7. Carpooling is seen as a _____ more environmentally friendly and sustainable way to travel.

(A) just   (B) very   (C) much   (D) almost

答案 **C**

原來是這樣

Carpooling is seen as a _____ more environmentally friendly and sustainable way to travel.

(A) just   (B) very   ❷ (C) much   (D) almost

中譯 共乘被視為更加環保和可續發展的旅行方式。

秒殺策略

❶ **判斷題型**

由 a _____ more environmentally friendly 得知，測驗點為「**修飾比較級的程度副詞**」。

❷ **驗證答案**

「修飾比較級的程度副詞」包括：much, far, even, still, rather, a lot, a little, a bit。

檢查

(A) 修飾原級的程度副詞，刪除

(B) 修飾原級的程度副詞，刪除

(C) 修飾比較級的程度副詞

(D) 修飾原級的程度副詞，刪除

故本題答案選 (C)

8. Compared with the service provided by Elite PR Group, ours is not _____ theirs.

  (A) junior to   (B) junior than   (C) inferior than   (D) inferior to

答案 D

原來是這樣

❷ 看全句

Compared with the service provided by Elite PR Group, ours is not _____ theirs.

❶ 看選項

  (A) junior to   (B) junior than   (C) inferior than   **❸** (D) inferior to

中譯　與 Elite 公關集團所提供的服務比較，我們所提供的不遜於他們。

秒殺策略 👑

❶ 判斷題型

看選項，測驗點為「junior / inferior」的用法。

❷ 驗證答案

由語意判斷，使用 inferior，並搭配 to，而非 than。junior to 比…資淺；比…年輕。👑

檢查

(A) 比…資淺；比…年輕，主詞應為人，刪除。

(B) 文法與語意皆不合，刪除。

(C) 應搭配 to，刪除。

(D) inferior to （品質）次的；較差的👑

故本題答案選 (D)

9. In terms of commuting costs, cycling is _____ the cheapest mean of transportation next to walking.

(A) quite   (B) very   (C) nearly   (D) almost

答案 A

原來是這樣

❶ 看全句 ❶
In terms of commuting costs, cycling is _____ the cheapest mean of transportation next to walking.

❷ (A) quite   (B) very   (C) nearly   (D) almost

中譯　以通勤費用來說,騎腳踏車是僅次於走路最便宜的交通方式。

秒殺策略

❶ 判斷題型

分析全句,由 cycling is _____ the cheapest mean of transportation...得知,測驗點為「**修飾最高級的程度副詞**」。

❷ 驗證答案

「修飾最高級的程度副詞」包括:much, by far, quite。

檢查

(A) 修飾最高級的程度副詞

(B) 修飾原級的程度副詞,刪除。

(C) 修飾原級的程度副詞,刪除。

(D) 修飾原級的程度副詞,刪除。

故本題答案選 (A)

10. _____ compete with A & M, our board of directors decided to cooperate with it.
　　(A) Instead　　　　(B) Except　　　　(C) More than　　　　(D) Rather than

答案 D

原來是這樣

❷ 看全句
_____ compete with A & M, our board of directors decided to cooperate with it.

❶ 看選項
　(A) Instead　　　　(B) Except　　　　(C) More than　　　　(D) Rather than

中譯　我們董事會決定與 A & M 合作，而不與他們競爭。

秒殺策略 👑

❶ 判斷題型

看選項得知，測驗點為「字詞片語使用」。

❷ 搭配語意，驗證答案

逐一判斷每個選項的語意與用法，帶入句子。

(A) instead (adv.) 然而 → 要符合本題語意，需搭配 instead of + competing

(B) except (prep) 除...之外（不包括）→ 少放句首，且後方多搭名詞

(C) more than (adj / adv) 多於；不但...也是；非常（=very）

(D) rather than (conj / prep) 而非 → rather than 連接 compete 與 cooperate 動作，原句：our board of directors decided to cooperate with A & M rather than (to) compete with it. 若 rather than 放句首，to 多半可省略。👑

檢查

(A) instead（adv）然而，刪除。

(B) except（prep）除...之外（不包括）文法不符，刪除。

(C) more than（ph）多於；不但...也是；非常，刪除。

(D) rather than（ph）而非 👑

故本題答案選 (D)

11-13 題參考下列通告

中譯

今天的商業新聞報導，Michael Hunter 先生，BEST 有限公司總裁，已經宣布明年退休。Michael Hunter 先生被視為台灣最具影響力的企業家之一，其擅長公共關係及企業聯繫，也協助打造 BEST 公司成為一個大型企業。在過去幾年中，BEST 比以前增加獲利更為明顯地多。BEST 經營團隊透露，Jim Hunter，也是 Michael Hunter 的兒子，被假定為指定接班人。Jim Hunter 極具資格且有經驗的實務，他被期待可以和其父親一樣優秀地引領 BEST 公司。

秒殺策略 ♛

11. 答案 **(A) most**

Mr. Michael Hunter, who..., is viewed as one of the **most** influential entrepreneurs in Taiwan.

解題 台灣最有影響力的企業家之一。... influential entrepreneurs in Taiwan 為一範圍且比較對象有三者以上，前又有 the 搭配，故使用最高級。♛

12. 答案 **(B) a lot more**

...has increased yields **a lot more** dramatically than it did before

解題 由 dramatically than 推得，需要比較級，用 more dramatically。再搭配修飾比較級的程度副詞（much, far, even, still, rather, a lot, a little, a bit）即可。♛

13. 答案 **(B) eminently**

...he is expected to lead the BEST Ltd. as **eminently** as his father

解題 修飾動詞 lead the BEST Ltd.，應使用副詞，as...as 應搭配原級副詞或形容詞，故選 eminently。♛

成為多益勝利組的字彙練功區

文法講解區	Mini Test 限時 5 分練習區
think up **v.** 想出 (點子)	eliminate [ɪ`lɪməˌnet] **v.** 消除
proposal [prə`pozl] **n.** 企劃案	toxin [`tɑksɪn] **n.** 毒素
earnings [`ɝnɪŋz] **n.** 收入，工資	previous [`priviəs] **a.** 以前的
efficient [ɪ`fɪʃənt] **a.** 有效率的	credible [`krɛdəbl] **a.** 可信的；可靠的
shortlisted [ʃɔrt`lɪstɪd] **a.** 篩選後的 (候選人名單)	coordinate [ko`ɔrdnɪt] **v.** 協調
tender offer **n.** 投標報價	distress area **n.** 災區
suspicious [sə`spɪʃəs] **a.** 可疑的	CV (curriculum vitae) **n.** 簡歷
superior to **a.** 優越的	retirement [rɪ`taɪrmənt] **n.** 退休
take over **v.** 接掌	legendary [`lɛdʒəndˌɛrɪ] **a.** 傳奇的
rumor [`rumɚ] **v.** 謠傳	carpooling [`karpulɪŋ] **n.** 共乘
supervisor [ˌsupɚ`vaɪzɚ] **n.** 上司	environmentally friendly **a.** 環保
operating cost **n.** 營運成本	sustainable [sə`stenəbl] **a.** 永續發展的
accommodating [ə`kaməˌdetɪŋ] **a.** 樂於助人的	commuting cost **n.** 通勤成本
	board of directors **n.** 董事會

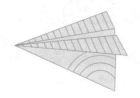

FAQ in TOEIC

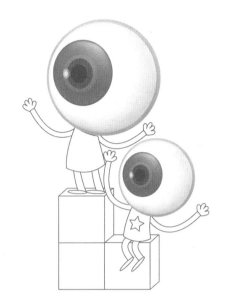

10
名詞與代名詞
(Nouns & Pronouns)

文法講解區

➓ 名詞與代名詞 (Nouns & Pronouns)

簡單看

　【名詞】是實詞的一種，指人、事、時、地、物、等實體或概念、情感、抽象事物的詞。

　【代名詞】是用來取代前面句中或對話已提過的人、事、物。

秒殺策略

(1) 根據選項，判斷題型

(2) 根據前後搭配的關鍵字詞判斷答案

❶ 名詞的功能與位置

〉名詞的功能

1 當主詞：	2 當受詞：	3 當補語：
[N] + V … S	(1) Vt + [N] 　　　　 O (2)介詞 + [N] 　　　　 O	(1)S + Be + [N] 　　　　　　 SC (2)S + Vt + O + [N] 　　　　　　　　 OC

> **EX** Your diagnosis of the machine problem was very helpful to us.
> （您對於機器問題的診斷對我們十分有幫助。）→當主詞

> **EX** The part-time worker distributed flyers to advertise the newly opened restaurant.
> （這兼職的員工發送傳單替新餐廳做宣傳。）→當動詞後的受詞

> **EX** According to the sales figures, our new promotional strategy seems workable.
> （根據銷售數據，我們新的促銷策略似乎可行的。）→ 當介係詞後的受詞

> **EX** Many distinguished guests at the party are talented performers from the UK.
> （在宴會上很多傑出的嘉賓都是來自英國的有才華的表演者。）→當主詞補語

> **EX** The manager appointed the experienced candidate counselor.
> （經理指派這有經歷的候選人為顧問。）→當受詞補語

〉名詞的位置

第一類：

⑴ 修飾語之後：修飾語包括了冠詞（a / an/ the）、所有格、形容詞

> **EX** Annie's background in investigation ensured her a position in the Customs.
> （Annie 調查的背景確保她在海關位置。）

⑵ 介係詞之後

> **EX** On the basis of an extensive survey, our office decided to bid for the project.
> （根據大規模調查後，我們公司決定競標這案子。）

⑶ 動詞之後：包括了及物動詞與連綴動詞

> **EX** The small company couldn't bear the brunt of the economic downturn and went bankrupt.
> （這小公司承受不了經濟衰然後就倒閉了。）

(2) 名詞之後：構成了複合名詞

EX According to our <u>return</u> policies, customers can return their items within 7 days.

（根據我們退貨政策，顧客必須在他們所購買的商店退還物品。）

第二類：

(1) 關係子句前

EX The casual manner <u>in which the manager announced the layoff</u> aroused employees' anger .

（總經理宣布解雇的隨意態度引起員工的氣憤。）

(2) 分詞片語前

EX We are sorry for a product defect <u>discovered in the first production run</u>.

（對於第一產量期間所發現的產品瑕疵，我們深感抱歉。）

(3) 介係詞片語前

EX Entries <u>in the agenda</u> were modified under the instruction of our president.

（在我們總裁指示下，議程條目被更正了。）

(4) 不定詞前

EX Our plans <u>to introduce new lines of luxury products</u> didn't work during economic recession.

（經濟衰退期時，我們推出高檔產品線的計畫似乎不奏效。）

2 名詞的種類：分為可數名詞與不可數名詞

可數名詞	不可數名詞
具體的普通名詞	抽象名詞 / 專有名詞 / 物質名詞
例：manual, skyscraper, branch	例：economy / Facebook / copper
單數前加冠詞 a / an，複數後加 s / es、或去 y 加 ies	只有單數型，前不加冠詞 a/an，但可加 the 與量詞
恆用複數型的複數名詞，例： clothes / thanks / looks + 複數動詞	恆用複數型的單數名詞，例： politics / diabetes / news + 單數動詞

搭配可數複數名詞的數量修飾詞		搭配不可數單數名詞的數量修飾詞	
a few/ few a great/good many a large/small number of a number of a couple of	可數複數 N + 複數 V	a great/good deal of a large/small amount of a little/ little an amount of a crumb/bit of	不可數單數 N + 單數 V

通用可數與不可數：plenty of / a lot of / a (great) wealth of / a large /small quantity of / some/ all / no / any

「可數用法」與「不可數用法」語意不同者，例：
works 作品 / work 工作；businesses 企業、商店 / business 生意、事務
damages 賠償金 / damage 損害；men 人們 / man 人類

③ 複合名詞：前一個名詞不能以形容詞或分詞取代

以下為多益常見的複合名詞：

bank account	銀行帳戶	delivery company	宅配公司
benefits package	福利制度	application form	申請表
fuel economy	低油耗	confirmation number	確認碼
consumer complaint	客戶投訴	course evaluation	課程評價
employee productivity	員工生產力	expiration date	到期日
installment payment	分期付款	interest rate	利息
market research	市場調查	expense report	支出報告
luggage allowance	行李限重	attendance record	出席紀錄
pay raise / increase	加薪	sales figures	銷售數字
public relations	公關	travel expenses	旅遊費用
return policy	退貨規定	time constraint	時間限制

4 代名詞種類：

代名詞	範例
人稱代名詞	I, me, my, you, your, he, him, his, she, her, it, its, we, us, our, they, them, their
所有格代名詞	mine, yours, his, hers, ours, theirs
反身代名詞	myself, ourselves, yourself, yourselves, himself, herself, itself, themselves
指示代名詞	this, that, these, those
不定代名詞	all, another, any, anybody, anyone, anything, both, each, everybody, everyone, everything, few, many, most, neither, nobody, none, nothing, oneself, other, some, somebody, someone, something
疑問代名詞	who, whom, whose, which, what, where
關係代名詞	who, whose, whom, which, that

5 人稱代名詞、所有格代名詞、反身代名詞的「數、性、格」

人稱	數	主格	受格	所有格	所有格代名詞	反身代名詞
第一人稱	單數	I	me	my	mine	myself
	複數	we	us	our	ours	ourselves
第二人稱	單數	you	you	your	yours	yourself
	複數	you	you	your	yours	yourselves
第三人稱	單數	he	him	his	his	himself
		she	her	her	hers	herself
		it	it	its	its	itself
	複數	they	them	their	theirs	themselves

6 人稱代名詞的位置與相對的「數」、「性」與「格」

下列三種「格」，可以表示代名詞與它們搭配的「動詞」、「介詞」與「其他名詞」的關係

格	功能	位置
主格	作為主詞或主詞補語	主格 +（助動詞）+ V
受格	作為及物動詞、不定詞、或介系詞的受詞	及物動詞 /不定詞 / 介係詞 + 受格
所有格	表示某人的所有權，後加 名詞 / 動名詞	所有格 +（形容詞）+ N

> **EX** James' ambition to be successful has surpassed **his** desire to have good interpersonal relationships in the office. Therefore, his colleagues don't want to befriend **him** even though **he** got recognized from the boss at work.
>
> （James 對成功的野心更甚於在辦公擁有好的人際關係。因此即使他在工作上得到老闆的肯定，他的同事也不想和他做朋友）

所有格代名詞 =人稱所有格 + 名詞，可放「主格」、「受格」或「補語」位置

> **EX** My supervisor seemed very satisfied with Linda's presentation, but not **mine** (=my presentation).
>
> （我上司似乎對於 Lina 的簡報很滿意，但對我的（簡報）確不是。）
> **注意：所有格代名詞已具名詞作用，故後面不可再接名詞**

7 反身代名詞的功能與作用：

(1) 反身用法：同一句子中，主詞與受詞為同一人或物時，受詞要用反身代名詞

EX Can you introduce yourself in one minute?

（您可以在一分鐘內自我介紹嗎？）

(2) 強調用法：加強主詞或受詞的語氣

EX The manager himself offered a verbal apology to the customer for his employee's rudeness.

（經理本身會對那顧客提出口頭道歉已標示。）

(3) 慣用法

by oneself 獨自	for oneself 為自己	in itself 本身	of itself 自動

EX Did Jerry do all the work by himself without anyone's assistance?

（Jerry 自己獨自完成所有的工作而無其他人的協助嗎？）

8 指示代名詞：

〉 this / these / that / those

• 為指示代名詞與指示形容詞，功能是用來指出特定的人或物。

> **EX** There are 5 items we have to check on this list.
> （這張單子有五個項目需要我們去確定。）

〉 that / those

• 除了上述用法外，**that** 和 **those** 還可用來代替前面提過的名詞，後加 **of** +名詞。

> **EX** The women shoes in our shop are much more stylish than those in the shop next door.
> （我們家女鞋的風格比隔壁家的藥來的流行的多。）

〉 慣用法 those people who 那些…的人

• **people** 可以省略成為 **those who** + 子句的句型

> **EX** Those who wish to join the club have to register in advance.
> （想要加入俱樂部的人要先登記。）

9 不定代名詞：

〉 some / any：兩者皆可代替單、複數名詞，與指示詞相同，兩者亦可當形容詞

• 兩者皆可代替單、複數名詞，與指示詞相同，亦可當形容詞。

　⑴ some（任何）：指「未定數中的一些」，用於肯定句及某些疑問句。

　⑵ any（一些）：指「未定數中的任何一個或多個」，用於否定、疑問及某些肯定句。

> **EX** Please do not hesitate to contact me if you have <u>any</u> further questions. I may offer <u>some</u> help.
> （若你有任何進一步的問題，別遲疑與我聯絡。我或許可以提供一些協助。）

〉 one / another / the other：

• 當數量有二或三個或群類時，會利用下面不定代名詞點出範圍。

　⑴ one（一個）：指一群人、事、物中的某一個，或是不特定的單數名詞。

　⑵ the other（剩餘的那一個）：兩者中的剩餘的另一個。

　⑶ another（另一個）：指提過的再一個，或是別的一個。

EX Twins as they are, <u>one</u> was much gorgeous than <u>the other</u>.

（雖然他們是雙胞胎，但其中一個比另一個來的漂亮。）

EX Body language differs from one culture to <u>another</u>.

（肢體語言因文化而異。）

〉others / the others：

• **當有搭配定冠詞 the 時，即指特定的剩下範圍。**

⑴ others（其他）：指提過的再好幾個人或物，或當「其他人」。

⑵ the others（剩餘的其他人或物）

EX For extended stays, our hotel proposes visitors three types of suites with extreme comfort.Some have 2 separated rooms for family, and <u>others</u> are one king bed suite for a couple.<u>The others</u> are two twin beds suite, the best value for those traveling in pairs.

（對於長期住宿，我們酒店提供遊客各類極度舒適的套房。有些設有兩個獨立的房間供家庭使用，有些則是給情侶或夫妻的一張特大號床套房。其他則是兩張床的套房，是給成對旅遊的遊客的最佳選擇。）

〉either / neither：

• **後面常搭配「of the + 名詞」，放主詞位置時，動詞都用單數。**

⑴ either（兩者之一）

⑵ neither（兩者皆不）

EX <u>Either</u> of the two marketing strategies is practical and acceptable. <u>Neither</u> of them is rejected by our manager.

（這兩個行銷策略皆可行且可被接受。兩者皆無被我們經理否決。）

6 假設語氣與條件句

7 不定詞與動名詞

8 分詞

9 比較句型

10 名詞與代名詞

Mini Test 練習區 限時 5 分

1. _____ sales clerks are not authorized to provide any discounts to customers.

   (A) We   (B) Our   (C) Us   (D) Ours

2. When taxpayers pay their taxes with a credit card, they can apply for an_____ payment plan, or periodic payment.

   (A) install   (B) installing   (C) installed   (D) installment

3. In a service firm like ___ , employee loyalty is always a focus that we have to create and keep.

   (A) we   (B) our   (C) us   (D) ours

4. Mr. Smith is more qualified than any _____ candidate in the interviews for the position.

   (A) a   (B) another   (C) other   (D) others

5. The cost of shipping rate this year is higher than _____ last year.

   (A) one   (B) it   (C) that   (D) those

6. It's a group project.Tom, you don't have to finish all the work by _____.

   (A) you   (B) yourself   (C) yourselves   (D) himself

7. BETTER & BEST Co. Ltd. plans to open two branches.One is in Taichung and _____ is in Kaohsiung.

   (A) Another   (B) other   (C) that   (D) the other

8. _____of the applicants are qualified for the position of Export Sales Manager. We need to post an employment notice again.

   (A) One   (B) No   (C) Either   (D) Neither

9. A good _____ record has a positive impact on one's performance and also shows if he or she can successfully achieve the outcomes of programs.

   (A) attend   (B) attending   (C) attendance   (D) attentive

10. Our manager was not satisfied with _____ of the planned activities in the incentive tour this year.

   (A) none   (B) any   (C) every   (D) almost

Question 11-13 refer to the following short notice

Attention R & D Dept. Members

This Friday the security department will be your department to get your picture taken. They will have you set a _____ number of your own. With the

> 11 (A) confirm
> (B) confirmed
> (C) confirmation
> (D) confirmational

taken photo and number

you set, they will make an identification card for you. _____ of you is

> 12 (A) Each
> (B) Some
> (C) Many
> (D) All

required to wear

the ID card at all times. The card can also unlock the doors of the building with higher security but more convenient access to other departments of the office. The new security system will surely make _____ company a safer

> 13 (A) us
> (B) we
> (C) our
> (D) ours

place to work.

1-10 Ans: 1.(B) 2.(D) 3.(D) 4.(C) 5.(C) 6.(B) 7.(D) 8.(D) 9.(C) 10.(B)

1. _____ sales clerks are not authorized to provide any discounts to customers.

(A) We　　　　　(B) Our　　　　　(C) Us　　　　　(D) Ours

答案 B

眼球追蹤

❷ 看全句

_____ sales clerks are not authorized to provide any discounts to customers.

❶ 看選項

(A) We　　　　　(B) Our　　　　　(C) Us　　　　　(D) Ours

中譯　我們的銷售人員無權提供任何折扣給客戶。

秒殺策略

❶ 判斷題型

看選項得知，測驗點為**人稱代名詞的「格」**。

❷ 根據前後搭配字詞，驗證答案

分析全句，由 sales clerks / are not authorized to provide…得知，主詞／動作皆完整敘述。空格應為修飾 sales clerks 的**冠詞（a / an / the）**、**所有格或形容詞**皆可。

檢查

(A) 主格，刪除。

(B) 所有格

(C) 受格，刪除。

(D) 所有格代名詞，刪除。

故本題答案選 (B)

2. When taxpayers pay their taxes with a credit card, they can apply for an _____ payment plan, or periodic payment.
   (A) install   (B) installing   (C) installed   (D) installment

答案 D

眼球追蹤

When taxpayers pay their taxes with a credit card, they can apply for an _____ ❷

payment plan, or periodic payment.

❶ 看選項

   (A) install   (B) installing   (C) installed   (D) installment

中譯 當納稅人使用信用卡繳納稅款，他們可以申請分期付款計劃，或分期付款。

秒殺策略

❶ 判斷題型

看選項得知，測驗點為「**詞類判斷**」。

❷ 根據前後搭配字詞，驗證答案

由 an _____ payment plan 得知，空格要搭配修飾 payment 的詞類，installment payment 為 N+N 的固定**複合名詞**搭配用法，選 installment。

檢查

(A) 動詞，刪除。
(B) 現在分詞，刪除。
(C) 過去分詞，刪除。
(D) installment payment 固定用法
故本題答案選 (D)

3. In a service firm like _____ , employee loyalty is always a focus that we have to create and keep.

   (A) we   (B) our   (C) us   (D) ours

答案 D

眼球追蹤

In a service firm like _____ ❷, employee loyalty is always a focus that we

have to create and keep.

❶ **看選項**

   (A) we   (B) our   (C) us   (D) ours

中譯 在像我們這樣的服務公司，員工忠誠度始終是一個重點，我們必須創造和保持。

秒殺策略

❶ **判斷題型**

看選項得知，測驗點為人稱代名詞的「**格**」。

❷ **根據前後搭配字詞，驗證答案**

由 In a service firm like _____ 得知，空格要可接在 like 之後的受格，考慮 us 與 ours。語意應為 in a service firm like our firm，故搭配所有格代名詞 ours。

檢查

(A) 主格，刪除。

(B) 所有格，刪除。

(C) 受格，但應指 our service firm，刪除。

(D) 所有格代名詞

故本題答案選 (D)

242

4. Mr. Smith is more qualified than any _____ candidate in the interviews for the position.

(A) a　　　　　　(B) another　　　　(C) other　　　　(D) others

答案 C

眼球追蹤

Mr. Smith is more qualified |than any _____ candidate in the interviews| for the
position.

❶ 看選項

(A) a　　　　　　(B) another　　　　(C) other　　　　(D) others

中譯　Smith 先生比面試中的其他任何候選人更有資格擔任此職務。

秒殺策略 👑

❶ **判斷題型**

看選項得知，測驗點為「**冠詞**」與「**不定代名詞**」。

❷ **根據前後搭配字詞，驗證答案**

由 than any _____ candidate in the interviews 得知，聯想到「**any other
+ 單數可數名詞**」的句型。👑

檢查

(A) a 不會與 any 同時出現，刪除。

(B) another 不會與 any 搭配，刪除。

(C) any other candidate 👑

(D) 後面還有 candidate，所以 other 應當形容詞，而非名詞使用，刪除。

故本題答案選 (C)

6 假設語氣與條件句

7 不定詞與動名詞

8 分詞

9 比較句型

10 名詞與代名詞

243

5. The cost of shipping rate this year is higher than _____ last year.
   (A) one　　　　　(B) it　　　　　(C) that　　　　　(D) those

答案 C

眼球追蹤

❷ 看全句
The cost of shipping rate this year is higher than _____ last year.

❶ 看選項
(A) one　　　　(B) it　　　　(C) that　　　　(D) those

中譯　今年出貨率的成本比去年高。

秒殺策略 ♛

❶ **判斷題型**

看選項得知，測驗點為「**代名詞**」。

❷ **根據前後搭配字詞，驗證答案**

分析全句，由 The cost of shipping rate this year/is/higher than/ _____ last year 得知，空格應為可以**代同一句前面出現過** the cost of shipping rate 的**指示代名詞**。

單數名詞用 that，複數名詞用 those。 ♛

檢查

(A) one 不定代名詞，刪除。
(B) it 人稱代名詞，會變成指同一物，刪除。
(C) that ♛
(D) those 指示代名詞，代替複數，刪除。
故本題答案選 (C)

6. It's a group project. Tom, you don't have to finish all the work by

_____.

(A) you   (B) yourself   (C) yourselves   (D) himself

答案 B

眼球追蹤

It's a group project. | Tom, you don't have to | finish all the work | by _____ .

❶ 看選項

(A) you   (B) yourself   (C) yourselves   (D) himself

中譯 這是一個團隊計畫。Tom，你不必自己來完成所有的工作。

秒殺策略

❶ 判斷題型

看選項得知，測驗點為「**反身代名詞的慣用語 by oneself**」。

❷ 根據前後搭配字詞，驗證答案

由 Tom, you don't have to 得知，本句為對 Tom 單一人所說的祈使句，主詞亦為**單數的** you，選 by yourself，表「你獨自一人」。

檢查

(A) 主格或受格，刪除。

(B) you 的反身代名詞

(C) 複數 you 的反身代名詞，刪除。

(D) he 的反身態名詞，人稱不符合，刪除。

故本題答案選 (B)

7. BETTER & BEST Co. Ltd. plans to open two branches. One is in Taichung and _____ is in Kaohsiung.

(A) Another   (B) other   (C) that   (D) the other

答案 D

眼球追蹤

❷ 看全句

BETTER & BEST Co. Ltd. plans to open ❷ two branches. ❷ One is in Taichung and ❷ _____ is in Kaohsiung.

❶ 看選項

(A) Anothe   (B) other   (C) that   (D) the other

中譯 BETTER & BEST 有限公司計畫開兩家分店。一個是在台中，另一種是在高雄。

秒殺策略

❶ 判斷題型

看選項得知，測驗點為「**不定代名詞中的數數**」概念。

❷ 根據前後搭配字詞，驗證答案

由前一句⋯plans to open two branches⋯得知，本句型為兩個對象時，「一個⋯另一個⋯」的句型，即 **one...the other** 的觀念。♛

檢查

(A) another 另一個，但無限定，刪除。

(B) other 沒有加 the 的 other，無限定，多半後方會與名詞搭配，刪除。

(C) that 指示代名詞，本句雖需限定，但無明確指出哪一家，刪除。

(D) the other 兩者的另一個 ♛

故本題答案選 (D)

8. _____ of the applicants are qualified for the position of Export Sales Manager. We need to post an employment notice again.

(A) One   (B) No   (C) Either   (D) Neither

答案　D

眼球追蹤

❷ _____ of the applicants are | qualified for the position of Export Sales Manager.

We need to post an employment notice again.

❶ **看選項**

(A) One   (B) No   (C) Either   (D) Neither

中譯　無申請者適合我們徵求的外銷部經理職位。我們需要再次發布就業公告通知。

秒殺策略

❶ **判斷題型**

看選項得知，測驗點為「**不定代名詞**」概念。

❷ **根據前後搭配字詞，驗證答案**

由 _____ of the applicants are…得知，空格應搭配可使用**複數**動詞的**代名詞**，即選 neither。

檢查

(A) one 搭配單數動詞，刪除。

(B) no 多數時為形容詞與副詞用法；當名詞時，為「否定」或「反對」，語意不符，刪除。

(C) either 搭配單數動詞，刪除。

(D) neither 後可搭配複數動詞

故本題答案選 (D)

9. A good _____ record has a positive impact on one's performance and also shows if he or she can successfully achieve the outcomes of programs.

(A) attend   (B) attending   (C) attendance   (D) attentive

答案 C

眼球追蹤

❷
| A good _____ record | has a positive impact on one's performance and also

shows if he or she can successfully achieve the outcomes of programs.

❶ 看選項
(A) attend   (B) attending   (C) attendance   (D) attentive

中譯 好的考勤記錄對一個人的表現有很正面的影響,也顯示了他或她是否能成功地實現計畫的成果。

秒殺策略

❶ **判斷題型**

看選項得知,測驗點為「**詞類判斷**」概念。

❷ **根據前後搭配字詞,驗證答案**

由⋯A good _____ record has a positive impact 得知,空格要搭配修飾 record 的詞類,**attendance record**「出席紀錄」為 N+N 的固定**複合名詞**搭配用法,選 attendance。

檢查

(A) attend 動詞,刪除。

(B) attending 現在分詞,刪除。

(C) attendance record 固定用法

(D) attentive (a) 注意的,留意的,刪除。

故本題答案選 (C)

10. Our manager was not satisfied with _____ of the planned activities in the incentive tour this year.

(A) none   (B) any   (C) every   (D) almost

答案 B

眼球追蹤

Our manager was |not satisfied with _____ of the planned activities| in the incentive tour this year.

❶ 看選項

(A) none   (B) any   (C) every   (D) almost

中譯 我們的經理並不滿意今年所舉辦的員工獎勵旅遊中的任何計畫活動。

秒殺策略

❶ 判斷題型

看選項得知，測驗點為「**不定代名詞**」概念。

❷ 根據前後搭配字詞，驗證答案

由 not...with _____ of the planned activities... 得知，空格為**可放否定句的**「**不定代名詞**」。any (a)任何的 (n)任一（人、事、物） (adv)少許，稍微any可當名詞或形容詞，多與**否定、疑問句與條件句搭配**。

檢查

(A) none 前已有否定，刪除。

(B) any 多與否定、疑問句與條件句搭配

(C) every 只能當形容詞，刪除。

(D) almost 副詞，刪除。

故本題答案選 (B)

11-13 請參考下列臨時通知

中譯

　　這個星期五的保全部門將會到貴部門替你拍照。此外，他們要求你設定自己的確認碼。照片和確認碼，會做成一張身分識別卡給你。你們每個人都必須隨時都佩戴著。該卡還可以解鎖所有的門但有較高的安全性，而且更方便地通到我們公司的其他部門。新的安全系統將使我們公司更安全。

秒殺策略

11. 答案　**(C) confirmation**
They will have you set a **confirmation** number of your own.
解題　confirmation number 確認碼，是多益常見的複合名詞。名詞修飾名詞，不能用形容詞或分詞代替。👑

12. 答案　**(A) Each**
Each of you is required to wear the ID card at all times.
解題　由 is required 得知，應用「單數」的不定代名詞。👑

13. 答案　**(C) our**
...system will surely make **our** company a safer place to work.
解題　company 為普通名詞，需放修飾語之後。修飾語包括了冠詞（a / an/ the）、所有格、形容詞，故選 (C) our 所有格。👑

250

成為多益勝利組的字彙練功區

文法講解區	Mini Test 限時 5 分練習區
diagnosis [ˌdaɪəɡˋnosɪs] **n.** 診斷	authorize [ˋɔθəˌraɪz] **v.** 授權
flyer [ˋflaɪɚ] **n.** 宣傳單	taxpayer [ˋtæksˌpeɚ] **n.** 納稅人
promotional strategy **n.** 促銷策略	periodic [ˌpɪrɪˋɑdɪk] **a.** 定期的
talented [ˋtæləntɪd] **a.** 有才華的	employee loyalty **n.** 員工忠誠度
appoint [əˋpɔɪnt] **v.** 指派	shipping rate **n.** 出貨率
counselor [ˋkaʊnslɚ] **n.** 顧問	an employment notice **n.** 就業通知
the Customs **n.** 海關	incentive tour **n.** （員工）獎勵旅遊
survey [sɚˋve] **n. v.** 調查	security department **n.** 安全部門
bid [bɪd] **v.** 競標	
economic downturn **n.** 經濟衰退	
go bankrupt **v.** 倒閉；破產	
arouse [əˋraʊz] **v.** 引起	
defect [dɪˋfɛkt] **n.** 瑕疵	
entry [ˋɛntrɪ] **n.** 條目；項目	
luxury product **n.** 高檔產品	
economic recession **n.** 經濟衰退	
surpass [sɚˋpæs] **v.** 甚於	
interpersonal relationship **n.** 人際關係	
get recognized **v.** 得到肯定	
verbal apology **n.** 口頭道歉	
stylish [ˋstaɪlɪʃ] **a.** 流行的	
register [ˋrɛdʒɪstɚ] **v.** 登記	
hesitate [ˋhɛzəˌtet] **v.** 遲疑	
propose [prəˋpoz] **v.** 推薦	

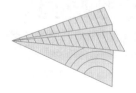

FAQ in TOEIC

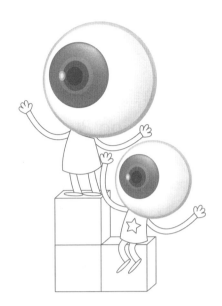

11

對等連接詞
(Coordinating & Correlative Conjunctions)

文法講解區

⑪ 對等連接詞 (Coordinating & Correlative Conjunctions)

簡單看

　　對等連接詞與對等連接詞片語是用來連接字與字、片語及片語或句子和句子的橋樑。TOEIC 會出現的題目，除了要根據前後句語意來挑出符合邏輯的連接詞之外，與轉承詞的區別或是附加結尾的考題時會出現。

秒殺策略

（1）判斷題型
（2）找關鍵詞語
（3）搭配語意

1 對等連接詞（片語）的功能

〉連接同詞性的單詞、片語與句子。

- 「單詞」＋**對等連接詞（片語）**＋「單詞」
- 「片語」＋**對等連接詞（片語）**＋「片語」
- 「句子」＋**對等連接詞（片語）**＋「句子」

EX Joining trade fairs is an <u>effective</u> and <u>efficient</u> way to build companies' reputations.

（參加商展是有效果與有效率建立公司名聲的方式。）

EX Dr. Kimberly is not only <u>a professional colleague</u> but also <u>a trustworthy friend</u>.

（Dr. Kimberly 不但是專業的同事也是值得信賴的朋友。）

EX <u>The manager closed the office door</u>, for <u>she needed to shut out all distractions</u>.

（經理關上辦公室門因為她需要杜絕所有分心的事。）

2 對等連接詞（片語）的種類

〉對等連接單詞

- and（而且）、but（但是）、or（或是）可連接單詞、片語與句子

EX Everyone in the company works hard, but our revenue is still declining.

（公司每個人都很努力工作，但營收仍逐漸衰退。）

- so（所以）、for（因為）、yet（但是；然而）可連接句子

EX Your performance at work is better, yet there is still room for improvement.

（你工作表現有比較好了，但仍有改善空間。）

〉對等連接片語

	對等連接片語	意義	連接主詞，單複數判斷
1	both A and B	A 與 B 兩者都	必為複數
2	not only A but also B	不只 A，B 也是	與 B 一致
3	either A or B	A 或 B 其中一個	與 B 一致
4	neither A nor B	既非 A 且非 B	與 B 一致

255

| 5 | not A but B | 不是 A，卻是 B | 與 B 一致 |
| 6 | A as well as B | A 和 B 都是 | 與 A 一致 |

EX Neither members of the Board of Directors nor <u>the president</u> <u>was</u> satisfied with the upcoming merger.

（所有董事成員與總裁都對即將進行的合併感到不滿意。）

EX <u>All the employees</u> as well as Mr. Blake <u>are</u> eligible to vote in to-day's election.

（所有員工與 Mr. Blake 一樣在今天的選舉中有資格投票。）

3 轉承詞

「轉承詞」是帶出句子與句子或段落間語意的起承轉合，但本身是**副詞**，而非連接詞，因此要用轉承詞連接句子時，若不使用句點隔開，則前方必須加上分號，後面搭配逗點。

轉承詞	中譯	類似語意的連接詞
moreover, further	此外	and
therefore, thus	因此	so
however	然而	but, yet

EX The bank sent a notice of overdue account to the client a month ago; however, the client said he hadn't received anything.

（銀行在一個月前就寄了催繳通知給那客戶，但他卻說沒有收到。）

4 附加結尾

為避免重複前方句子內容，連接詞後面的句子可用 so, too, either, neither 來形成附加結尾。要注意的是，動詞的時態須和前方句子一致。此譯為「也」的附加結尾用法如下。

〉too / either
• 肯定的用 **too**，否定的用 **either**。
• 兩者均是放在句尾，且其前加逗號。

EX The media center is all open to all the faculty, and the conference hall is, too.

（多媒體中心對所有教職員是開放借用，會議中心也是。）

EX The digital camera doesn't come with a warranty, and those DVD players don't, either.

（這數位相機沒有附有保固期，那些 DVD 也是沒有。）

〉so / neither

• 肯定的用 **so**，否定的用 **neither**。

• 兩者均置於在句首或句中，其後的子句須倒裝。

EX The media center is all open to all the faculty, and so is the conference hall.

（多媒體中心對所有教職員是開放借用，會議中心也是。）

EX The digital camera doesn't come with a warranty, and neither do those DVD players.

（這數位相機沒有附有保固期，那些 DVD 也是沒有。）

Mini Test 練習區 限時 5 分

1. The lease determines who is responsible for fixing any damage both for "normal wear and tear" _____ for other types, whether intentional or accidental.
   (A) and   (B) or   (C) but   (D) for

2. Based on its launch history, new iFad will release unexpectedly _____ on Christmas Day or on Christmas Eve.
   (A) as   (B) both   (C) neither   (D) either

3. Next, either your phone numbers or ID card number _____ required for verification.
   (A) is   (B) are   (C) be   (D) was

4. We offer not only seniors (65+) _____ persons with disabilities travel at half the regular passenger fare rate.
   (A) nor   (B) as well as   (C) in addition   (D) but also

5. We will correct the bad situation immediately; _____, you will be provided with a full refund.
   (A) and   (B) while   (C) moreover   (D) however

6. BEST company reserves the right to modify _____ discontinue this offering, during the promotional period.
   (A) and   (B) or   (C) any   (D) for

7. Jill Abramson got fired _____ for being a woman but for being bad at her job.
   (A) is   (B) because   (C) not   (D) X

8. Water shortage problems arose with little rain during the rainy season; _____, rationing of water may become necessary in a week.
   (A) and   (B) so   (C) therefore   (D) for

9. To our depression, gross profit didn't increase last quarter, and neither _____ revenue.
   (A) was   (B) wasn't   (C) did   (D) didn't

10. At first, Amanda always complained that she had to go on a business trip twice a month, _____ after one year, she seemed to get accustomed to it.
    (A) yet   (B) however   (C) though   (D) despite

11.對等連接詞 ｜ 迷你練習區

11 對等連接詞

12 形容詞子句

13 副詞子句

14 名詞子句

15 介係詞

Question 11-13 refer to the following report

Ten o'clock news. This is your late-morning traffic update. Traffic is moving smoothly throughout the area with the exception of Xinyi _____ Zhong

11 (A) or
    (B) but also
    (C) either
    (D) as well as

-shan Road near the approach to the Ketagalan Boulevard. More than 10 thousand people participated in the "Appleflower Student Movement" held between Presidential Building and the East Gate, _____ the area is closed

12 (A) so
    (B) for
    (C) but
    (D) yet

and all traffic is being rerouted down Civic Boulevard to the Taipei Train Station. Expect delays in this area of up to 40 minutes during the morning and afternoon. This situation may continue for several weeks, _____ the

13 (A) yet
    (B) for
    (C) as a result
    (D) as a result of

movement may not end until early October. Tune in for the next traffic update at 12:00.

1-10 Ans: 1.(A) 2.(D) 3.(A) 4.(D) 5.(C) 6.(B) 7.(C) 8.(C) 9.(C) 10.(A)

1. The lease determines who is responsible for fixing any damage both for "normal wear and tear" _____ for other types, whether intentional or accidental.

(A) and   (B) or   (C) but   (D) for

答案 A

眼球追蹤

The lease determines who is responsible for fixing any damage for | both "normal wear and tear" _____ for other types, | whether intentional or accidental.

❶ 看選項

(A) and   (B) or   (C) but   (D) for

中譯 租約決定誰負責修復「正常磨損」與其他類型的任何損壞，不論是有意還是無意的損害。

秒殺策略

❶ 判斷題型

看選項得知，測驗點為「**連接詞（片語）**」。

❷ 找關鍵詞語

由…both / for"normal wear and tear"/ _____ /for other types 得知，空格搭配 both A and B 的對等連接片語。

檢查

(A) 搭配 both A and B

(B) 搭配 either…or 刪除。

(C) 搭配 not A but B 刪除。

(D) 當 conj，後加句子；當介係詞，後加名詞，刪除。

故本題答案選 (A)

2. Based on its launch history, new iFad will release unexpectedly
_____ on Christmas Day or on Christmas Eve.

(A) as   (B) both   (C) neither   (D) either

答案 D

眼球追蹤

Based on its launch history, new iFad will release unexpectedly _____ on

Christmas Day or on Christmas Eve.

❶ 看選項

(A) as   (B) both   (C) neither   (D) either

中譯 根據發表的歷史，新的 iFad 將會不預期地在聖誕節或前夕發行。

秒殺策略 👑

❶ 判斷題型

看選項得知，測驗點為「**連接詞（片語）**」。

❷ 找關鍵詞語

由 _____ on Christmas Day/or/on Christmas Eve 得知，空格搭配 either A
or B 的對等連接片語。👑

檢查

(A) 連接詞 (conj) 當；因為；正如。介係詞 (prep) 身分 語意與文法皆不合，刪除。

(B) 搭配 both A and B 刪除。

(C) 搭配 neither A nor B 刪除。

(D) 搭配 either A or B 👑

故本題答案選 (D)

3. Next, either your phone numbers or ID card number _____ required for verification.

(A) is　　　　(B) are　　　　(C) be　　　　(D) was

答案 A

眼球追蹤

❸ 看全句

❷
Next, either your phone numbers or ID card number _____ required for verification.

❶ 看選項

(A) is　　　　(B) are　　　　(C) be　　　　(D) was

中譯　　進行驗證需要你的電話號碼或身份證號碼。

秒殺策略 👑

❶ 判斷題型

看選項得知，測驗點為「**主要動詞**」。

❷ 找關鍵詞語與主詞

由 Either your phone numbers or ID card number _____ 得知，either A or B + 主要動詞，**主要動詞看 B 決定**，考慮 is 或 was。

❸ 時態

看全句句意，本句為**指示操作**，則使用**現在或未來簡單式**，故選 is。👑

檢查

(A) 現在簡單式 👑

(B) 複數動詞，刪除。

(C) 原形動詞，刪除。

(D) 時態不符合，刪除。

故本題答案選 (A)

4. We offer not only seniors (65+) _____ persons with disabilities travel at half the regular passenger fare rate.

(A) nor　　　　　(B) as well as　　　　(C) in addition　　　　(D) but also

答案 D

眼球追蹤

We offer ❷ | not only seniors (65+) _____ persons with disabilities | travel at half the regular passenger fare rate.

❶ **看選項**

(A) nor　　　　　(B) as well as　　　　(C) in addition　　　　(D) but also

中譯　我們不僅提供 65 歲以上的老年人也提供殘障人士定期客運半價票卷旅程。

秒殺策略 👑

❶ **判斷題型**

看選項得知，測驗點為「**連接詞（片語）**」。

❷ **表示「方法」、「手段」，搭配介係詞 by**

由 not only seniors (65+) / _____ persons with disabilities 得知，空格搭配 not only A but also B 的對等連接片語。

檢查

(A) 搭配 neither A nor B，刪除。

(B) 搭配 A as well as B，刪除。

(C) adv 此外，不可連接名詞（片語），刪除。

(D) 搭配 not only A but also B 👑

故本題答案選 (D)

5. We will correct the bad situation immediately; _____, you will be provided with a full refund.

 (A) and   (B) while   (C) moreover   (D) however

答案 C

眼球追蹤

❸ 看全句

We will correct the bad situation immediately **②** ; _____, you will be provided with a full refund.

❶ 看選項

 (A) and   (B) while   (C) moreover   (D) however

中譯 　我們將立即改正不良的情況；此外，您將獲得全額退款。

秒殺策略

❶ **判斷題型**

 看選項得知，測驗點為「**連接詞與轉承詞**」。

❷ **找關鍵詞語**

 由**分號**與**逗點**得知，空格需要**轉承（副）詞**，而非連接詞，即考慮 moreover 與 however。

❸ **判斷題型**

 由全句句意，correct the bad situation 與 you will be provided with a full refund 得知，moreover 符合語意。

檢查

(A) conj 且，文法不合，刪除。

(B) conj 當，文法不合，刪除。

(C) adv 此外

(D) adv 然而，語意不合，刪除。

故本題答案選 (C)

11.對等連接詞｜秒殺實戰區

11 對等連接詞

12 形容詞子句

13 副詞子句

14 名詞子句

15 介係詞

6. BEST company reserves the right to modify _____ discontinue this offering, during the promotional period.

(A) and　　　　(B) or　　　　(C) any　　　　(D) for

答案 B

眼球追蹤

❸ 看全句 ─── ❷

BEST company reserves | the right to modify _____ discontinue | this offering, during the promotional period.

❶ 看選項

(A) and　　　　(B) or　　　　(C) any　　　　(D) for

中譯 於推廣期內，BEST 公司保留修改或終止本次活動發行的權限。

秒殺策略

❶ 判斷題型

看選項得知，測驗點為「**連接詞與不定詞 any**」

❷ 找關鍵詞語

由 the right to modify _____ discontinue this offering 得知，空格前後為**兩對等的動詞**，空格應搭配**連接詞**

❸ 搭配語意

由全句句意，modify 與 discontinue 不可能同時存在，故選 or👑

檢查

(A) conj 且，語意不合，刪除。

(B) conj 或👑

(C) adj；n 任何（…人/物），文法不符合，刪除。

(D) conj 因為，只連接句子與句子，刪除。

故本題答案選 (B)

7. Jill Abramson got fired _____ for being a woman but for being bad at her job.

   (A) is   (B) because   (C) not   (D) X

答案 C

眼球追蹤

Jill Abramson got fired ❷ _____ for being a woman but for being bad at her job.

❶ 看選項

  (A) is   (B) because   (C) not   (D) X

中譯　Jill Abramson 被炒魷魚不是因為是女性，而是無法將工作做好。

秒殺策略

❶ **判斷題型**

看選項得知，本題須逐一將答案帶入來判斷與檢測。

❷ **找關鍵詞語**

看由 _____ for being a woman / but / for being bad at her job 得知，

有 for being a woman 與 for being bad at her job 兩對等介係詞片語，再

次檢測選項。空格應搭配 not A but B 的對等連接片語。

檢查

(A) is 帶入，全句會有兩個主動詞，刪除。

(B) because 後，需搭配子句，刪除。

(C) 搭配 not A but B

(D) 需有 not 來搭配連接兩個介係詞片語。

故本題答案選 (C)

266

8. Water shortage problems arose with little rain during the rainy season; _____, rationing of water may become necessary in a week.
   (A) and　　　　　(B) so　　　　　(C) therefore　　　　　(D) for

答案 C

眼球追蹤

Water shortage problems arose with little rain during the rainy season **;** _____ , ❷
rationing of water may become necessary in a week.

❶ 看選項
   (A) and　　　　　(B) so　　　　　(C) therefore　　　　　(D) for

中譯 少雨的雨季使得缺水問題出現；因此，有可能一週內會限水。

秒殺策略 👑

❶ **判斷題型**

看選項得知，測驗點為「**連接詞與轉承詞**」。

❷ **找關鍵詞語**

由分號與逗點得知，空格需要**轉承（副）詞**，而非連接詞，選 therefore。👑

檢查

(A) conj 且，文法不合，刪除。

(B) conj 所以，文法不合，刪除。

(C) adv 因此 👑

(D) conj 因為，前方需要逗點，語意與文法皆不合，刪除。

故本題答案選(C)

9. To our depression, gross profit didn't increase last quarter, and neither _____ revenue.

  (A) was   (B) wasn't   (C) did   (D) didn't

答案 C

眼球追蹤

To our depression, gross profit │ didn't increase last quarter, and neither _____

revenue.

❶ 看選項

  (A) was   (B) wasn't   (C) did   (D) didn't

中譯   令我們沮喪的是，最後一季淨利並沒有增加，而營收入也無增加。

秒殺策略

❶ 判斷題型

看選項得知，測驗點為「〈也（不）〉的附加結尾」。

❷ 找關鍵詞語

由 gross profit didn't increase last quarter/neither 得知，空格應搭配 did。

檢查

(A) 主動詞為 increase，即不考慮 Be 動詞，刪除。

(B) 主動詞為 increase，即不考慮 Be 動詞，刪除。

(C) 與 didn't 時態一致，肯定的助動詞

(D) 有 neither 出現，無須再加 not，刪除。

故本題答案選 (C)

11.對等連接詞｜秒殺實戰區

11 對等連接詞

12 形容詞子句

13 副詞子句

14 名詞子句

15 介係詞

10. At first, Amanda always complained that she had to go on a business trip twice a month, _____ after one year, she seemed to get accustomed to it.

(A) yet　　　　(B) however　　　　(C) though　　　　(D) despite

答案　A

眼球追蹤

❷ 看全句

At first, Amanda always complained that she had to go on a business trip twice a month, ❸ _____ after one year, she seemed to get accustomed to it.

❶ 看選項

(A) yet　　　　(B) however　　　　(C) though　　　　(D) for

中譯　起初，Amanda 總是抱怨說她必須每月出差兩次，但一年後，她似乎習慣了。

秒殺策略 👑

❶ 判斷題型

看選項得知，測驗點為「**連接詞、轉承詞與介係詞**」。

❷ 找關鍵詞語

分析全句，空格前後，為兩個完整子句，且**只有逗點分開**，故**空格應搭配連接詞**，而非副詞或是介係詞考慮 yet 與 though。

❸ 驗證答案

將選項帶入空格驗證，yet「然而，但是」，語意符合；though「雖然」，語意不符。👑

檢查

(A) conj 然而，但是 👑

(B) adv 然而　文法不符，刪除。

(C) conj 雖然，語意不符，刪除。

(D) prep 雖然，文法不符，刪除。

故本題答案選 (A)

11-13 題請參考下列報導

中譯

　　十點整新聞。這是你的晚晨的交通更新。除了近凱達格蘭大道的信義與中山路外，整個區其他交通順暢。　超過一萬多人參加了在總統府和東門中間舉辦的「蘋果花學運」，因此該地區被封閉，且所有車輛必須由市民大道繞到台北火車站。預計上午與下午在此區域都會延誤 40 分鐘。這情況可能會持續幾個星期，因為運動可能直到十月初才會結束。請繼續鎖定 12 點路況更新。

秒殺策略

11. 答案　**(D) as well as**

　　with the exception of Xinyi **as well as** Zhongshan Road...

解題　with the exception 後的道路應處同樣情況，用 as well as 符合語意。

12. 答案　**(A) so**

　　..."Appleflower Student Movement"..., **so** the area is closed...

解題　movement 造成交通阻塞，是因果關係，依語意，選 so。

13. 答案　**(B) for**

　　This situation may continue..., **for** the movement may not end

解題　情況會繼續是因為學運會持續到十月，依語意，可選(B)或(D)，但空格後為一完整句，故須對等連接詞 for 來連接，即選 for。

成為多益勝利組的字彙練功區

文法講解區	Mini Test 限時 5 分練習區
reputation [ˌrɛpjəˋteʃən] **n.** 名聲	lease [lis] **n.** 租約
trustworthy [ˋtrʌstˌwɝðɪ] **a.** 值得信賴的	normal [ˋnɔrml] **a.** 正常的
revenue [ˋrɛvəˌnju] **n.** 營收	wear and tear **n.** 磨損
decline [dɪˋklaɪn] **v.** 衰退	verification [ˌvɛrɪfɪˋkeʃən] **n.** 驗證
merger [mɝdʒɚ] **n.** (公司等的）合併	refund [rɪˋfʌnd] **n.** 退款
eligible [ˋɛlɪdʒəbl] **a.** 有資格的	discontinue [ˌdɪskənˋtɪnju] **v.** 停止，中斷
overdue [ˋovɚˋdju] **a.** 未兌的	promotional period **n.** 促銷期間
faculty [ˋfæklṭɪ] **n.** 教職員	shortage [ˋʃɔrtɪdʒ] **n.** 缺少，不足
conference hall **n.** 會議中心	rationing [ˋræʃənɪŋ] **n.** 定量配給、限量
warranty [ˋwɔrəntɪ] **n.** 保固	gross profit **n.** 毛利
	quarter [ˋkwɔrtɚ] **n.** 付款的季度
	a business trip **n.** 出差
	get accustomed to + Ving 習慣
	approach [ˋkwɔrtɚ] **n.** 通道
	boulevard [ˋbuləˌvɑrd] **n.** 大道
	reroute [riˋrut] **v.** 改道
	tune in **v.** 收聽或收看

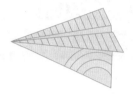

FAQ in TOEIC

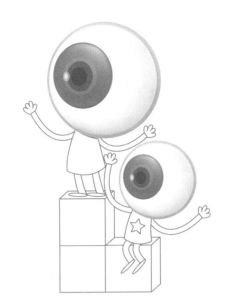

12

形容詞子句
(Adjective Clauses)

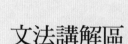
文法講解區

12 形容詞子句 (Adjective Clauses)

簡單看

　　形容詞子句即是關係子句，是具有形容詞的功能的句中句，是結構體較大的形容詞，用來修飾前面的名詞或代名詞（稱為先行詞）。

　　關係詞帶出關係子句雖然繁多複雜，但 TOEIC 試題多半測驗最基礎的觀念，即選擇適當的關係代名詞、關係副詞與介詞後面應搭配的關係代名詞（只能接 whom/which/whose +名詞，不能接 that/where/when)的考題。

秒殺策略

（1）判斷題型，是否測試形容詞子句觀念，
　　　是否需要關係詞。
（2）判斷關係詞是否有先行詞：
　　　yes → that, who, which, whose, whom,
　　　關係副詞（where, when, why, how)
　　　no→ what, whatever, whichever,
　　　whoever, whomever, 關係副詞（where,
　　　when, why, how)
（3）依語意或個別選項判斷答案（如所帶句子
　　　是否缺主詞或受詞）。
（4）檢查是否有特殊限定用法（如：關係詞前
　　　有介係詞或逗點時）。

❶ 關係代名詞的形式

關係代名詞是兼具連接詞與代名詞的功能，所帶的子句，為形容詞作用，修飾前方的先行詞。

> 先行詞，就是置於關代前，代替的人或事物。

要注意的是：
- 關代的「格」**與先行詞無關**，是要看其在**關係子句**內的所扮演角色決定。
- 關代當受格，可以省略；但前有介係詞不可省。
- 關代為主格時，接在後面的動詞，必須要和先行詞的「人稱與數」相一致。

	主格	所有格	受格
人	who	whose	whom
物、動物	which	whose(of which)	which
人、物、動物	that	*	that

〉關代為主格

EX The candidates <u>who</u> were late for the interview are not eligible for that position.

（面談遲到的候選人無資格擔任那職務。）

〉關代為受格

EX Lancer Corporation is the company <u>which</u> we look forward to co-operate with.

（Lancer Corporation 是我們期盼的合作公司。）

〉關代為所有格

EX Most of the clients <u>whose</u> data got hacked have suffered fraudulent charges.

（資料被駭客取得的少數顧客已經被盜刷了。）

2 關係詞的種類

1	關係代名詞	who, whose, whom, which, that
2	關係副詞	why, when, where, how
3	關係形容詞	which, what, whichever, whatever...
4	複合關係代名詞	what, whoever, whosever, whomever, whichever, whatever
5	複合關係副詞	wherever, whenever, however
6	複合關係形容詞	whatever, whichever
7	準關係代名詞	as, but, than

〉關係代名詞 **that**

• 常用 that 作為關代之時機（但並非絕對）

    (1) 先行詞前面有「最高級」

    (2) 先行詞包括「人」與「非人」

    (3) 先行詞前面有「序數」，如 **the first**、**the last**（最後）

    (4) 先行詞前面有 **all**，**no**，**every**，**any**，**the only**，**the same**，**the very**（正是）

    (5) 疑問句的開頭是 **who**，**which**，**what** 等，常用 **that**，避免重複

EX This is the most demanding work that I have ever carried out.

    （這是我曾執行過要求最嚴謹的工作了。）

EX Which showroom is the one that is exhibiting Peggy Ahwesh's works?

    （在展示 Peggy Ahwesh 作品的，是哪一間展示廳?）

• 不能用 that 作為關代之時機

    (1)「介系詞」後面

    (2)「逗點」後面

    (3) 先行詞為 people, those（那些人），關係代名詞用 who

EX We plan to invite Alexander Jenkins, who travels extensively for the fashion and modeling industries, to be our guest speaker.

    （我們計劃邀請 Alexander Jenkins 當我們的主講嘉賓，其為時尚業和模特行業閱歷豐富。）

〉關係代名詞 **what**

    • what = the thing(s) + which 或 = all that。

- what 本身已含先行詞，故在句中，無先行詞出現時，則用 what。
- what 之後的關係子句內，缺主詞或是受詞，是不完整的子句。
- what 所帶的句子，用法與名詞子句相同。

EX Mr. Chernock has apologized to me for <u>what he said</u>.

（Mr. Chernock 以對我道歉他所説的話。）

注意：此 what 關係子句，無先行詞 ，身分為「**關係子句內的受詞**」與「**for 後面的受詞**」

3 形容詞子句的數量表示

形容詞子句若要用來表達先行詞的特定數量時，用以下公式

one / each / two several / some both / all / half many / much / most any / none / the rest	+ of + 關係代名詞 (whom/which/whose +名詞)

EX There are twenty people in the IT Department, most of whom are males.

（資訊部門有 20 人，多數都是男性。）

4 關係副詞

〉關係副詞種類

	地方	時間	理由	方法程度
關係副詞	where	when	why	how
	in/at/on	in/at/on	for	in/by
	which	which	which	which
先行詞	the place	the time	the reason	the way（搭配 in） the means （搭配 by）

- 關係副詞 = 介系詞 + 關係代名詞，具有副詞與連接詞的功用。
- 完整的子句：關係副詞後為完整的子句。
- 不應有再有介係詞：其所帶的形容詞子句前不應再有介係詞。
- 先行詞可以省略。

• 關係副詞形成過程

This is the bank. I opened my account in the bank.

→ This is the bank <u>and</u> I opened my account in <u>it</u>.

→ This is the bank <u>which</u> I opened my account <u>in</u>.

→ This is the bank <u>in which</u> I opened my account.

→ This is the bank <u>where</u> I opened my account.

5 主詞、動詞的一致性

　　關代本身無單數與複數的分別，其人稱、動詞的數必須和先行詞一致。

〉 先行詞（單數）＋關係代名詞（當主詞）＋單數動詞

EX A & P is a full-service investment <u>company</u> that <u>specializes</u> in offering financial guidance to high net.

(A & P 是個全方位專精於提供高淨利財務指導的投資公司。)

〉 先行詞（複數）＋關係代名詞（當主詞）＋複數動詞

EX The <u>employees</u>, who <u>were</u> taken to the hospital, suffered from smoke inhalation.

（被帶至醫院的員工都遭受到濃煙吸入嗆傷）

NOTES

Mini Test 練習區 限時 5 分 ⏱

1. The senior consultant has provided the marketing department with insightful advice on _____ can increase the effectiveness of marketing campaigns.
   (A) where　　　(B) that　　　(C) what　　　(D) whose

2. The enterprise _____ long-term mortgage loans on land were quite costly decided toexpand its market size business for higher profits.
   (A) which　　　(B) that　　　(C) what　　　(D) whose

3. Labor Day, _____ workers are eligible to take a day off, pays tribute to the contributions and achievements of all workers.
   (A) which　　　(B) when　　　(C) what　　　(D) whose

4. _____ launches a new project should present an outline of marketing strategy in advance.
   (A) However　　　(B) Whatever　　　(C) Whenever　　　(D) Whoever

5. Any employee with two language certificates _____ eligible for the application.
   (A) is　　　(B) can　　　(C) are　　　(D) should

6. The client with _____ I talked on the phone was very anxious about the outstanding payments.
   (A) who　　　(B) that　　　(C) whom　　　(D) what

7. Miss Brenda is the very skilled negotiator _____ is qualified for the position of public relations managers.
   (A) that　　　(B) who　　　(C) whom　　　(D) whose

8. We will add relevant information regarding the workshop to our website theparticipants can easily refer to at home.
   (A) which　　　(B) where　　　(C) when　　　(D) how

9. All the food ingredients are required by law to list on the product packaging _____consumers can see them easily.
   (A) which　　　(B) that　　　(C) where　　　(D) whose

10. The speaker at the seminar gave a great presentation, most of _____ was about retail management and strategic planning.
    (A) which　　　(B) it　　　(C) what　　　(D) whom

Question 11-13 refer to the following letter

Part-Time Office Assistant Needed

The BEST Logistics Company in central Taichung seeks an organized indi-vidual to provide part-time support in charge of customer accounts. The as-sistant will be expected to perform a wide range of tasks, some of _____

        11 (A) that
           (B) them
           (C) who
           (D) which

require project management skills.

The candidate _____ working experience in a similar role is over three

    12 (A) who
       (B) with
       (C) which
       (D) whose

years is preferred.

In addition, excellent verbal and written communication skills are necessary. Hours will be 9:00 A.M., to 5:00 P.M., three days a week. The candidate must be able to start on February 1. The salary offer will be commensurate with the office regulations.

Anyone _____ has interest can send an e-mail with their resume to Derek

    13 (A) who
       (B) that
       (C) whose
       (D) X

Jeter, Director of Human Resources, at djeter@bestlogistics.ie.

1-10 Ans: 1.(C) 2.(D) 3.(B) 4.(D) 5.(A) 6.(C) 7.(A) 8.(A) 9.(C) 10.(A)

1. The senior consultant has provided the marketing department with insightful advice on_____ can increase the effectiveness of marketing campaigns.
   (A) where   (B) that   (C) what   (D) whose

答案 **C**

眼球追蹤

The senior consultant has provided the marketing department with｜insightful **②**

advice on _____ can increase the effectiveness of marketing campaigns.

❶ 看選項
　(A) where   (B) that   **③** (C) what   (D) whose

中譯 資深顧問已經提供行銷部門精闢的建議於如何增加行銷宣傳的效力。

秒殺策略 👑

❶ 判斷題型

看選項得知，測驗點為「**關係詞**」。

❷ 判斷關係詞前是否有先行詞

由 insightful advice on/ _____ can increase the effectiveness …得知，**空格關係詞前無先行詞**，即考慮 what 與關係副詞 where。

❸ 搭配語意，驗證答案

將(C)what = the thing(s) that 帶入，符合語意與文法。👑

檢查

(A) 代地方的副詞，刪除。

(B) 當關代，前無先行詞，文法錯，當名詞子句連接詞，後應加完整子句，刪除。

(C) what = the thing(s) that 👑

(D) 前應有先行詞，後應搭配一名詞，刪除。

故本題答案選 (C)

2. The enterprise _____ long-term mortgage loans on land were quite costly decided toexpand its market size business for higher profits.
(A) which　　　　(B) that　　　　(C) what　　　　(D) whose

答案　D

眼球追蹤

❷
The enterprise _____ ❸ long-term mortgage loans on land were quite costly

decided to expand its market size business for higher profits.

❶ 看選項
(A) which　　　　(B) that　　　　(C) what　　　　(D) whose

中譯　此企業有很高的長期土地貸款，決定擴大其市場規模以獲取更高收益。

秒殺策略 👑

❶ 判斷題型

看選項得知，測驗點為「**關係詞**」。

❷ 判斷關係詞前是否有先行詞

由 the enterprise/ _____ long-term mortgage loans on land were quite costly 得知，**關係詞前有先行詞 enterprise**，即考慮 that, which, whose。

❸ 判斷後方是否接完整形式的句子

「long-term mortgage loans on land were quite costly」，**為完整句子**，則選 whose。👑

檢查

(A) 後方應接不完整形式句子或選擇性用法, 刪除。

(B) 當關代，後方應接不完整形式句子，刪除。

(C) 前無須有先行詞，刪除。

(D) 關係所有格，後面搭配完整形式的句子👑

故本題答案選 (D)

3. Labor Day, _____ workers are eligible to take a day off, pays tribute to the contributions and achievements of all workers.
   (A) which   (B) when   (C) what   (D) whose

答案 B

眼球追蹤

②   ③

Labor Day, _____ workers are eligible to take a day off, pays tribute to the

contributions and achievements of all workers.

❶ 看選項

   (A) which   (B) when   (C) what   (D) whose

中譯 勞工節是讚揚所有工人的貢獻和的成就，是他們有資格放一天假的時候。

秒殺策略

❶ 判斷題型

看選項得知，測驗點為「**關係詞**」。

❷ 判斷關係詞前是否有先行詞

由**關係詞前有先行詞 Labor Day,** 即考慮 which, whose 與關係副詞 when。

❸ 判斷後方是否接完整形式的句子

「workers are eligible to take a day off」，**為完整句子**，即考慮 whose 與關係副詞 when **再搭配語意**，選 when，代表 on Labor Day。

檢查

(A) 當關代，後方搭配非完整句子, 刪除。

(B) 關係副詞，代表 on Labor Day

(C) 前有先行詞，刪除。

(D) 語意不合，刪除。

故本題答案選 (B)

4. _____ launches a new project should present an outline of marketing strategy in advance.

(A) However　　　(B) Whatever　　　(C) Whenever　　　(D) Whoever

答案 D

眼球追蹤

❷ 看全句

_____ launches a new project should present an outline of marketing strategy in advance.

❶ 看選項

(A) However　　　(B) Whatever　　　(C) Whenever　　　(D) Whoever

中譯 任何發起一個新計畫的人都應事先提出行銷策略。

秒殺策略 👑

❶ 判斷題型

看選項得知，測驗點為「**複合關係代名詞／複合關係副詞**」。

❷ 搭配語意，驗證答案

全部選項接無需考慮先行詞，因此分析全句，利用語意判斷答案即可。

_____ launches a new project/should present an outline of marketing strategy.... 得知 **launches a new project 應是人當主詞**，選 Whoever，代表 Anyone who。👑

檢查

(A) 複合關係副詞，無論如何，語意不合, 刪除。

(B) 複合關係代名詞，無論什麼，語意不合，刪除。

(C) 複合關係副詞，無論如何，語意不合，刪除。

(D) 複合關係代名詞，無論任何人 👑

故本題答案選 (D)

5. Any employee with two language certificates _____ eligible for the application.

   (A) is   (B) can   (C)are   (D) should

答案 A

眼球追蹤

❷ 看全句

Any employee with two language certificates _____ eligible for the application.

❶ 看選項

   (A) is   (B) can   (C) are   (D) should

中譯 任何只要有兩張語言證書的員工都有資格申請。

秒殺策略

❶ 判斷題型

看選項得知，測驗點為「**主詞與動詞的一致**」。

❷ 判斷動詞所對應主詞的單複數

分析全句，由 Any employee / with two language certificates / _____ eligible for application 得知，「that owns over two language certificates」是形容詞子句，全句主詞為 Any employee，**主要動詞為單數**。

檢查

(A) 單數動詞

(B) 後面需再搭配動詞，刪除。

(C) 複數動詞，文法錯誤，刪除。

(D) 後面需再搭配動詞，刪除。

故本題答案選 (A)

6. The client with _____ I talked on the phone was very anxious about the outstanding payments.

(A)who   (B) hat   (C) whom   (D) what

答案 C

眼球追蹤

❷

The client | with _____ I talked on the phone | was very anxious | about the

outstanding payments.

❶ **看選項**

(A) who   (B) that   (C) whom   (D) what

中譯 我電話上交談的客戶對於未付款項十分擔心。

秒殺策略 👑

❶ **判斷題型**

看選項得知，測驗點為「**關係詞**」。

❷ **判斷關係詞前是否有先行詞**

由 The client / with _____ I talked on the phone / was very anxious payments 得知，**關係詞前有先行詞且有介係詞**，只考慮 whom 與 which。

❸ **搭配語意，驗證答案**

由 with _____ I talked on the phone 得知，空格應為**人**非事物，選 whom。
👑

檢查

(A) 介係詞後, 要受格，刪除。

(B) 不放介系詞後，刪除。

(C) 代替人的受格關代 👑

(D) 前無須有先行詞，刪除。

故本題答案選 (C)

7. Miss Brenda is the very skilled negotiator _____ is qualified for the position of public relations managers.

(A) that   (B) who   (C) whom   (D) whose

答案 A

眼球追蹤

Miss Brenda is | the very ③ skilled negotiator _____ is qualified for the position

of public relations managers.

❶ 看選項

(A) that   (B) who   (C) whom   (D) whose

中譯 Miss Brenda 就是那適合公關經理位置的有技巧的談判者。

秒殺策略

❶ 判斷題型

看選項得知，測驗點為「**關係詞**」。

❷ 判斷關係詞前是否有先行詞

由 the very skilled negotiator/ _____ is qualified for the position 得知，**關係詞前有先行詞 negotiator 且後面直接搭配動詞 is qualified for the position**，即考慮**主格關代** that 與 who。

❸ 搭配 that 用法

先行詞 skilled negotiator 前有 the very 來修飾，故搭配 that。

檢查

(A) 有 the very 修飾先行詞，多半使用關代 that

(B) 有 the very 修飾先行詞，刪除。

(C) 當受格的關代，刪除。

(D) 當所有格的關代，刪除。

故本題答案選 (A)

288

8. We will add relevant information regarding the workshop to our website _____ the participants can easily refer to at home.
   (A) which   (B) where   (C) when   (D) how

答案 A

眼球追蹤

We will add |relevant information regarding the workshop| to our website ❷

_____ the participants can easily refer to at home. ❸

❶ 看選項
(A) which   (B) where   (C) when   (D) how

中譯 我們將會把關於研討會的相關訊息登到網站，參加人員可容易在家參考。

秒殺策略

❶ 判斷題型

看選項得知，測驗點為「**關係詞**」。

❷ 判斷關係詞前是否有先行詞

關係詞前有先行詞 relevant information regarding the workshop （注意：先行詞非 our website），即考慮 which 與 關係副詞 where, when, how。

❸ 搭配語意，驗證答案

搭配語意，且 refer to 後缺受詞，故空格應為 which。還原句子為 the participants can easily refer to relevant information regarding the workshop at home。

檢查

(A) 當受格關代，代 relevant information regarding the workshop ♛
(B) 代地方的關係副詞，刪除。
(C) 代時間的關係副詞，刪除。
(D) 但方法的關係副詞，刪除。
故本題答案選 (A)

289

9. All the food ingredients are required by law to list on the product packaging _____ consumers can see them easily.

(A) which   (B) that   (C) where   (D) whose

答案 C

眼球追蹤

All the food ingredients are required by law to list on ❷ the product packaging

❸ _____ consumers can see them easily.

❶ 看選項

(A) which   (B) that   (C) where   (D) whose

中譯 所有的成份依法都要被列在消費者容易看的到的產品包裝上。

秒殺策略

❶ **判斷題型**

看選項得知，測驗點為「**關係詞**」。

❷ **判斷關係詞前是否有先行詞**

關係詞前有先行詞 product packaging，四者 that, which, whose, 關係副詞 where 都可考慮。

❸ **判斷後方是否接完整形式的句子**

「consumers can see them easily」，**為完整句子**，考慮 whose 與 where。

搭配語意，選 where，**代表 on the product packaging。**

檢查

(A) 後應為非完整句子，刪除。

(B) 當關係代名詞時，後應為非完整句子，刪除。

(C) 代地方的關係副詞

(D) 語意不合，刪除。

故本題答案選 (C)

10. The speaker at the seminar gave a great presentation, most of _____ was about retail management and strategic planning.

(A) which   (B) it   (C) what   (D) whom

答案 A

眼球追蹤

❷ 看全句

The speaker at the seminar gave | a great presentation, | most of _____ | was

about retail management and strategic planning.

❶ 看選項

(A) which   (B) it   (C) what   (D) whom

中譯 在研討會上這演講人做了很好的報告，多數與零售管理與策略規劃有關。

秒殺策略

❶ 判斷題型

看選項得知，測驗點為「**關係詞**」。

❷「形容詞子句表示先行詞的數量」句型

分析全句，主要句 The speaker at the seminar gave a great presentation 與 most of _____ was...**無連接詞**，故(B)刪除。同時也聯想「**形容詞子句表示先行詞的數量**」句型。

❸ 判斷先行詞

「**形容詞子句表示先行詞的數量**」句型，故考慮 which 與 whom 依語意與文法，先行詞為 presentation，選 which，代表 and...it(the great presentation)。

檢查

(A) 代替事物的關係代名詞，受格

(B) 句中無連接詞，文法錯誤，刪除。

(C) 前有先行詞，刪除。

(D) 先行詞為 presentation 事物，非人，刪除。

故本題答案選 (A)

11-13 請參閱下列一則廣告

中譯

誠徵兼職公司助理

位於台中中部的 BEST 物流公司尋求一名有組織能力的工作者，兼職負責客戶賬戶事宜。該助手盼可執行各種任務，其中一些需要管理項目的技能。

有類似三年以上的工作經驗的候選人，優先考量。此外，良好的口頭和書面溝通技巧是必要的。時間為上午 9:00 到下午 5:00，每週 3 天。候選人必須能夠從 2 月 1 日開始工作。薪資將依照公司規定。有興趣者可以發送電子郵件與他們的簡歷至 djeter@bestlogistics.ie，人力資源總監 Derek Jeter 收即可。

秒殺策略

11. 答案　**(D) which**
　　 ...to perform a wide range of tasks, some of **which** require project management skills
　 解題　原句為...tasks , and some of them require project...關代可有 and（連接詞）與 them（代名詞）的功能，且放在 of 後面，故用 which。

12. 答案　**(D) whose**
　　 The candidate **whose** working experience in a similar role is over three years is preferred.
　 解題　whose 代替前方的 candidate's，與後方 working experience in a similar role is over three years 句子做連結。

13. 答案　**(B) that**
　　 Anyone **that** has interest can send an e-mail ...
　 解題　先行詞為 anyone，搭配關代 that。

成為多益勝利組的字彙練功區

文法講解區	Mini Test 限時 5 分練習區
look forward to **v.** 期盼	consultant [kən`sʌltənt] **n.** 顧問
cooperate [ko`ɑpə͵ret] **v.** 合作	insightful [`ɪn͵saɪtfəl] **a.** 有見解的
hack [hæk] **v.** 非法闖入電腦網絡	campaign [kæm`pen] **n.** 活動
fraudulent [`frɔʒələnt] **a.** 欺詐的	enterprise [`ɛntə͵praɪz] **n.** 企業
demanding [dɪ`mændɪŋ] **a.** 使人吃力的；高要求的	long-term **a.** 長期的
carry out **v.** 執行	pay tribute to **v.** 讚揚
showroom [`ʃo͵rum] **n.** 陳列室	launch [lɔntʃ] **v.** 開辦；發起
industry [`ɪndəstrɪ] **n.** 行業	certificate [sə`tɪfəkɪt] **n.** 證照
guest speaker **n.** 主講嘉賓	application [͵æplə`keʃən] **n.** 申請
IT Department **n.** 資訊部門	outstanding [`aʊt`stændɪŋ] **a.** 未償付的
* IT= information technology	negotiator [nɪ`goʃɪ͵etə] **n.** 交涉者、談判者
opened one's account **v.** 開戶	public relations manager **n.** 公關經理
full-service **a.** 全套服務的	regarding [rɪ`gɑrdɪŋ] **prep.** 關於
specialize [`spɛʃəl͵aɪz] **v.** 專精	workshop [`wɜk͵ʃɑp] **n.** 專題討論會
financial [`spɛʃəl͵aɪz] **a.** 財務的	refer to **v.** 參考
net [nɛt] **n.** 淨利	ingredient [ɪn`gridɪənt] **n.** 成分
inhalation [͵ɪnhə`leʃən] **n.** 吸入	packaging [`pækɪdʒɪŋ] **n.** 包裝
	consumer [kən`sjumə] **n.** 消費者
	seminar [`sɛmə͵nɑr] **n.** 研討會
	retail [`ritel] **n. a.** 零售
	strategic [strə`tidʒɪk] **a.** 策略的
	organized [`ɔrgən͵aɪzd] **a.** 有組織力的
	in charge of **prep.** 負責
	verbal communication **n.** 口語溝通
	commensurate [kə`mɛnʃərɪt] **v.** 相稱
	office regulation **n.** 公司規定
	résumé [͵rɛzʊ`me] **n.** 履歷
	Human Resources **n.** 人力資源

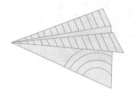

FAQ in TOEIC

13

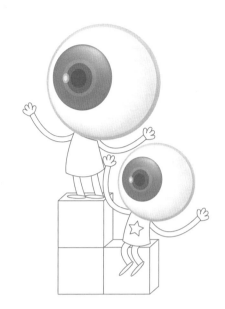

副詞子句 (Adverbial Clauses)

文法講解區

⑬ 副詞子句 （Adverbial Clauses）

簡單看

　　副詞子句是具有副詞的功能的句中句，是結構體較大的副詞，功能修飾主要子句，用於表示主要子句發生的原因、時間、條件、讓步、目的等。

秒殺策略

（1）判斷需要連接詞、介係詞還是副詞
（2）符合前後句邏輯的連接詞

1 副詞子句的形式

〉副詞子句位置彈性，可放主要子句後（無須逗號），或放主要子句前（須逗號）。

- 「副詞子句連接詞 + 主詞 + 動詞」，主要子句。
- 主要子句，「副詞子句連接詞 + 主詞 + 動詞」。

EX Because working overtime everyday took a toll on his health, Mr. Alexis decided to take a few days off.

= Mr. Alexis decided to take a few days off because working overtime everyday took a toll on his health.

（因為天天加班造成健康損害，Mr. Alexis 決定休幾天假。）

2 副詞子句的種類

1	表「時間」	when, whenever , while, before, after, since, until, once, as soon as
2	表「條件」	if, once, unless, as long as, in case (that), providing that, provided that
3	表「原因」	because, since, as, in that, now that
4	表「目的」	so (that), in order that
5	表「讓步」	although, though, even if, even though, while, whereas
6	表「結果」	so + adj /adv + that such + N + that

〉表「時間」的從屬連接詞：時間副詞子句要用現在式代替未來式

when, whenever , while, before, after, since, until, once, as soon as

EX We will let you know ASAP <u>when</u> new products arrive.

（當新貨到達時，我們會盡快讓您知道。）

〉表「條件」的從屬連接詞：條件副詞子句要用現在式代替未來式

if, once, unless, as long as, in case (that), providing that, provided that

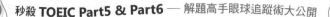
> **EX** Providing that the company keeps a close eye on emerging trends, its products can quickly meet changing market demands.
>
> （只要那公司密切注意新興潮流。其產品可以很快符合變動市場的需求。）

〉表「原因」的從屬連接詞：不可與對等連接詞 so 一起使用

because, since, as, in that, now that

> **EX** Because the delivery date had to be pushed back, Maerskline suffered huge losses .
>
> （由於運送日期被迫延期，Maerskline 船運公司損失慘重。）

〉表「目的」的從屬連接詞：

so (that), in order that

> **EX** Mr. Smith will establish a trust so that his family can be well taken care of after he passes away.
>
> （為了去世後家人可以得到完善照顧，Mr. Smith 將會成立信託基金會。）

〉表「讓步」的從屬連接詞：不可與對等連接詞 but 一起使用

although, though, even if, even though, while, whereas, whether...or not

> **EX** Mergers wouldn't be in the company's best interest whereas the Board of Directors aims to enhance shareholder value.
>
> （雖然董事會意在提高股東價值，但合併不是對公司最有利的做法。）

〉表「結果」的從屬連接詞：

so + adj /adv + that 與 such + N + that

> **EX** Cloud computing can save us so much money and time that productivity at our office has increased by 10 percent.
>
> （雲端科技可以節省我們如此多的金錢和時間以致於我們辦公室生產力增加了一成。）

3 保留連接詞的分詞構句（修飾性副詞片語）

分詞構句，即是「副詞子句」精簡來的副詞片語，旨在「修飾整個主要子句」，形成分詞構句步驟在第八章已經提過，現在再複習一次，加強功力！

Step 1 去連接詞（亦可保留連接詞，使語意更鮮明）

Step 2 判斷主詞：

(1) 副詞子句的主詞與主要子句相同，去掉副詞子句的主詞（本節重點）。

(2) 副詞子句的主詞與主要子句不同，副詞子句主詞需保留（獨立分詞構句）

Step 3 變化動詞形式：

(1) 主動：改為 Ving（現在分詞）

(2) 被動：改為 Vpp（過去分詞）

EX After <u>the repair technicians</u> troubleshot for hours, <u>they</u> eventually fixed all the network   and computer problems.

→<u>After troubleshooting for hours</u>, the repair technicians eventually fixed all the network and computer problems.

（經過檢測抓錯數小時後，維修人員終於解決的所有網絡與電腦問題。）

④ 副詞子句連接詞與介係詞

在英文文句中，可以用不同文字表示相同意思。以下的副詞子句連接詞與介係詞可以表達出意義類似的文句，但用法不同。**連接詞後搭配的是句子，介係詞後搭配的名詞。**

語意	介係詞	副詞子句連接詞
即使	despite, in spite of	though, although, even though / if
因為	because of, owing to, due to	because, since, now that
萬一	in case of	in case that
在…期間	for, during	while
除…之外	except, apart from	except that
除非有	without	unless

EX Though <u>there was increasing competition from new market entrants</u>, the company still expanded quickly.

= Despite <u>increasing competition from new market entrants</u>, the company still expanded quickly.

（雖然市場新進對手增加，此公司仍擴張快速）

Mini Test 練習區　限時 5 分

1. Passengers are advised to take only carry-on luggage for short trips _____ it is less likely to be lost or stolen than check-in luggage.

   (A) as　　　　(B) if　　　　(C) so　　　　(D) unless

2. Before _____ gift certificates, we will evaluate the cost-effectiveness.

   (A) issue　　　(B) issued　　　(C) issuing　　　(D) we issuing

3. _____ you do not agree to these terms, your account will be terminated.

   (A) When　　　(B) If　　　(C) For　　　(D) In case of

4. Our company carefully develops a mutually-beneficial relationship with many of our clientele _____ our revenues can grow steadily as expected.

   (A) due to　　(B) while　　(C) provided that　　(D) so that

5. _____ the current condition of the market improves, the retail chain won't expand.

   (A) Except　　(B) Unless　　(C) If　　(D) For

6. _____ the location of the mall is excellent, it's still difficult to yield a profit with high rents.

   (A) Because　　(B) Apart from　　(C) Even though　　(D) As long as

7. The customers' responses have always been excellent _____ new promotional mailers were sent out last month.

   (A) while　　(B) whereas　　(C) since　　(D) so that

8. Vehicle advertising works so effectively and economically _____ it's worth investing in.

   (A) so　　(B) for　　(C) since　　(D) that

9. Shipping and handling fees are not refundable, _____ in certain states and countries where these items are refundable.

   (A) in case　　(B) except　　(C) although　　(D) however

10. _____ around a table and chatting, each colleague waited for Mr. Johnson to congratulate him on his promotion.

    (A) Seat　　(B) Seated　　(C) Seating　　(D) Seats

Question 11-13 refer to the following email

To： Debbie Talbert <dtalbert@gmail.com>

From： Nancy Norling <nnorling@marriottcopley.com>

Date： August 3

Subject： RE：tickets

Dear Ms. Talbert,

I received your e-mail dated August 2 indicating that you would like to pur-chase tickets for the Emma Girard's performance scheduled for August 8 at Marriott Copley.Unfortunately, ＿＿＿＿ Emma's live performance is so

　　　　11 (A) for
　　　　　　(B) since
　　　　　　(C) though
　　　　　　(D) because of

amazing and fabulous, all tickets have been sold out just in one hour.

I am sorry that we were not able to accommodate your request; ＿＿＿＿, there

　　　　　12 (A) but
　　　　　　 (B) although
　　　　　　 (C) however
　　　　　　 (D) despite

are still a few tickets available for a singing training program.Emma Girard will be the main instructor in the program from August 10 to 13.＿＿＿＿ that

　　　　　13 (A) If
　　　　　　 (B) Once
　　　　　　 (C) Provided
　　　　　　 (D) As long as

you would like to purchase tickets for this program, please call me at 111-515-0032 as soon as possible.

Sincerely,

Nancy Norling, Manager Boston Marriott Copley

1-10 Ans: 1.(A) 2.(C) 3.(B) 4.(D) 5.(B) 6.(C) 7.(C) 8.(D) 9.(B) 10.(B)

1. Passengers are advised to take only carry-on luggage for short trips _____ it is less likely to be lost or stolen than check-in luggage.
   (A) as   (B) if   (C) so   (D) unless

答案 A

眼球追蹤

❷ 看全句

Passengers are advised to take only carry-on luggage for short trips _____ it is less likely to be lost or stolen than check-in luggage.

❶ 看選項

| (A) as | (B) if | (C) so | (D) unless |

中譯　乘客被建議短途旅行只要攜帶隨身行李，因為相較於檢查托運行李，它不太可能被弄丟或被竊取。

秒殺策略

❶ **判斷題型**

看選項得知，測驗點為「**連接詞**」，用以連接兩個句子。

❷ **搭配語意，驗證答案**

分析全句，由 take only carry-on luggage 與 less likely to be lost or stolen than check-in luggage 得知，空格應找表「原因」的連接詞。

---

as (conj) 大觀園

· 如…一般
The application procedure is not so complex as you think .
· 當…時
As the tenant moved out, he left the flat in bad condition..
· 隨著
As time goes by, we get older .
· 因為
Mr. Lin went to Paris as a new branch opened there.
· 雖然
Exhausted as he was , he still completed all the work.

11 對等連接詞

12 形容詞子句

13 副詞子句

14 名詞子句

15 介係詞

2. Before _____ gift certificates, we will evaluate the cost-effective-ness.

(A) issue   (B) issued   (C) issuing   (D) we issuing

答案　C

眼球追蹤

Before ❷ _____ gift certificates, we will evaluate the cost-effectiveness.

❶ 看選項

(A) issue   (B) issued   (C) issuing   (D) we issuing

中譯　在發行禮卷時，我們會先評估成本效益。

秒殺策略

❶ 判斷題型

看選項得知，測驗點為「**動詞變化或獨立分詞構句**」

❷ 判斷主被動

由語意推知，Before 後的主詞應為 we，所以 (we) / issue，為主詞 / 動詞 的主動關係，故 issue 轉化成現在分詞 issuing

註：此時若改成分詞構句，則 before 後的 we 必須省略，不能保留。

複習：分詞構句形成步驟

❶ 去連接詞（亦可保留連接詞，使意義更顯明）
❷ 判斷主詞：主詞同，可省略其一；主詞不同，兩者須都保留（獨立分詞構句）
❸ 動詞分詞化 ：主動 → Ving；被動 → p.p.

303

3. _____ you do not agree to these terms, your account will be terminated.

(A) When   (B) If   (C) For   (D) In case of

答案 **B**

眼球追蹤

❷ 看全句

_____ you do not agree to these terms, your account will be terminated.

❶ 看選項

(A) When   (B) If   (C) For   (D) In case of

中譯 如果您不同意這些條款，你的帳戶將被終止。

秒殺策略 ♛

❶ **判斷題型**

看選項得知，測驗點為「**連接詞**」，用以連接兩個句子。

❷ **搭配語意，驗證答案**

分析全句，you do not agree to these terms 與 your account will be terminated 語意得知，空格應找表「條件」的連接詞。♛

---

if (conj) 大觀園

· 如果（表示條件）

The president will consider the merger if the price is fair .

· 要是（表示假設）

If you were the manager, I would make the same decision.

· 即使（表示讓步）

The squatter still occupied the lot even if he was reported.

· 每一次……時（表示因果關係）

If his proposal is rejected, he feels depressed.

· 是否

The CEO wondered if he should make a takeover bid for the small firm.

4. Our company carefully develops a mutually-beneficial relationship with many of our clientele _____ our revenues can grow steadily as expected.

(A) due to　　　(B) while　　　(C) provided that　　(D) so that

答案 D

眼球追蹤

❷ 看全句

Our company carefully develops a mutually-beneficial relationship with many of our clientele _____ our revenues can grow steadily as expected.

❶ 看選項

(A) due to　　　(B) while　　　(C) provided that　　(D) so that

中譯 我們公司用心地與客戶發展互惠關係，是為了讓營收如預期般地穩步增長。

秒殺策略

❶ **判斷題型**

看選項得知，測驗點為「**連接詞**」，用以連接兩個句子。

❷ **搭配語意，驗證答案**

分析全句，由 carefully develops a mutually-beneficial relationship 與 revenues..grow steadily 語意得知，空格應找表「**目的**」的連接詞。

---

so that (conj) 大觀園

· 為的是
The line was closed so that we can cut down on labor costs.
· 具有相同意思的用法還有：
in order that +S +V =in order to V = so as to V= for the purpose of Ving
· 注意：so...that S V 表示「如此⋯以至於」
The price of property has risen so enormously that we can't afford a house.

11 對等連接詞
12 形容詞子句
13 副詞子句
14 名詞子句
15 介係詞

5. _____ the current condition of the market improves, the retail chain won't expand.

(A) Except   (B) Unless   (C) If   (D) For

 答案 B

眼球追蹤

❷ 看全句

_____ the current condition of the market improves, the retail chain won't expand. our revenues can grow steadily as expected.

❶ 看選項

(A) Except   (B) Unless   (C) If   (D) For

中譯 除非目前市場情況改善，不然這家零售連鎖不會展店。

秒殺策略

❶ **判斷題型**

看選項得知，測驗點為「**連接詞**」，用以連接兩個句子。

❷ **搭配語意，驗證答案**

分析全句，由 the current condition…improves 與 the retail chain won't expand 得知，空格應找 表「**條件**」的連接詞。

unless (conj) 大觀園

· 除非
Unless FB takes over the game company, it can't survive on the app store.
· 亦可當介係詞 表示「除…之外，除非」
There is no way out unless compromise of both parties.

6. _____ the location of the mall is excellent, it's still difficult to yield a profit with high rents.

(A) Because   (B) Apart from   (C) Even though   (D) As long as

答案 C

眼球追蹤

❷ **看全句**

_____ the location of the mall is excellent, it's still difficult to yield a profit with high rents.

❶ **看選項**

(A) Because   (B) Apart from   (C) Even though   (D) As long as

中譯 儘管商場的地理位置十分優越，但因高租金，要獲利仍很難。

秒殺策略 👑

❶ **判斷題型**

看選項得知，測驗點為「**連接詞**」與「**介係詞（片語）**」。

❷ **搭配語意，驗證答案**

分析全句，由 the location of the mall is excellent 與 it's still difficult to… 得知，兩部分皆為句子，所以需要「**連接詞**」；再者，前後子句有矛盾的關係，需要表「**讓步**」的「**連接詞**」。👑

even though (conj) 大觀園

‧ 即使（表示讓步）= even if （語氣較強烈）
Even though it's nine in the late evening, a number of diners are still in that fancy restaurant.

11 對等連接詞

12 形容詞子句

13 副詞子句

14 名詞子句

15 介係詞

7. The customers' responses have always been excellent _____ new promotional mailers were sent out last month.

(A) while   (B) whereas   (C) since   (D) so that

答案 C

眼球追蹤

❷ 看全句

The customers' responses have always been excellent _____ new promotional mailers were sent out last month.

❶ 看選項

(A) while   (B) whereas   (C) since   (D) so that

中譯 自從新的促銷郵寄上個月發送出去後,客戶的反應一直是很好的。

秒殺策略

❶ 判斷題型

看選項得知,測驗點為「**連接詞**」,用以連接兩個句子。

❷ 搭配語意,驗證答案

分析全句,由由 responses have always been excellent 與 mailers were sent out last month 得知,後一句為前一句的時間標記。空格應找 表「時間」的連接詞,搭配時態觀念,會搭配 **have always been 完成式時態**的從屬連接詞,為 since

---

since (conj) 大觀園

· 自⋯以來,從⋯至今
The product has been sold like hot cakes since we launched a promotion.
· 既然;因為
Since the issue is so controversial, let's avoid.

11 對等連接詞

12 形容詞子句

13 副詞子句

14 名詞子句

15 介係詞

8. Vehicle advertising works so effectively and economically _____ it's worth investing in.

(A) so   (B) for   (C) since   (D) that

答案 D

眼球追蹤

Vehicle advertising works | ❷ so effectively and economically _____ it's worth

investing in.

❶ **看選項**

(A) so   (B) for   (C) since   (D) that

中譯 車輛廣告是如此有效且經濟，所以它值得投資的。

秒殺策略 👑

❶ **判斷題型**

看選項得知，測驗點為「**連接詞**」，用以連接兩個句子。

❷ **找關鍵詞語**

由關鍵詞語 so effectively and economically … 得知，空格需要表示「**結果**」的連接詞故套用 so + adj / adv + that S V 句型 即可。👑

so...that (conj) 大觀園

· 如此…以至於（中間可加形容詞或副詞）
The marketing manager is so experienced that he has been headhunted by many companies.

· 相同意思的用法有 such+ N + that S + V
The marketing manager has such great experience that he has been headhunted by many companies.

9. Shipping and handling fees are not refundable, _____ in certain states and countries where these items are refundable.

(A) in case　　(B) except　　(C) although　　(D) however

答案　B

眼球追蹤

Shipping and handling fees are not refundable, _____ ❷ in certain states and

countries where these items are refundable.

❶ 看選項

(A) in case　　(B) except　　(C) although　　(D) however

中譯　除了在某些州和國家之外，運輸與裝卸費用概不退還。

秒殺策略 👑

❶ 判斷題型

看選項得知，測驗點為「**分辨使用連接詞與介係詞的時機**」。

❷ 搭配語意，驗證答案

由 in certain states and countries where these items are refundable 得知，空格需要**介係詞**，選 except。👑

---

except (prep) 大觀園

· 除...之外 後面可加「名詞」、「副詞」、「介係詞片語」、「子句」
　Air travel across much of Asia has been disrupted except Taiwan.

· except for 表示對局部的否定，對主要多數的肯定，用於不同事物間的比較
　The meeting was very effective and productive except for the CEO's attitude.

· except that + S + V
　The party was great except that refreshments were served late.

10. _____ around a table and chatting, each colleague waited for Mr. Johnson to congratulate him on his promotion.

(A) Seat   (B) Seated   (C) Seating   (D) Seats

答案 B

眼球追蹤

❷ 看全句

_____ around a table and chatting, each colleague waited for Mr. Johnson to congratulate him on his promotion.

❶ 看選項 ❸

(A) Seat   (B) Seated   (C) Seating   (D) Seats

中譯 圍著一張桌子坐著聊天，每個同事等待 Mr. Johnson 到來以祝賀他晉升。

秒殺策略 👑

❶ 判斷題型

看選項得知，測驗點為「**動詞變化**」。

❷ 確定分詞構句用法

分析全句，逗點後，為主要子句；逗點前無連接詞與主詞，立即聯想「**分詞構句**」。

❸ 判斷主被動

「坐著」的用法：

be seated = seat oneself = take/have a seat = sit down。

(each colleague) / was seated **為被動**，故選過去分詞 seated。👑

驗證分詞構句流程

· 先試著推回原來的完整句（連接詞只要合乎邏輯即可）

推得句子 Each colleague was seated around a table and chatting, and they waited for Mr. Johnson to congratulate him on his promotion.

· 將推得句子再做一次簡化成分詞構句的步驟

❶ 去連接詞and

❷ 主詞colleague同，省略前方主詞

❸ was seated 動詞分詞化，即得 seated

311

11 對等連接詞

12 形容詞子句

13 副詞子句

14 名詞子句

15 介係詞

11-13 請參閱下列電子信件

中譯

收件人　Debbie Talbert <dtalbert@gmail.com>
寄件人：Nancy Norling <nnorling@marriottcopley.com>
日期：八月三日
主題：回覆：票

親愛的 Talbert 女士，

我收到您的 8 月 2 日電子郵件，您表示想購買八月三日 Emma Girard 在 Marriott Copley 的表演票卷。不幸的是，由於 Emma 的現場表演是如此驚人和美妙，所有門票早在一小時內完售。對於我們無法滿足您的要求我十分抱歉；然而，有一場唱歌訓練課程的票還有幾張可得。Emma Girard 將會在 8 月 10 日至 13 日在這課程裡擔任主講師。只要你想購買這訓練課程的票，請盡快給我打電話，電話是 111-515-0032。

誠摯敬上，
Nancy Norling，波士頓 Marriott Copley 經理

秒殺策略

11. **答案** **(B) since**
　　Unfortunately, **since** Emma's live performance is..., all tickets have been sold out just in one hour.
　　解題　since (conj) 因為、既然，文意與文法接符合，故選 (B)。
　　(A) for +N ；(D) because of + N

12. **答案** **(C) however**
　　...to accommodate your request; **however,** there are still...
　　解題　however (adv) 然而，語氣轉承詞。分號後，單一子句前，可搭配副詞，無須連接詞。故選 (C)。
　　(D) despite + N

13. **答案** **(C) Provided**
　　Provided that you would like to purchase tickets for this program, please call me...
　　解題　provided that (conj) 只要、倘若，文意與文法接符合，故選 (C)。

成為多益勝利組的字彙練功區

文法講解區	Mini Test 限時 5 分練習區
take a toll **v.** 造成重大損失（或毀壞等）	carry-on luggage **n.** 隨身行李
ASAP = as soon as possible 盡快	gift certificate **n.** 禮券
keep a close eye on sb/sth **v.** 密切注意	evaluate [ɪˋvæljʊˌet] **v.** 評價、評估
emerging trend **n.** 新興潮流	cost-effectiveness **n.** 成本效益
meet demand **v.** 符合需求	issue [ˋɪʃʊ] **v.** 發給，配給
delivery date **n.** 運送日期	term [tɝm] **n.** 條款
trust [trʌst] **n.** 信託基金會	terminate [ˋtɝməˌnet] **v.** 終止
shareholder [ˋʃɛrˌholdə] **n.** 股東	mutually-beneficial **a.** 互利
cloud computing **n.** 雲端科技	clientele [ˌklaɪənˋtɛl] **n.** 顧客
productivity [ˌprodʌkˋtɪvətɪ] **n.** 生產力	retail chain **n.** 零售連鎖
repair technician **n.** 維修人員	yield a profit **v.** 獲利
troubleshoot [ˋtrʌblˌʃut] **v.** 解決問題	rent [rɛnt] **n.** 租金
entrant [ˋɛntrənt] **n.** 競爭對手	promotional mailer **n.** 促銷郵件
	vehicle advertising **n.** 車身廣告
	economically [ˌikəˋnɑmɪklɪ] **adv.** 節約地
	handling fee **n.** 手續費
	refundable [rɪˋfʌndəbl] **a.** 可退款的
	fabulous [ˋfæbjələs] **a.** 極好的
	accommodate [əˋkɑməˌdet] **v.** 滿足（某人要求）
	instructor [ɪnˋstrʌktə] **n.** 指導者

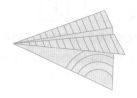

FAQ in TOEIC

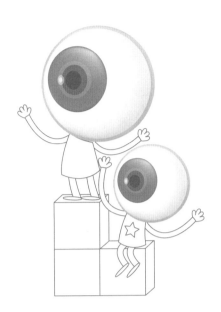

14
名詞子句 (Noun Clauses)

文法講解區

⑭ 名詞子句 (Noun Clauses)

簡單看

　　名詞子句是具有名詞的功能的句中句，與一般的名詞詞組用法相同，只是結構較大，因此名詞子句可在主要句子裡當作主詞、受詞、與補語。

秒殺策略

（1）判斷題型：是否需要名詞子句

（2）子句中，是否為完整句子

　　　yes → that 子句 或 if/whether 子句 或 wh- 間接問句 (where, when, why, which, how)

　　　no → wh- 間接問句 (who, what, which, how much, how many)

（3）依語意或個別選項判斷答案

1 名詞子句的功能

名詞子句可在主要句子裡當作主詞、受詞、與補語。

要注意的是：

- 名詞子句非倒裝句，子句中的語序為：先主詞，後動詞。
- 名詞子句放句首當主詞時，**連接詞絕不可省**，而後面須接**「單數動詞」**。

〉當主詞

EX Whether the president will hold the meeting **or not matters a lot.**

（總裁是否主持會議室很重要的。）

〉當受詞

EX **Check to see** if we can use cooking facilities **before you sign the lease.**

（在你簽租約前，確定我們是否可使用烹飪設備。）

〉當補語

EX **The main point is** that we can't aquire so much currency together in a short time.

（重點就是我們無法在短時間內湊齊如此大筆現金。）

2 名詞子句連接詞的種類

TOEIC 常考名詞子句大致分為 that 子句、 if/whether 子句、wh- 間接問句

名詞子句	that S + V
	if / whether S + V
	wh-疑問詞 S + V

〉that S + V

EX That last month's salary will be delayed **has shocked many employees.**

（上個月的薪水會延遲震驚很多員工。） →當主詞

EX **We are sorry to inform you** that we may have to return our order.

（我們很抱歉通知您我們可能需要退回訂單。） →當受詞

EX **The argument is** that the delivery date is not within the grace period.

（爭論在於交貨日並不在寬限期內。） →當補語

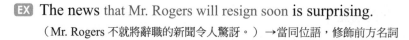

EX The news that Mr. Rogers will resign soon **is surprising.**

（Mr. Rogers 不就將辭職的新聞令人驚訝。）→當同位語，修飾前方名詞

- that 名詞子句注意事項
  (1) 名詞子句中，that 為連接詞作用，後接完整的句子。
  (2) 不當介係詞的受詞。
  (3) 放句首當主詞，that 不可省略。
- BE 動詞 +（感情／知覺／確信的）adj + that + S + V
  (1) 此時 that 名詞子句當補語。
  (2)「感情的」形容詞：pleased, glad, happy, delighted, sad, regretful 等。
  (3)「知覺/確信的」形容詞：aware, sure, certain, convinced, positive 等。

  EX The dealers were not happy that we have increased our prices on most models.

  （經銷商對於我們對大多貨品提高價錢不高興。）

〉if / whether S + V

EX Whether the small banks will consolidate **or not concerns the locals.**

（這些小銀行是否將合併讓地方人憂慮。）→當主詞

EX I don't know if our new designs will get a good reception in the market.

（我不知道我們家的新款式是否在市場能得到好反應。）→當受詞

EX The main problem is that if your application will be accepted (or not).

（主要的問題就是你的申請是否會被接受。）→當補語

EX They discussed the problem whether wages should keep pace of inflation or not.

（他們在討論工資是否應該隨通膨同步。）→當同位語

〉wh-疑問詞 S + V

EX Why the manager flung money away on the risk investment **irritated most board directors.**

（經理浪費錢去冒那個險的原因惹惱了董事會。）→當主詞

EX The report has shown where our financial pressures come.

（該報告顯示我們財政壓力來自何方。）→當受詞

EX Complete compliance with the guests wishes and needs is why the hotel can make high earnings year after year.

（努力滿足顧客需求是此家飯店可以年復一年賺取高受益的原因。）→當補語

EX Do you have any ideas how much you should be paid for a starting salary?

（你對你起薪應該多少有任何想法嗎?）→當同位語

3 if 與 whether 的共同點與差異點

〉共同點：

- if 與 whether 皆可當名詞與副詞子句連接詞。當名詞子句連接詞時，翻譯為「是否」。
- whether 和 if 後面都可以接 or not，但 if … or not 不常使用。

〉差異點：if 名詞子句有些事情不可以做：

- 當主詞或 Be 動詞的補語

EX Whether our company will embark on a new business **depends on the president.** (O)

If our company will embark on a new business depends on the president. (X)

（本公司是否投資新事業端看總裁。）

EX The problem is whether Mr. Johnson is authorized to act for the president or not. (O)

The problem is if Mr. Johnson is authorized to act for the president or not. (X)

（問題是 Mr. Johnson 是否有被授權代行總裁的職務。）

- 當名詞的同位語

EX It's your decision whether you stay or job hop. (O)

It's your decision if you stay or job hop. (X)

（要繼續待著或是跳槽是你的決定。）

- 放介係詞之後

EX What we will invest depends on whether we can maximize our earning from it or not. (O)

What we will invest depends on if we can maximize our earning from it or not. (X)

（我們所會投資的端看是否能從中獲得最大收益而決定。）

④ that 與 what 名詞子名兩者的區分

〉**that** 名詞子句：that 之後所接子句是完整的句子，即「主詞 + 動詞 + （受詞/補語）」。

> **EX** We believe that we can continue to cooperate with you in the future.

〉**what** 後面接的是不完整句（即缺乏主詞或受詞）

> **EX** Our current task is to find out what caused a great deficit this year.
> （我們當今任務就是找出是什麼造成今年巨大的虧損。）→ what 代主詞

> **EX** High-quality products and services are what our customers ask for.
> （高品質的產品與服務是我們的顧客所要求的。）→ what 代受詞

⑤ 名詞子句作為建議性動詞之受詞

下列含有「要求」、「命令」、「建議」、「主張」的動詞，之後所接的名詞子句，主要動詞都用「原形動詞」，以強調內容的重要性。

〉**S + 此類 V + that + S + (should) + 原 V**

「要求」：ask, require, demand, request
「命令」：command, order
「建議」：advise, propose, suggest, recommend
「主張」：insist, urge, maintain

> **EX** The other party suggested that a new clause (should) be annexed to the treaty.
> （對方要求條約上附加一條新條款。）

⑥ 名詞子句作為建議、懇求理性判斷形容詞之補語

〉**It is + 此類 adj + that + S + (should) + 原 V**

「重要的」：important, vital
「必要的」：necessary, essential, imperative
「適當的」：proper, advisable
「急迫的」：urgent

> **EX** It is necessary that a parent company provide sufficient support for its subsidiary.
> （母公司對於子公司應該要提供足夠的支柱是必要的。）

NOTES

Mini Test 練習區 限時5分

1. _____ a tour guide's duties are depends on their location and employer.
   (A) That   (B) Which   (C) What   (D) Whether

2. It is vital that each product, before sold, _____ to conform to the regulations it is subject to.
   (A) tests   (B) is tested   (C) has tested   (D) be tested

3. The CEO of the company is still thinking over _____ the proposed merger plan should be accepted or not.
   (A) if   (B) that   (C) why   (D) whether

4. Before processing his clients' applications, the bank clerk expressed strong regrets that he couldn't tell them exactly _____ they would receive.
   (A) that   (B) whether   (C) how much   (D) how come

5. A long-term contract for five-year engagement with your company is _____ we are looking forward to.
   (A) that   (B) what   (C) this   (D) while

6. _____ Mr. Johnson can mediate all the disputes between the two departments well remains to be seen.
   (A) If   (B) What   (C) Whether   (D) All

7. The supervisor requires that all clauses _____ clearly stated when the contract is made.
   (A) be   (B) is   (C) are   (D) have

8. You will need to contact our office to see _____ we are able to waive our request.
   (A) if   (B) that   (C) what   (D) which

9. The potential investors have to be convinced _____ the business plan is carefully constructed and has significant market potential.
   (A) of   (B) that   (C) if   (D) what

10. The company's response to your complaint is _____ you will be offered a full refund plus 20% off in your next purchase.
    (A) that   (B) if   (C) what   (D) X

Question 11-13 refer to the following email

To: Rachel Ashton < rachel@ ashtongym.com >
From: Samantha Ronson <ronson@ gmail.com >
Date: May 21
Subject: club resignation letter

Dear Ms. Ashton

I regret to inform you _____ I am resigning from my membership with

          11 (A) if
              (B) what
              (C) which
              (D) whether

BEST Gym. I wish to let you know why I have to do so.

At the beginning of being a member, the cost was NT$ 800 per month, but now it is NT$ 1,000 per month. Aside from this significant increase in cost, _____ I have been dissatisfied with is the aerobics classes at the gym.

12 (A) how
    (B) that
    (C) what
    (D) which

The scheduled classes often seemed to be canceled temporarily. For busy members with hectic schedules and full-time jobs, _____ we can attend

          13 (A) if
             (B) that
             (C) what
             (D) whether

these classes at will DOES matter a lot. I expect to know your future improvement in these matters.

Sincerely,

Samantha Ronson

1-10 Ans: 1.(C) 2.(D) 3.(D) 4.(C) 5.(B) 6.(C) 7.(A) 8.(A) 9.(B) 10.(A)

1. _____ a tour guide's duties are depends on their location and employer.

(A) That   (B) Which   (C) What   (D) Whether

答案 C

眼球追蹤

❶ 看全句

_____ a tour guide's duties are depends on | their location and employer.
                            ❷

(A) That   (B) Which   ❸ (C) What   (D) Whether

中譯 導遊的職責是什麼依他們的位置和雇主而定。

秒殺策略 👑

❶ **判斷題型**

分析全句，測驗點為「**名詞子句**」，帶全句的「**主詞**」。

❷ **判斷空格後是否為完整形式句子**

由 _____ a tour guide's duties are/depends on 得知，a tour guide's duties are 非完整形式句子，即考慮 which 與 what 所帶的間接問句。

❸ **搭配語意，驗證答案**

(B)which 需搭配選擇性的內容；(C)what 符合語意。👑

檢查

(A) 無意義，名詞子句的連接詞，後面需接完整句子, 文法不符，刪除。

(B) 哪一個，語意不合，刪除。

(C) 什麼，代表 the thing(s) that 👑

(D) 是否，後面需接完整句子，刪除。

故本題答案選 (C)

2. It is vital that each product, before sold, _____ to conform to the regulations it is subject to.

　　(A) tests　　　　　(B) is tested　　　　(C) has tested　　　　(D) be tested

答案　D

眼球追蹤

It is │vital│ that each product, before sold, _____ to conform to the regulations it

is subject to

❶ 看選項

　　(A) tests　　　　　(B) is tested　　　　(C) has tested　　　　(D) be tested

中譯　這是重要的，就是每個產品，在銷售之前，應該被測試以符合它必須符合的規定。

秒殺策略 👑

❶ 判斷題型

　　看選項得知，測驗點為「**動詞變化**」。

❷ 搭配關鍵字 vital 用法，驗證答案

　　見關鍵字 vital，聯想句型，It is + 建議、懇求、理性判斷的形容詞 + that + S + (should) + 原 V。故 _____ 應為 should be tested，省略 should，得 (D)。👑

檢查

(A) 非原 V，刪除。

(B) 非原 V，刪除。

(C) 非原 V，刪除。

(D) should be tested，should 省略👑

故本題答案選 (D)

3. The CEO of the company is still thinking over _____ the proposed merger plan should be accepted or not.

(A) if   (B) that   (C) why   (D) whether

答案 D

眼球追蹤

❶ 看全句

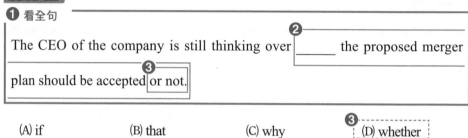

The CEO of the company is still thinking over _____ the proposed merger plan should be accepted or not.

(A) if   (B) that   (C) why   ❸ (D) whether

中譯　該公司的 CEO 仍然思考提議的合併計劃是否應該接受與否。

秒殺策略 👑

❶ **判斷題型**

分析全句，測驗點為「**名詞子句**」，當 think over 的「**受詞**」。

❷ **判斷空格後是否為完整形式句子**

the proposed merger plan should be accepted 為完整形式句子，即考慮 that 子句 或 if / whether 子句或 why 所帶的間接問句。

❸ **搭配語意，驗證答案**

關鍵字 or not，則必搭配 whether。👑

檢查

(A) 不搭配 or not，刪除。

(B) 不搭配 or not，刪除。

(C) 不搭配 or not，刪除。

(D) whether...or not 無論...是否 👑

故本題答案選 (D)

4. Before processing his clients' applications, the bank clerk expressed strong regrets that he couldn't tell them exactly _____ they would receive.

(A) flex   (B) flexible   (C) flexibly   (D) flexibility

答案  C

眼球追蹤

❶ 看全句

Before processing his clients' application, the bank clerk expressed strong

❷

regrets that he |couldn't tell them exactly _____ they would| receive.

❷

(A) that   (B) whether   ❸ (C) how much   (D) how come

中譯 在處理客戶們的申請前，銀行職員表示十分抱歉，他不能告訴他們精確會收到多少錢。

秒殺策略 👑

❶ 判斷題型

分析全句，測驗點為「**名詞子句**」，當 tell 的「**受詞**」。

❷ 判斷空格後是否為完整形式句子

they would receive 為非完整形式句子，即考慮 how much 的間接問句。

❸ 搭配語意，驗證答案

驗證答案(C)how much 多少錢，當 receive 的受詞，符合語意。👑

檢查

(A) 非 wh- 間接問句（who, what, which, how much, how many），刪除。

(B) 非 wh- 間接問句（who, what, which, how much, how many），刪除。

(C) 多少錢，語意與文法皆符合 👑

(D) 怎麼會，語意與文法皆不合，刪除。

故本題答案選 (C)

5. A long-term contract for five-year engagement with your company is _____ we are looking forward to.

   (A) that   (B) what   (C) this   (D) while

 答案 **B**

眼球追蹤

❶ 看全句

❸

A long-term contract for five-year engagement with your company is _____

❷

we are looking forward to.

   (A) that   **❸** (B) what   (C) this   (D) while

中譯 與貴公司為期五年的長期合同正是我們深切期盼的。

秒殺策略 👑

❶ 判斷題型

分析全句，測驗點為「**名詞子句**」，當「**主詞補語**」。

❷ 判斷空格後是否為完整形式句子

we are looking forward to 為非完整形式句子，即考慮 what 間接問句。

❸ 搭配語意，驗證答案

驗證答案(B)what 當 we are looking forward to 的受詞，符合語意。👑

檢查

(A) 非 wh- 間接問句（who, what, which, how much, how many），刪除。

(B) 代表期待的事物 👑

(C) 非 wh- 間接問句（who, what, which, how much, how many），刪除。

(D) 非 wh- 間接問句（who, what, which, how much, how many），刪除。

故本題答案選 (B)

6. _____ Mr. Johnson can mediate all the disputes between the two departments well remains to be seen.

(A) If   (B) What   (C) Whether   (D) All

答案 C

眼球追蹤

❶ 看全句

❸ ❷

_____ Mr. Johnson can mediate all the disputes between the two departments

well remains to be seen.

(A) If ❸   (B) What   ❸ (C) Whether   (D) All

中譯 Johnson 先生是否可以調解兩部門之間的所有糾紛有待觀察。

秒殺策略 👑

❶ 判斷題型

分析全句，測驗點為「**名詞子句**」，當全句的「**主詞**」。

❷ 判斷空格後是否為完整形式句子

主動詞 remains 前 Mr. Johnson can mediate all the disputes...well 為完整形式句子，即考慮 if 或 whether 子句。

❸ if 子句當名詞子句時，不可以做的事

驗證答案 if 子句，不可當主詞／Be 動詞的補語／名詞的同位語／放介係詞之後，故本題為當主語的名詞子句，故可用 if，故選(C)。👑

檢查

(A) if 子句，不可當主詞，刪除。   (B) 後需搭配非完整形式句子，刪除。

(C) whether 子句當主詞 👑   (D) 後需搭配非完整形式句子，刪除。

故本題答案選 (C)

11 對等連接詞

12 形容詞子句

13 副詞子句

14 名詞子句

15 介係詞

7. The supervisor requires that all clauses _____ clearly stated when the contract is made.

  (A) be   (B) is   (C) are   (D) have

答案 A

眼球追蹤

The supervisor | requires | ❷ that all clauses _____ clearly stated when the contract is made.

❶ 看選項

  (A) be   (B) is   (C) are   (D) have

中譯 　主管要求在合同訂立時，所有條款應明確說明。

秒殺策略

❶ 判斷題型

看選項得知，測驗點為「**動詞變化**」。

❷ 搭配關鍵字 require 用法，驗證答案

見關鍵字 require，聯想句型 S + 建議性 V + that + S + (should) + 原 V。
所以 that all clauses (should) be clearly stated，should 省略，得(A)。

檢查

(A)（should）**be** clearly stated，should 省略

(B) 非原 V，刪除。

(C) 非原 V，刪除。

(D) 非原 V，刪除。

故本題答案選 (A)

8. You will need to contact our office to see _____ we are able to waive our request.

(A) if   (B) that   (C) what   (D) which

答案 A

眼球追蹤

❶ 看全句   ❸   ❷

You will need to contact our office to | see _____ | we are able to waive our request.

(A) if ❸   (B) that   (C) what   (D) which

中譯 您需要聯繫我們的辦公室，看看我們是否能夠撤回我們的要求。

秒殺策略

❶ 判斷題型

分析全句，測驗點為「**名詞子句**」，當 see 的「**受詞**」。

❷ 判斷空格後是否為完整形式句子

由 _____ 後得知，we are able to waive our request 為完整形式句子，即考慮 that 子句 或 if 子句 或 which 所帶的間接問句。

❸ 依主動詞，驗證答案

主動詞 see (=ask)，後面多搭配 if / whether 子句。♛

檢查

(A) 是否，多放 see 後方搭配成名詞子句♛

(B) 無語意，較少放在詢問性動詞後面，刪除。

(C) 後應為不完整形式的句子，刪除。

(D) 應在其後搭配選擇的項目，刪除。

故本題答案選 (A)

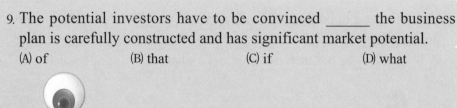

9. The potential investors have to be convinced _____ the business plan is carefully constructed and has significant market potential.

  (A) of   (B) that   (C) if   (D) what

答案 B

眼球追蹤

❶ 看全句

❸ ———————— ❷ ————————

The potential investors have | to be convinced _____ | the business plan is carefully constructed and has significant market potential.

  (A) of   ❸ (B) that   (C) if   (D) what

中譯 潛在投資者必須確信，商業計劃是經過精心構造，且具有顯著的市場潛力。

秒殺策略

❶ 判斷題型

分析全句，測驗點為「**名詞子句**」，當 be convinced 的「**受詞**」。

❷ 判斷空格後是否為完整形式句子

the business plan 後至 market potential 為完整形式句子，即考慮 that 子句或 if 子句。

❸ 依主動詞，驗證答案

主動詞 be convinced，**後接內容明確真實的肯定的 that 子句**，非 if/whether 子句。

檢查

(A) be convinced of＋N 而非句子，刪除。

(B) be convince that S V 確信某事

(C) be convinced，後不搭配 if/whether 子句，刪除。

(D) what 後接不完整形式句子，刪除。

故本題答案選 (B)

10. The company's response to your complaint is ＿＿＿＿ you will be offered a full refund plus 20% off in your next purchase.

(A) that　　　　　(B) if　　　　　(C) what　　　　　(D) X

答案 A

眼球追蹤

❶ 看全句

The company's response to your complaint is ＿＿＿＿ **❷** you will be offered a full refund plus 20% off in your next purchase.

❸ 看選項

(A) that　　　　(B) if　　　　(C) what　　　　(D) X

中譯 該公司的對你投訴的回應是，你將獲得全額退款，另加 20%的折扣到您的下次購買。

秒殺策略 ♛

❶ 判斷題型

分析全句，測驗點為「**名詞子句**」，當「**主詞補語**」。

❷ 判斷空格後是否為完整形式句子

you will be offered 後為完整形式句子，即考慮 that 子句 或 if 子句。

❸ 依選項判斷，驗證答案

依選項逐一判斷(A)與(B)，驗證答案。 that 子句，可當主詞補語，**且不可省略**，故選(A)。♛

檢查

(A) that 子句，帶後方子句，當主詞補語 ♛

(B) if 子句，不可以當主詞補語，刪除。

(C) what 後接不完整形式句子，刪除。

(D) 需要有名詞連接詞 that，且不可省略。

故本題答案選 (A)

11-13 請參考下列電子信件

中譯

收件人: Rachel Ashton < rachel@ ashtongym.com >
寄件人: Samantha Ronson <ronson@ gmail.com >
日期: 五月二十一日
主題: 退俱樂部會員信

親愛的 Ashton女士：

我很遺憾地通知您，我將終止 BEST 健身房的會員。我希望讓你知道我為什麼要這麼做。剛開始是成員時，費用為 800 元每月，但現在是 1000 元每月。除了月費顯著增加，我一直感到不滿的是健身房的事有氧課程似乎經常臨時取消。對於行程滿檔和忙碌全職工作者來說，我們是否可以隨意參加這些課程真的很重要。我在這些事情上期待您的進步。

真誠的，
Samantha Ronson

秒殺策略

11. 答案 **(B) that**
I regret to inform you **that** I am resigning from my membership with BEST Gym.
解題 inform sb that +子句 通知某人某事。

12. 答案 **(C) what**
... **what** I have been dissatisfied with is the aerobics classes at the gym.
解題 空格前無先行詞，因此 what (= the things that)，可以帶 I have been dissatisfied with，成為其受詞，形成 what 名詞子句，當全句的主詞。

13. 答案 **(D) whether**
... **whether** we can attend these classes at will DOES matter a lot
解題 後面的名詞子句不缺乏主詞或受詞時，不考慮 what 與 which，whether「是否」可帶名詞子句，當全句主詞或受詞皆可，此題即帶全句的主詞；但 if 帶的名詞子句，不能當主詞或 Be 動詞的補語。

成為多益勝利組的字彙練功區

文法講解區	Mini Test 限時 5 分練習區
cooking facilities **n.** 烹飪設備	be subject to **v.** 依照
acquire [əˋkwaɪr] **v.** 取得	think over **v.** 仔細考慮
currency [ˋkɝənsɪ] **n.** 貨幣	contract [kənˋtrækt] **n.** 合同；合約
inform [ɪnˋfɔrm] **v.** 通知	engagement [ɪnˋgedʒmənt] **n.** 僱用
the grace period **n.** 寬限期	mediate [ˋmidɪˏet] **v.** 調解
dealer [ˋdilɚ] **n.** 經銷商	dispute [dɪˋspjut] **n.** 糾紛
consolidate [kənˋsɑləˏdet] **v.** 合併	waive [wev] **v.** 放棄；撤回
inflation [ɪnˋfleʃən] **n.** 通膨	potential [pəˋtɛnʃəl] **n.** 潛力
fling [flɪŋ] **v.** 擲、拋、丟	aside from **prep.** 除了...之外
irritate [ˋɪrəˏtet] **v.** 使...惱怒	hectic [ˋhɛktɪk] **a.** 忙亂的
compliance [kəmˋplaɪəns] **n.** 順從；屈從	temporarily [ˋtɛmpəˏrɛrəlɪ] **adv.** 暫時地
embark on **v.** 著手；開始	
act for **v.** 代表；代理	
deficit [ˋdɛfɪsɪt] **n.** 虧損	
annex [əˋnɛks] **v.** 附加	
treaty [ˋtritɪ] **n.** 條約	
subsidiary [səbˋsɪdɪˏɛrɪ] **n.** 子公司	

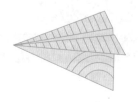

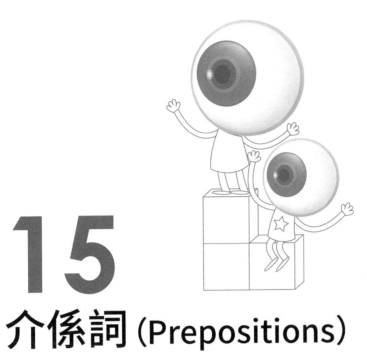

15

介係詞 (Prepositions)

文法講解區

⓯ 介係詞（Preposition）

簡單看

　　簡單來說，介係詞是用來介紹關係的詞語，是用來表示它後面的「受詞」與句子中其他字詞之間的關係。介系詞基本搭配即是「介係詞＋名詞／動名詞／名詞子句／代名詞（受格）」。

　　介系詞基本觀念簡單，但像機器中的螺絲釘，多、雜，且要表達出精確的語意時，缺其不可，因此須要用心去背誦，就容易養成語感。

秒殺策略 👑

（1）搜尋關鍵字，判斷需要搭配的介係詞：
　　　「時」、「地」、「原因」、「目的」、
　　　「方式」、「贊同」還是「反對」
（2）帶入慣用法或公式，用語意驗證答案

1 介係詞片語的類型與功能

〉當形容詞片語

(1) 修飾名詞

EX In Lululemon shops, you can find clothes made for women <u>of all</u> <u>sizes</u>.

（在 Lululemon 商店，你可以找到適合各種身形的女裝。）→ of all sizes 修飾 woman

(2) 當主詞補語

EX Mr. William is <u>on another line</u>. Would you like to hold?

（William 先生正在講電話，你要等等嗎？）→ on another line 修飾 Mr. William

〉當副詞片語

(1) 修飾動詞

EX The value of a stock is not always judged <u>by the current price</u>.

（股票的價值並不總是由現價來判斷。）→ by the current price 修飾 is judged

(2) 修飾形容詞

EX Mr. Fox is very efficient and accurate <u>in his decision</u>.

（Mr. Fox 對於他的決定很有效且精準。）→ in his decision 修飾 efficient and accurate

(3) 修飾整句

EX <u>Because of your excellent service</u>, we've decided to cooperate with you again.

（由於您絕佳的服務，我們已決定再次與您合作。）→ Because of your excellent service 修飾後面整句

② 表示「時間」或「期間」的介係詞

at （點）	時刻，正午，夜半，何時，目前，最初，最後，年齡等
	at two o'clock, at noon, at night, at midnight, at present, at first, at last, at that moment, at lunch, at once, at sunrise, at the age of
on （特定日子）	特定日子，日期，星期，特定日的上、下午及晚上
	on New Year's Day, on June 4th, on Sunday, on Saturday mornings, on the morning of May 15
in （較長時間）	周，月份，季節，年，世紀，上午，下午，晚上，過去的期間，未來的期間
	in the morning (afternoon, evening), in May, in spring, in 1988, in the 21st century, in the morning, in the past, in the future, in five minutes
until/till	表示「持續一段時間」，作「直到……止」解
	The theme pub usually opens until 6 a.m.
by	表示「動作完成的期限」，作「在……以前」解
	Ms. Bridget will finish the project by the end of this month.
since	表示「從過去某時到現在 止」，作「從……以來」解
	Facebook has acquired more than 40 companies since 2005.
for	表示「一段時間」，後面常搭配有數字的時間
	Josh has performed in front of live audiences for ten years.
during	表示「狀態的繼續中」，作「在……期間中」解
	Eric Hofmeister is the acting supervisor during my absence.
through	表示「整體時間」，作「從頭到尾」解
	The director guided and assisted the new actor through the whole process.
over	表示「涵蓋所有期間」，強調期間內某動作的變化
	The music business has been a war of attrition over the past 10 decades.
within	表示「在……期間」，強調動作很短促
	The new accountant has to learn this accounting software within 10 days.

3 表示「地點」或「方位」的介係詞

at （點）	地址，開放空間的一點，場合等
	at 100 King Street, at the airport, at work, at the meeting
on （面）	在…的表面
	on the platform, on the second floor, on the wall, on page 10, on board
in （空間／區域）	在空間內的概念，大區域範圍（城市、國家、地區）
	in my hand, in the office, in the sky, in Paris
over	在…的正上方 （可能接觸、部分或全部地覆蓋、或指移動）
	over the river, over your face, all over the world
under	在…的正下方（可能接觸、部分遮蓋或隱藏、或指移動）
	under your chair, under an umbrella, under a brick arch
above	在…之上 （上方、未接觸）
	above sea level, above average
below	在…之下 （下方、未接觸）
	below the horizon, below average
by / beside next to	在…旁邊
	by the sea, beside the advisor, next to the post office
around	圍繞在……四周，四處（移動、看）
	around the table, around the corner, walk around Moscow
between	在…之間 （指二者之間）
	between the two of us, between 12 to 13 p.m., between meals
among	在…之間 （指三者以上、或為……所圍繞）
	among my clients, among trees
across from opposite	在…對面
	across from the bank, opposite the shop

4 表示「原因」或「目的」的介係詞

for	為了（後方多為一般的理由或目的，常與 famous, noted, blame, punish, reward 連用，表示「著名、處罰、獎賞等的理由」）
	The movie carried off the Academy Awards for best play.
from	因 （表示外在原因）
	Jay called in sick. He got ill from overeating.
of	因 （表示內在原因）
	Mr. Anson was really ashamed of such failure.
at	因 （表示情感原因，後方多搭「驚訝、或喜悅等感情」的動詞或形容詞）
	The president was surprised at the rumor.

5 表示「方式」的介係詞

by	用於交通、傳輸、工具、手段
	by taxi, by plane, by sea, by air, by phone, by email, by hand
in	用於交通、工具、語言
	in a taxi, in a boat, in pencil, in ink, in English
on	用於交通
	on foot, on a bus, on a train, on a bike, on a ship
with	用於工具、附帶狀態、with +（代）名詞+補語 （介詞片語副詞、形容詞、分詞）
	with a knife, with a key, with a gun. with tears rolling down

6 表示「贊同」與「反對」的介係詞

for, with	贊同、支持
	Are you for or against equal pay for equal work?
against	反對、防備
	Dr. Wu was very much against commencing drug treatment.

7 慣用語 1 — 介係詞片語

in accordance with	依照	in advance of	在...之前
in charge of	負責	in favor of	贊同
in honor of	紀念、慶祝	in terms of	就...而言
in regard to	關於	in reference to	關於
in possession of	擁有	in place of	替代

8 慣用語 2 — 動詞 + 介係詞

allow for	斟酌、考慮	apologize for	道歉
apply for	應徵、申請	apply to	適用、應用
account for	說明、佔（比率）	agree to/with	同意
cut down/back on	減少	convince A of B	使 A 相信 B
cater to	迎合的口味	compensate for	補償
contribute to	捐贈、貢獻	deal in	交易
incorporate A into B	將 A 納入 B	inform A of B	向 A 通知 B
remind A of B	使 A 想起 B	notify A of B	向 A 通知 B
sign up for	報名、投保	subscribe to	訂閱、綁約

comply with = conform to = abide by= adhere to 遵守

9 慣用語 3 — 名詞 + 介係詞

advance in	在…方面的進步	benefit from	從…得到利益
increase / decrease in	…的增加／減少	interest in	對…的興趣
interest on	…的利息	access to	利用、接觸
demand for	對…的需求	information on	關於…的資訊
influence/ effect/ impact on	對…的影響	request for	對…的要求／申請
respect for	對…的尊重	confidence in	對…有信心

tax, damage, solution, approach to 對…的稅、損失、解決方法、方式

10 慣用語 4 — Be 動詞 + 形容詞 + 介係詞

be entitled to	有資格	be equipped with	有…配備、能力
be equal to	等同於	be consistent with	與…一致
be devoted/dedicated/ committed to	致力於	be faced with	面對
be subject to	容易受到	be compared with	比較
be compared to	比較、比喻	be concerned with	關心、關係
be comparable to	與…不相上下	be compatible with	和…相容

NOTES

Mini Test 練習區 限時5分

1. Before the interview, Antony sat outside _____ his eyes closed.
   (A) in   (B) off   (C) with   (D) about

2. Randy did product demonstrations twice _____ the last electronics convention.
   (A) in   (B) on   (C) at   (D) for

3. Personnel Department will send you an appointment notice _____ the official announcement.
   (A) in favor of   (B) in possession of   (C) in charge of   (D) in advance of

4. Derartu Tulu rose to fame and became the national hero _____ winning a gold medal in the 10,000m event at the 1992 Barcelona Olympic Games.
   (A) at   (B) in   (C) by   (D) with

5. As a chief executive, Robson was _____ certain courtesies rarely accorded others.
   (A) entitled to   (B) compared with   (C) devoted to   (D) concerned with

6. The sales department has been discussing how to improve the strategies to fight _____ sharp decline in sales.
   (A) for   (B) with   (C) to   (D) against

7. The company didn't have successful expansion in Asia because it did little to alter design to _____ Asian tastes.
   (A) cater to   (B) account for   (C) contribute to   (D) compensate for

8. Subscribers will have free access _____ our connected text-to-speech capabilities.
   (A) in   (B) for   (C) to   (D) in

9. Experts indicate the growing gap _____ rich and poor, resulting from fast technological change and globalization of the economy, is likely to persist and widen.
   (A) about   (B) within   (C) along   (D) between

10. The investment incorporates financial assets _____ market conditions into its combination.
    (A) equipped with   (B) equal to   (C) subject to   (D) committed to

Question 11-13 refer to the following letter

Dear Mr. Doug Armstead,

Welcome to Hayes Pharmaceuticals I am glad that you have joined our sales team and I look forward to working with you in the weeks and months ahead.

Over the next few days, we have arranged _____ a series of lectures

11 (A) for
   (B) with
   (C) in
   (D) to

training sessions to help you learn about our company policies and departmental procedures. _____ company policy, participants must attend and

12 (A) Next to
   (B) In case of
   (C) In regard to
   (D) In accordance with

participate in all sessions!

Tim McKinney will provide you with a detailed schedule when he visits you later today. Once again, welcome to our team! If you have any questions, please feel free to call me _____ extension 5566.

13 (A) in
   (B) at
   (C) by
   (D) on

Sincerely,

Atsushi Noguchi, Manager Sales Department

1-10 Ans: 1.(C) 2.(C) 3.(D) 4.(C) 5.(A) 6.(D) 7.(A) 8.(C) 9.(D) 10.(B)

1. Before the interview, Antony sat outside _____ his eyes closed.
   (A) in   (B) off   (C) with   (D) about

 **答案** C

眼球追蹤

Before the interview, Antony sat outside ❷——❶ his eyes closed.

中譯 要以最佳狀態接受面談，Antony 在面試前坐在外面。

秒殺策略 ♛

❶ 尋找關鍵詞語

由關鍵詞語 his eyes closed，立即聯想是「**受詞**」**+ 補語**（修飾）」的句型。

❷ 搭配句型，驗證答案

此為表附帶動作的片語，用來修飾前方動作的附加狀態。

句型：**with + O + Ving / Vpp**。♛

複習：with +（代）名詞+補語

· 在此句型中，修飾 with 後受詞的補語可以是現在分詞、過去分詞、介系詞片語和形容詞。
· The supervisor gave the presentation with the figures demonstrating our financial problems.
  上司正用數字來陳述我們的財政問題。→ 現在分詞
· He will accept my help only with no strings attached.
  只有在沒有附帶條件下, 他才會接受我的幫助。→ 過去分詞
· After knowing getting promoted, he whistled on the street, with his hands in his pockets.
  在知道升遷後，他將手插在口袋哩，在街上吹著口哨。→ 介係詞片語
· The two parties disputed for hours with the meeting chaotic.
  雙方爭執數小時，讓會議混亂著。→ 形容詞

2. Randy did product demonstrations _____ the last electronics convention.

　(A) in　　　　　(B) on　　　　　(C) at　　　　　(D) for

答案　C

眼球追蹤

Randy did product demonstrations 　②|_____| 　 the last electronics |convention|.　①

中譯　Randy 已經在上次的電子展上做了產品演示。

秒殺策略 ♛

❶ 尋找關鍵詞語

　　由關鍵詞語 convention 會議，大會，立即聯想與 meeting 相同。

❷ 表示「場合」，搭配介係詞 at

　　表示「場合」，搭配介係詞 at。♛

複習：【表示「地點」或「方位」的介係詞 – at, on, in】

・ **AT**：at college, at the top, at door, at the corner, at the bus stop, at the bank, at reception
・ **ON**：on the bus, on the bike, on the way, on the menu, on the radio, on television, on the left
・ **IN**：in a taxi, in a row, in a lift (elevator), in the newspaper

3. Personnel Department will send you an appointment notice
_____ the official announcement.

(A) in favor of   (B) in possession of   (C) in charge of   (D) in advance of

答案 D

眼球追蹤

❶ 看全句

Personnel Department will send you an appointment notice _____ official announcement.

中譯 人事部門會在正式聲明發布前寄送委任通知給您。

秒殺策略 👑

❶ 依語意，驗證答案

(A) in favor of 贊同   (B) in possession of 擁有

(C) in charge of 負責   (D) in advance of 在…之前

依語意，Personnel Department will send you an appointment notice <u>in
advance of</u> official announcement.人事部門通常會在正式聲明前做個人私下
通知。👑

介係詞片語：介係詞+名詞+介係詞

· in agreement with	與…一致	· in recognition of	為肯定；褒獎
· in appreciation of	感謝	· in the interests of	為了…利益
· in comparison with	比較	· in case of	倘使；萬一
· in contact with	與…聯絡	· in violation of	違反
· on behalf of	代表	· on condition of	假使
· for fear of	因恐	· for the purpose of	為…目的

4. Derartu Tulu rose to fame and became the national hero _____ winning a gold medal in the 10,000m event at the 1992 Barcelona Olympic Games.

(A) at   (B) in   (C) by   (D) with

答案  C

眼球追蹤

Deraru Tulu rose to fame and became the national hero  |_____| winning a gold

|medal| in the 10,000m event at the 1992 Barcelona Olympic Games.

中譯 藉由在 10000 米的運動項目與 1992 年巴塞羅那奧運會贏得金牌，Derartu Tulu 快速成名並成為民族英雄。

秒殺策略

❶ **尋找關鍵詞語**

由**關鍵詞語** winning a gold medal 需要某「方式」或「手段」達到，立即聯想 by。

❷ **表示「方法」、「手段」，搭配介係詞 by**

by「藉由」贏得金牌，使得 Derartu Tulu 竄起並成為民族英雄。

---

by 介係詞

· 方式（藉由…工具或方法）：by email, by hand, by MRT, by air
· 時間（在…之前）：by noon, by the end of the month, by Friday
· 地點（在…旁邊）：by the sea, by the door, by the
· 方向（經過）：drive by many shops, run by us, walk by your house

5. As a chief executive, Robson was _____ certain courtesies rarely accorded others.

(A) entitled to　　　　　　　　(B) compared with

(C) devoted to　　　　　　　　(D) concerned with

答案 **A**

眼球追蹤

❶ 看全句

As a chief executive, Robson was _____ certain courtesies rarely accorded others.

中譯　作為首席執行官，Robson 享有某種極少給予別人的禮遇。

秒殺策略 👑

❶ 依語意，驗證答案

由 as a chief executive, courtesies 等字，可以猜得 Robson 享有別人鮮有的禮遇。

(A) (be) entitled to 有資格　　　　(B) (be) compared with 比較

(C) (be) devoted to 致力於　　　　(D) (be) concerned with 關心、關係

依語意，As a chief executive, Robson was <u>entitled to</u> certain courtesies rarely accorded others. 作為首席執行官，Robson <u>享有某種極少給予別人的</u>禮遇。👑

Be 動詞 + 形容詞 + 介係詞－Part 1

- be grateful for 感激
- be absent from 缺席
- be prohibited from 被禁止
- be attentive to 注意
- be confined to 受限於
- be content with 滿意
- be familiar with 熟悉

- be fit / perfect / suitable for 適合於
- be far from 一點也不
- be derived from 由…得來
- be superior / inferior to 優／劣於
- be similar to 類似於
- be consistent with 與…一致
- be provided with 備以

15.介係詞｜秒殺實戰區

11 對等連接詞

12 形容詞子句

13 副詞子句

14 名詞子句

15 介係詞

6. The sales department has been discussing how to improve the strategies to fight _____ sharp decline in sales.
 (A) for　　　　(B) with　　　　(C) to　　　　(D) against

答案　D

眼球追蹤

The sales department has been discussing how to |improve the strategies to ❷

| fight |❶ _____ | sharp decline |in sales.

中譯　銷售部門一直在討論如何改善策略對抗急遽下降銷售額。

秒殺策略 👑

❶ **尋找關鍵詞語**

由**關鍵字** fight 得知，可以搭配 for, with, over/about, against 三種介係詞。
fight for + 奮鬥的目標或對象　　　fight over/about + 爭吵的事務
fight with + 一起奮鬥的夥伴　fight against + 要抗爭的人事物

❷ **表示「反對」、「防備」，搭配介係詞 against**

由 improve the strategies... to fight...decline 得知，要選擇 against 「防備」意味。👑

against 介係詞

· 對抗、違反：fight against evil, against my will,
· 防 備： against a poor crop, take medicine against the cold
· 以⋯為背景： green against the gold
· 緊靠著、毗連：lean against the door, the house against the church

7. The company didn't have successful expansion in Asia because it did little to alter design to _____ Asian tastes.
   (A) cater to
   (B) account for
   (C) contribute to
   (D) compensate for

答案 A

眼球追蹤

❶ 看全句
The company didn't have successful expansion in Asia because it did little to alter design to _____ Asian tastes.

中譯 這公司在亞洲擴張沒有成功，因為它並未改變設計以迎合亞洲人的口味。

秒殺策略 👑

❶ **依語意，驗證答案**

由 didn't have successful expansion, little to alter design to 等字，可猜得無「迎合的口味」之意

(A) cater to 迎合的口味
(B) account for 說明、佔（比率）
(C) contribute to 捐贈
(D) compensate for 補償

依語意，The company didn't have successful expansion in Asia because it did little to alter design to <u>cater to</u> Asian tastes. 這公司在亞洲擴張沒有成功，因為它並未改變設計以<u>迎合</u>亞洲人的口味。 👑

搭配用法 cater to sb招待某人；cater one's needs/wishes/tastes

動詞 + 介係詞

- appeal to 訴諸於；吸引
- attribute to 歸因於
- associate with 結交；聯想
- dispose of 處理；除去
- preside over 管理；領導
- amount to 相當於
- take to 喜歡；開始從事某事
- dispense with 省卻；無需
- enroll for 報名上課
- inquire about 詢問有關

8. Subscribers will have free access ＿＿＿＿ our connected text-to-speech capabilities.
(A) in　　　　　　(B) for　　　　　　(C) to　　　　　　(D) in

答案 C

眼球追蹤

Subscribers will |have free |access| ＿＿＿＿ our connected text-to-speech capa-bilities.

中譯 用戶將可以免費使用我們文字轉語音的功能。

秒殺策略

❶ 尋找關鍵詞語

由**關鍵字 access** 得知，搭配介係詞 to

❷ 搭配慣用法，驗證答案

have free access to our connected text-to-speech capabilities 用戶「可免費使用」…的功能。

名詞 + 介係詞

- admiration for 對…的讚美
- approval of 對…的贊同
- authority on 對…的權威
- objection to 對…的異議
- responsibility for 對…的責任
- appreciation of 對…的感激或欣賞
- attempt at 在…的努力
- capacity for 對…的能力
- protection from 對…的防備
- substitute for 取代

9. Experts indicate the growing gap _____ rich and poor, resulting from fast technological change and globalization of the economy, is likely to persist and widen.

(A) about   (B) within   (C) along   (D) between

答案  D

眼球追蹤

Experts indicate the growing ❶ gap _____ rich and poor, ❷ resulting from fast

technological change and globalization of the economy, is likely to persist and widen.

中譯 專家指出，由經濟的快速技術變革和全球化造成的貧富差距鴻溝，很可能會持續和擴大。

秒殺策略 👑

❶ 尋找關鍵詞語

由 the growing gap... rich and poor 得知，**關鍵字 gap**「差距」一定是兩者之間的，介於 rich and poor。

(A) (be) entitled to 有資格   (B) (be) compared with 比較

(C) (be) devoted to 致力於   (D) (be) concerned with 關心、關係

❷ 表示兩者之間的距離、差距」，搭配介係詞 between

the growing gap between rich and poor，代表貧富兩者之間的鴻溝差距。👑

---

between 介係詞

- 在 A 與 B 之間（指時間，空間，順序等）：between the school and home
- 介乎 A 與 B 之間（指數量，距離，程度等）：a man between sixty and seventy
- 來往於 A 與 B 之間（指空間）：air service between cities
- 由於 A 與 B 的共同影響：between work and studies
- 區別 A 與 B 不同：difference between good and bad

10. The investment incorporates financial assets _____ market conditions into its combination.
   (A) equal to   (B) equipped with   (C) subject to   (D) committed to

答案 B

眼球追蹤

❶ 看全句
The investment incorporates financial assets _____ market conditions into its combination.

中譯 這投資把容易受到市場環境支配的金融資產納入它的組合。

秒殺策略 👑

❶ 尋找關鍵詞語

由 financial assets, market conditions 等字，可猜得，是「容易受到」市場情況所影響的金融資產。

(A) (be) equal to 等同於   (B) (be) equipped with 有...配備、能力
(C) (be) subject to 容易受到   (D) (be) committed to 致力於

依語意：The investment incorporates financial assets <u>subject to</u> market conditions into its combination. 這投資把<u>容易受到</u>市場環境支配的金融資產納入它的組合。👑

Be 動詞 + 形容詞 + 介係詞－Part 2

· be based on 以...為基礎	· be familiar with 熟悉的
· be critical of 挑剔	· be faithful to 忠心於
· be dependent on 依靠	· be supportive of 支持
· be equivalent to 相當於	· be tolerant of 容忍
· be essential to 對…很重要	· be sure of/about 確定

357

11-13 請參閱下列一則信件

中譯

Doug Armstead 先生 您好

歡迎來到 Hayes 藥業！我很高興你加入我們的銷售團隊，我期待著與您在今後幾週和幾個月的工作。在接下來的幾天裡，我們已經安排了一系列的講座與培訓課程，以幫助您學得我們公司的政策和部門程序。按照公司規定，參加者必須出席和參加所有的會議！Tim McKinney 在今天稍後拜訪你時將為您提供詳細的時間表。再次，歡迎加入我們的團隊！如果您有任何問題，請隨時給我打電話至分機 5566。

誠摯敬上，
Atsushi Noguchi，銷售部經理

秒殺策略

11. 答案　**(A) for**

we have arranged **for** a series of lectures

解題　arra　for sb / sth 為（某人／某事）作安排，作準備。

12. 答案　**(D) In accordance with**

In accordance with company policy, participants must attend...

解題　(A) next to 僅次於　　　　　(B) in case of　如果；萬一
(C) in regard to 關於　　　　　(D) in accordance with 根據；與...一致

13. 答案　**(B) at**

please feel free to call me **at** extension 5566

解題　extension 分機，搭配 at。

成為多益勝利組的字彙練功區

文法講解區	Mini Test 限時 5 分練習區
value [`vælju] **n.** 價值	electronics [ɪlɛk`trɑnɪks] **n.** 電子學
stock [stɑk] **n.** 股票	convention [kən`vɛnʃən] **n.** 會議；大會
current price **n.** 現價	appointment notice **n.** 委任通知
acquire [ə`kwaɪr] **v.** 併購	official [ə`fɪʃəl] **a.** 官方的
acting [`æktɪŋ] **a.** 代理的	rise to fame **v.** 成名
attrition [ə`trɪʃən] **n.** 損耗；磨損	courtesy [`kɝtəsɪ] **n.** 殷勤
carry off **v.** 贏得；獲得（獎章等）	accord [ə`kɔrd] **v.** 給予；贈予
call in sick **v.** 請病假	sharp [ʃɑrp] **a.** 急劇的
equal pay for equal work **n.** 同工同酬	subscriber [səb`skraɪbɚ] **n.** 用戶
commence [kə`mɛns] **v.** 開始；著手	capability [ˌkepə`bɪlətɪ] **n.** 功能
drug treatment **n.** 藥物治療	incorporate [ɪn`kɔrpəˌret] **v.** 把⋯合併
	financial asset **n.** 金融資產
	session [`sɛʃən] **n.** 講習會
	extension [ɪk`stɛnʃən] **n.** 電話分機

Leader 004

秒殺新多益Part 5 & Part 6 -
解題高手眼球追蹤術大公開

作　　者　陳力曼
發 行 人　周瑞德
企劃執行　劉俞青
封面設計　高鍾琪
內文排版　菩薩蠻數位文化有限公司
校　　對　徐瑞璞、陳欣慧

印　　製　大亞彩色印刷製版股份有限公司
初　　版　2014 年 10 月
出　　版　力得文化
電　　話　（02）2351-2007
傳　　真　（02）2351-0887
地　　址　100 台北市中正區福州街 1 號 10 樓之 2
E m a i l　best.books.service@gmail.com
定　　價　新台幣 369 元

港澳地區總經銷　泛華發行代理有限公司
地　　址　香港筲箕灣東旺道 3 號星島新聞集團大廈 3 樓
電　　話　（852）2798-2323
傳　　真　（852）2796-5471

國家圖書館出版品預行編目(CIP)資料

秒殺新多益Part 5 & Part 6：解題高手眼球追蹤術大公開 /
陳力曼著. -- 初版. -- 臺北市：力得文化, 2014.10
　　面；　公分. -- (Leader；4)
　ISBN 978-986-90759-3-0(平裝)

　　1. 商業英文 2. 會話
805.1895　　　　　　　　　　　　　　　103018600